The
Sisters
of
Luna Island

ALSO BY STACY HACKNEY

Forever Glimmer Creek

The
Sisters
of
Luna Island

Stacy Hackney

Simon & Schuster Books for Young Readers
NEW YORK • LONDON • TORONTO • SYDNEY • NEW DELHI

SIMON & SCHUSTER BOOKS FOR YOUNG READERS

An imprint of Simon & Schuster Children's Publishing Division

1230 Avenue of the Americas, New York, New York 10020

This book is a work of fiction. Any references to historical events, real people, or real places are used fictitiously. Other names, characters, places, and events are products of the author's imagination, and any resemblance to actual events or places or persons, living or dead, is entirely coincidental.

Text © 2022 by Stacy Hackney

Jacket illustration © 2022 by Jennifer Bricking

Jacket design by Krista Vossen © 2022 by Simon & Schuster, Inc.

SIMON & SCHUSTER BOOKS FOR YOUNG READERS

and related marks are trademarks of Simon & Schuster, Inc.

For information about special discounts for bulk purchases, please contact Simon & Schuster Special Sales at 1-866-506-1949 or business@simonandschuster.com.

The Simon & Schuster Speakers Bureau can bring authors to your live event. For more information or to book an event, contact the Simon & Schuster Speakers Bureau at 1-866-248-3049 or visit our website at www.simonspeakers.com.

Interior design by Hilary Zarycky

The text for this book was set in Goudy Old Style.

Manufactured in the United States of America

0322 FFG

First Edition

2 4 6 8 10 9 7 5 3 1

CIP data for this book is available from the Library of Congress.

ISBN 9781534488694

ISBN 9781534488717 (ebook)

For my sister, Sarah,
who has saved me a million times over

RULES OF AROMAGIC:

Gather flowers before a rainstorm.

Enchant spices beneath a sliver of moon.

Blend charms with the clearest intent.

But beware the price of fate.

CHAPTER ONE

Cinnamon will attract prosperity and wealth.

The knock came at midnight. Sharp and staccato, it cracked open the silence of the house. Marigold Lafleur nestled farther under the blankets, but her eyes popped open all the same, her heart keeping pace with the rap-tap-tap that had awoken her.

Someone was here.

The stillness of sleep gave way to the softest of sounds behind the thin walls—covers rustling, arms stretching, heads lifting. Lou groaned from the room next door, and Birdie exhaled a tiny breath. Mama's footsteps pattered past. All the while, Marigold wondered who dared to turn up on their stoop.

No one came to Lilac Cottage in the daylight. In truth, no one had come much at all ever since the earthquake. Whoever was at the door needed something, and they needed it badly.

Marigold slid off the edge of her mattress. Through her open window the moonlight was a ribbon of silver rippling over her dresser tucked under the eaves, and the single bed that just fit inside the narrow walls. Tiptoeing across the room, Marigold shrugged on a robe. She crept down the hall, careful to avoid the creaky floorboards on the other side of her bedroom door.

Staying pressed against the wall, Marigold snuck halfway down the stairs and stopped before the landing where the stairs turned toward the front door. She peeked her head around the corner and spied Tara Ricketts in the doorway. Her brown hair was messy and tangled, and her face was streaked with tears. Behind her, the night stretched out like the ocean behind it, dark and full of secrets.

"He'll never straighten up. It doesn't matter what I do. He can't hold a job to save his sorry life. We're broke. We might lose the house." Tara was sobbing so hard, her face had disintegrated into the wrinkles and folds of a crushed flower petal.

Mama clucked in sympathy, ushering Tara into the front hall. "You could look for opportunity elsewhere, leave Luna Island."

"I've got nowhere to go," Tara said.

Mama took a deep, slow breath, her shoulders rising with the movement. It was a telltale sign. She was smelling Tara's fears. "I'm guessing you're most worried about that baby daughter of yours."

Tara nodded. "I want her to get off this island someday."

"I might have something to help, but it comes at a price," Mama said.

Marigold shrank back, her stomach dropping like a stone in water. Mama was tampering in someone else's life. Again.

"I'll pay, whatever it is. My mama gave me some money. You can have it all." Tara's voice creaked out, high-pitched and clogged with tears.

"The cost I'm referring to isn't related to money. There's a price for changing one's future, and I can't predict what it will be," Mama said.

Mama called them vexes—the consequences for altering fate. She could fix one part of Tara's life, but a vex might make something awful happen to another part. It was the unpredictability and danger of aromagic.

"I don't care," Tara said in a defiant tone. She held out several crumpled green bills.

Mama plucked the money from Tara's hand. "You'd better come on back, then."

Marigold's mouth flooded with a sour taste. Sure, they needed the money, but what Mama did to get it—Marigold couldn't excuse it, not after last spring. She pushed back into a corner of her mind the memory of the ground shaking and a pale, still face.

Mama cleared her throat and called up the stairs, "I wouldn't count on winning the role of a spy anytime soon."

Stupid. Marigold should have known Mama would catch her. Mama couldn't remember to lock their back door, but she always knew when someone was watching. Marigold stepped out from behind the wall.

"Since you're awake, why don't you come on down?" A half smile tugged at Mama's lips.

Marigold's nose flooded with the scent of wildflowers and herbs, memories of the past overwhelming her senses. She pictured Mama beaming at her above the burner, the tingling of Marigold's fingertips as she concentrated on the flame. It was powerful and exciting and . . . wrong. Marigold pressed her heels into the wooden floorboards and reminded herself she wanted nothing to do with aromagic anymore.

Birdie appeared beside her on the landing, hands on her hips. Her pajamas hung in a creaseless line on her thin frame, and her auburn hair was swept up in a perfect ponytail even though she'd just been asleep. "Marigold needs her rest. It's the first day of school tomorrow."

"As far as I can see, she's already awake," Mama said.

"'Cause of all the commotion," Lou said, pushing past Birdie on long legs corded with muscle. She sat down on the bottom step. "Half the island could hear you carrying on down here."

"I'm sorry," Tara said quickly.

Birdie didn't even look at Tara, her gaze burning into Mama as she strode down the remaining stairs. "Marigold needs to get back to bed like any other normal seventh grader. Not that there's anything normal about this family."

Mama closed her eyes a second too long at Birdie's jab. Marigold tried to think of something to say to dissolve the tension blanketing the room. Yet Mama was already shuffling Tara down the narrow hallway covered in peeling flowered wallpaper and past the crooked stairs stretching up in a maple-patterned jigsaw puzzle.

"I'm sorry for getting up, but we haven't had a visitor in a while." Marigold scampered down to where Birdie and Lou stood. She couldn't wait to tell Sam about this the next day.

"You go on to bed, M," Birdie said. "I'll keep watch over Mrs. Ricketts. I don't know what Mama is thinking. Heading into the basement to work and planning to leave some woman we barely know alone in our kitchen in the middle of the night."

"Stop worrying for once," Lou said, exasperated. "We all need sleep, and Tara Ricketts isn't going to hurt anything. She's too much of a mess."

"Exactly. She's in no shape to make a reasonable decision. Someone needs to keep an eye on her," Birdie said.

Lou rolled her eyes. "Fine, I'll come with you. I'm not going to stick you alone with Mama's latest bad decision."

"If you're both going, I'm going too," Marigold declared. Now that her sisters were awake and staying up, she didn't want to miss any of the action.

Birdie held up her hand to stop Marigold.

"I'll go to bed right after." Marigold clasped her hands together in a plea. "I know it's late, but at least we're all up late together. It's an adventure." If this were a movie and Marigold were the star, she'd sweep into the kitchen with her white nightgown swirling behind her. With the power of her own persuasion she'd convince Tara to dump her no-good husband.

Marigold deflated as Birdie frowned instead of answering. Sometimes it seemed as though Birdie helped Marigold, only to boss her around a minute later.

Lou cuffed Birdie on the arm. "Oh, let her stay. No one can fall asleep now. Although . . ." She tapped her lip, pretending to think. "We could wrap this up early by locking Mama in the basement."

"Yeah right. Mama would kill us," Birdie scoffed.

They all knew not to mess with Mama's aromagic. The only time Marigold could remember Mama yelling at her was when Marigold spilled all their rose water while attempting a friendship charm without permission.

"Don't worry. We'll let her out by morning," Lou said, winking at Marigold.

"I'll even throw down a pillow," Marigold said, and grinned. "And maybe a blanket."

"Well, sure. We don't want her to get cold," Lou added.

Birdie sighed. "You two are hilarious. Can we get this over with?"

"You're no fun," Lou said, sticking her tongue out at Birdie.

"So you're always telling me. All right, M, you can come," Birdie relented.

Marigold linked her arm through Birdie's and nestled close to her side. "I'd never really lock Mama in the basement."

Lou linked herself to Birdie's other side. "I definitely would but only if you weren't home."

Birdie looked at Lou, her mouth twitching. She began giggling. Lou and Marigold joined in as they pulled one another down the hall.

By the time they reached the kitchen, Mama was

already gone. Tara was slumped over at the kitchen table, her head in her hands. Their small kitchen was tattered and peeling, with splintered cabinets and chipped paint, but it had gleaming wooden countertops that Birdie polished with lemon oil every night, and vibrant green herbs lined the window in terra-cotta pots. Lou had hung her game schedule on the refrigerator beside Birdie's *Highest Grade Point Average* certificate. Several photos of the three sisters decorated the remaining space of the metal doors. The room might have been ragged, but Marigold loved it all the same.

Birdie grabbed the dinged-up kettle from the stove, bustled over to the sink, and filled it with water for tea. Behind her the back porch lantern glowed, and fractured fingers of gold light reached into the shadows. There was a banging downstairs, and the rich scent of cinnamon rose through the floorboards.

"Prosperity charm," Lou whispered. "Got to be."

Marigold shivered. Faint echoes of lilac-tinged smoke followed the pungent cinnamon as it curled up from the basement; the tendrils wound their way around Tara's calves and seeped into her skin. Though Tara couldn't see or smell Mama's charm yet, it was already working its way into her life. She shifted in her seat, uncomfortable but not knowing why.

Tara had said she needed money, but prosperity charms

were notoriously difficult to control. The outcomes were unpredictable at best and horrible at worst. Greed and money were usually intertwined, and changing fate because of greed never led to anything good.

"If you need money, you should borrow it," Marigold urged Tara. "A lot can go wrong if you use Mama's charm for money."

"I didn't ask for money," Tara said, her eyes bloodshot and bleary. "I'm trying to help Ray get a job. That's all I want."

But at Tara's words, an acrid scent hit Marigold's nostrils. She froze and breathed out, trying to dispel the smell and stay calm. Yet the burning aroma only grew stronger until it filled her brain. Not now. But her nose wouldn't listen.

"Gambling," Marigold blurted out.

Birdie sighed. "Not again."

"Gambling?" Lou asked, and peered closer at Tara. "Yep, I can see it."

"What are y'all talking about?" Tara asked in a tight voice.

"It's nothing," Birdie reassured Tara while frowning at Marigold.

"I'm sorry. I tried to stop," Marigold rushed. Her gift always surfaced at the exact wrong time. "I'm an utter failure!"

"More like, dramatic failure," Lou said, her mouth quirking up at the corners.

"That's not true," Birdie said, her eyes softening in Marigold's direction. "But you need to try harder. We'll work on it. The goal is normal, right?"

"Right," Marigold said, hanging her head. "Normal" was good grades and Daddy back on Luna Island. "Normal" was not blurting out the secrets you smelled.

"What did you mean by 'gambling'?" Tara asked, looking guiltier by the second.

Silence thickened in the room. The kettle screamed into the quiet, and Birdie hurried to take it off the stove. "Where is Mama?" she mumbled, glancing at the basement door.

"Whatever you heard, it's not true." Tara's throat worked to swallow. "I don't gamble."

Tara was lying. Marigold pushed aside the image of Tara playing poker online. Sometimes the smell of someone's secret was so strong, it conjured up a picture as clear as her own face in the mirror.

"It's none of our business." Birdie set a mug of tea in front of Tara.

Mama finally appeared, halting the conversation. She carried a glass spray bottle filled to the brim with golden liquid. Marigold knew it contained a charm of cinnamon for wealth, mint for success, and honeysuckle for good fortune. It also was full of Mama's intentions; her best guess at what Tara needed and wanted. While Marigold knew it was a part of her mother's nature to help others, Mama recognized the need to pay their bills, especially with Daddy gone and fewer townspeople seeking her charms. Yet even now Marigold could see the nearly invisible smoke wafting from the edges of the bottle and crawling up Tara's arms, entwining around her throat, forever altering her future. An unsettling feeling stirred deep down inside Marigold.

Tara's eyes went wide. "What's that?"

"A special blend of spices and herbs. Ray will get that job. All you have to do is spritz this into the air around him, and you'll have what you want." Mama smiled and held out the bottle.

Birdie's mouth tightened, and she gestured to her sisters. Lou pulled Marigold out of her seat and pushed her toward the door. None of them looked at Mama.

"We're going to bed," Birdie said in a crisp voice.

Mama's smile faded. "If you'll give me a minute here, I could make us some more tea."

"No need," Lou added.

Mama looked at her two eldest daughters, their gazes turned toward the hallway, and sighed at the warning she saw on their faces. "All right, then."

Marigold followed her sisters back up to their room. The twin beds were nearly touching, but there was a small space in the middle that was the perfect size for Marigold.

"Can I sleep in here tonight?" Marigold asked.

Birdie and Lou exchanged a glance. Then Lou was shoving her field hockey equipment under the bed and Birdie was grabbing her extra quilt and spreading it on the floor.

Birdie surveyed Marigold's spot between the beds. "You'll sleep better in your own room. You have a big day tomorrow, and all the research says we go into REM sleep faster—"

"Birdie, no one cares." Lou flopped down onto her blue-and-white-striped comforter.

"Hey, some people think research is cool," Marigold said with mock seriousness, sinking down into her cozy nest.

"Oh man, I'm really in trouble if you two start telling me how to be cool," Lou said, smiling wickedly and clicking off the light.

The front door closed with a distinct thump. Tara was gone, but Marigold couldn't help wondering what would happen to her. What about Ray and her daughter and the secret gambling? What kind of price would fate require?

Marigold pulled the covers up past her chin, over her nose, until only her eyes peeked out. The image of Tara at her computer seared into her mind once again. Marigold closed her eyes and listened to her sisters' breathing deepen. She smelled Birdie's sweet gardenia and Lou's spiced vanilla scents. Her limbs relaxed, her lashes fluttered. Slowly everything faded to black. No use thinking about Tara anymore tonight. She was safe here in the darkness between Birdie and Lou, cozy and warm, sharing the same breaths, the same smells, the same heartbeat.

Marigold always felt safest with her sisters.

CHAPTER TWO

Clove can produce a powerful protection charm with unintended consequences.

The three sisters left the house together the following morning. Leaves canopied the sky above and tinted the light a greenish hue. Thick bushes and brambles crept into the path as though the overgrowth intended to overtake it entirely someday. Though Luna Island was crescent shaped and surrounded by the Atlantic Ocean on all sides, a dense forest had carved its way right down the middle of the island.

Marigold had been dreading this day for months. Not

even her first-day-of-school outfit could cheer her up. She'd rolled up the waistband of Birdie's skirt and borrowed Lou's cool denim shirt. Though she'd only had five minutes in front of the bathroom mirror because her sisters had been arguing over the hair dryer, she'd managed to twist her hair into a pretty french braid. Still, she kicked at the forgotten branches littering the dusty path. The fallen oak leaves smelled like cider mixed with ocean brine, and the last of the honeysuckle sweetened the air. It was the particular smell of Luna Island, except there was a faint rotting scent chasing it today.

The rise of voices from around the bend grew. Marigold's throat went dry, and she stopped.

"Marigold?" Birdie asked.

"Actually, I don't feel well," Marigold announced. "Maybe I should go back home."

"What's wrong with you?" Lou asked, hands on her hips.

"My stomach hurts and my head kills. I'm achy all over and I might throw up or pass out. It could be the flu, or worse!" Marigold hugged her stomach, hoping she looked sick.

Birdie shook her head. "You're going to school. The first day is important for making a good impression on your teachers."

"I can't make a good impression if I puke on someone," Marigold pointed out.

"I watched you eat three frozen waffles for breakfast," Lou said.

"Would you believe swine fever?" Marigold asked hopefully.

"Not unless you grow a snout," Lou said.

Marigold stared at the ground and blew out a long breath. "It's just . . . no one talks to me anymore. I'm the middle school outcast—it's embarrassing."

"You have Sam," Birdie reminded her.

Marigold brightened a little. That was true. Sam Fitch was her best friend and the one person who'd stuck by her, even after the events of last spring. They had spent their summer going to Scoops to split the signature strawberry chocolate chip sundae, and he'd taken her fishing nearly every day.

"Besides, your classmates will be too busy figuring out their schedules to worry about you," Birdie said.

"But it's not fair," Marigold complained. "You both go to high school on the mainland where everyone isn't whispering behind our backs." And truthfully, it was sometimes so close behind her back that she could hear every word while she stood in line at Moon Market. They hissed under their breath like scalded cats, words like "hurt," "witch," and "evil."

"People have always talked about us," Lou said, shrugging.

"But it's gotten much worse," Marigold whispered. She wanted to add, "since the earthquake," but knew she didn't need to.

"Most of the gossip has died down, same way it always does." Birdie put a hand on Marigold's shoulder. "No one cares about what happened in the cafeteria anymore."

Marigold shuddered at the memory of her epic meltdown.

"This is part of the reason why I could kill Mama for continuing to practice," Birdie said, more to herself than to her sisters. "How she can even consider aromagic after what happened is beyond me."

"But don't you secretly like your gift of smelling when people break the rules, so you can tattle on them?" Lou asked in a teasing voice.

"It's a weakness, not a gift," Birdie snapped. "Your ability to smell what people want is just as bad. It's distracting and an invasion of privacy."

Lou twisted her mouth into a frown. "We didn't ask for this, and I personally don't mind knowing what someone really wants. You wouldn't believe how much people lie."

Marigold looked down, thinking about the way her aromagic had erupted before she'd been able to stop it the night before. It *was* wrong. She would push it deep down inside herself, no matter what it took. Her gift for smelling secrets had only emerged a year ago. Birdie and Lou had practiced long enough to control their aromagic. Marigold was still figuring out ways to control hers.

"It's hardest for you right now," Lou said. "But we won't live on Luna Island forever."

"I'll live in New York City," Marigold said.

"And before you head off to become a Broadway star, we'll all go to colleges where no one knows anything about us," Birdie said.

Marigold's head popped up at Birdie's comment, a panic cycling through her like a tornado. "But you're not going to college next year. You said you were taking online courses."

"I am," Birdie said in a reassuring voice. She would graduate from high school at the end of this school year, but she'd promised not to leave Luna Island just yet.

"I can't imagine either of you leaving me," Marigold said. "It's bad enough with Daddy gone. I wish he would hurry up and come home." As soon as Marigold said his name, her chest tightened like someone had tied a thick rope around her and pulled.

"It won't be too much longer," Birdie finally said.

"I miss him," Marigold said softly. "Remember how he always made blueberry pancakes on the first day of school? He would bang all the pots in the kitchen to wake us up." Mama hadn't even gotten out of bed that morning, same as every day since Daddy had left.

"Blueberry pancakes give you pimples," Lou said, shoving Marigold gently in the shoulder. "They're called blimples."

Marigold cracked a smile. "Blimples is not a real thing."

They continued on, and the path opened up to the Captain Scar Marina, full of restaurants and shops that hugged the edge of the water. Golf carts lined the road in front of the buildings.

They passed Miss Lizzie and Miss Eugenie, two of the town council members, sitting at their usual table on the wooden deck beside the pale-pink brick storefront of Dream Pies Bakery. The ladies turned and stared for a long time at the sisters, before drawing their heads close together and whispering. Mrs. Linder left the Dogwood Coffee Shop, holding the hands of her twin daughters, whom Birdie had once babysat. Yet when Birdie waved today, Mrs. Linder turned and dragged her daughters to the other side of the marina. Even Miss Iris, who used to stop by their house for tea, now hurried into the Dolphin Gift Shop as they passed. Marigold sighed. Despite what Birdie hoped, the gossip hadn't totally died down. Marigold missed greeting her neighbors and feeling like a part of the town.

Gazing around the peaceful marina, Marigold could almost forget the awful events that had soured the town's feelings toward her family. The sun dappled the water with golden tiger stripes, and gentle waves broke against the bulkhead, causing the ships to sway in their slips. Luna Island looked like the perfect seaside town where nothing odd could ever happen, but that was only its surface. Once you lingered on the island, you noticed that underneath, a strangeness had always been there, lurking in the shadows.

Legend said that the five founding families of Luna Island had had pirate allegiances and magic in their blood. Yet the pirates were gone and the magic that used to run through the founding families had long faded away, all except for Marigold's family. These days, magic wasn't to be trusted, never mind indulged in. The town had only just finished repairing the damage from last spring, so perhaps Marigold and her sisters still deserved their scorn.

After all, the earthquake had been their fault.

"We need to hurry or we'll be late," Birdie said, her body already twisting in the direction of the ferry. She thrust a bag into Marigold's hand, filled with oatmeal chocolate chip cookies—Birdie's specialty and Marigold's favorite. "Here, I thought you might need something sweet today."

Marigold clutched the bag and smiled. "When did you find time to make these?"

"I packed my backpack with new school supplies over a week ago. I was looking for things to do," Birdie replied.

Lou crouched down beside Marigold and looked her right in the eye. "If anyone is mean to you today, kick them right in the shin."

Birdie coughed out a noise of protest. "Absolutely not! She'll get suspended."

"Fine," Lou said. "I'll go to their house and kick them myself."

Birdie swatted Lou's arm. "I swear it's like you're determined to get us all in trouble."

Birdie pulled Marigold to her side and hugged her close. On Marigold's other side, Lou wrapped her arm around them both. For a second, the three sisters stood in place, linked together. Maybe it really would all be fine.

The ferry horn blared, the arms dropped, and Lou and Birdie were racing toward the boat. At the water's edge the bright blue flags of the Crossbones Restaurant fluttered in the sea breeze as if waving goodbye.

Marigold tore her gaze from the water and continued down the path alone. The glow of her sisters' earlier encouragement faded with each step closer to school. Up until last year, she'd had plenty of friends. But everything had changed after Daddy's accident. A tree had fallen on his golf cart during the earthquake. Marigold had spent three straight weeks at the hospital with him. That's why it had taken her a while to learn that the town blamed Mama for the earthquake, and maybe Marigold too. She stopped getting texts from friends, and no one came by to check on her except for Sam. People shoved threatening notes into their mailbox; egged Lilac Cottage twice; and threw a rock at the front window, cracking it down the side. Her teachers suggested she was better off finishing sixth grade at home. It was the loneliest few months of her life.

Now branches snapped under her shoes and leaves crackled in the breeze, as if nature were already taunting her before her classmates had the chance. Smoothing her hair, Marigold lifted her chin. She had to stop worrying. The school had sent Marigold her class schedule in the mail. Everyone expected her back, which meant back to normal. Nothing ever turned out as bad as she imagined. Besides, there was always Lou's shin-kicking idea.

Up ahead Sam waited for her at the curve in the road at their usual spot halfway between their two houses. At least she didn't have to walk in by herself. Marigold broke into a relieved smile and took off at a jog.

"Pushing it on the time today," Sam said, tapping his watch.

"Sorry," Marigold said. "I tried to get out of going at all."

"But Birdie wouldn't let you?"

"Yep," Marigold said, and examined her friend. "New hair color for the first day?"

Sam's dark hair was a ferocious purple along the tips. It had been yellow for most of the summer, and pink before that.

"I thought school could use some livening up." Sam's guitar was in a case slung over his shoulder. On his skinny frame he wore his Dirk Thomas and the Wailers T-shirt, for an underground band Marigold had never heard of before Sam had made her listen to them. His skin was tanned golden brown from the summer sun.

"I like it," Marigold decided.

The redbrick building rose in front of them. A large gray-and-blue sign—LUNA ISLAND MIDDLE SCHOOL— was flanked by two dolphins and hung above the double front doors.

"How are you feeling about today?" Sam asked, side-eyeing her from beneath his hair.

"You mean how am I feeling about facing a crowd of seventh graders who spent all summer talking about me behind my back? . . . I feel great," Marigold said sarcastically.

"Hey, I called you every day," Sam said.

"Your mama probably made you."

"Course she made me. But don't I still get credit for hanging with the town outcast? Some might call it noble. I'm like a hero in a lot of ways."

Marigold pushed him. "Only if your superpower is scaring away all the fish."

"I caught that Spanish mackerel last week."

"It took you three months," Marigold teased.

Sam stopped walking, his face suddenly serious. "Look, don't get down about the other kids. Everyone acts like weirdoes when they can't explain stuff."

"Yeah. . . . Maybe no one remembers the cafeteria," Marigold said hopefully. "It was a quiet summer, and we haven't gotten a mean note in two months."

"Who cares what they say anyway? The important thing is what you think about yourself."

"Right. I'll pretend like I don't care. I'm an actress, after all. I can do this."

"Yeah, you can," Sam said, and fist-bumped Marigold.

They reached the schoolyard and edged their way through the crowds of students streaming into the front of the building like a school of fish. Inside, the gray walls were decorated with construction paper drawings, and the speckled linoleum floors stretched out in front of her. She breathed in the smell of pencil shavings and the stale grease of cafeteria french fries. Same old walls, same old floors, same old smells. When they reached the middle of the main hallway, Sam and Marigold headed in opposite directions for their first classes.

Alone in the school for the first time in months, Marigold felt daunted by the crowd around her, with their faces melding together. Were all the kids staring at her, or was that only in her head? Had two sixth graders crossed the hall to avoid her? Had she heard that group of eighth-grade boys whisper "witch"? Birdie's words surfaced in Marigold's mind—everyone was too busy to worry about her. She hoped it was true. Eyes trained on the ground, she walked forward, and bumped right into Lauren Spelling.

"Ouch," Lauren said, rubbing her arm. She stood beside Kendall Barrett. They were wearing matching purple backpacks, turquoise braided bracelets, and short jean skirts. Marigold instantly wished she'd worn a jean skirt instead of the white skirt she'd borrowed from Birdie.

"Sorry," Marigold said, forcing out a small laugh. "I didn't see you."

Marigold's hands fluttered at her side, so she clenched her backpack straps to keep them still. There was no reason to feel nervous. Lauren and Kendall had been her friends since kindergarten. She'd spent nights at their houses. The three of them had made dance videos they'd all sworn never to show anyone, and had practiced applying mascara. They were all friends—maybe not best friends like her and Sam, but good friends—or they had been.

"It's okay," Lauren said, and turned to leave. Her long and silky white-blond hair spilled over her shoulders.

"Wait," Marigold said. "How—how was your summer?"

Lauren exchanged a look with Kendall. "Fine. I was at camp."

"I visited my grandma," Kendall added. Rather than looking at Marigold, she fiddled with the blue beads on her bracelet, which glinted against her brown skin.

"I texted you but never heard back. I guess you were both gone awhile," Marigold said, trying to keep the conversation going.

They traded another meaningful look that made Marigold's cheeks burn. Still, neither of them walked away. That was surely a good sign.

Kendall cleared her throat. "We wanted to give you some space."

"After the cafeteria," Lauren clarified.

At their words Marigold was transported back to the previous April.

She was sitting at a table with Lauren and Kendall when the smell of clove, carnation, and juniper stung her nostrils with its sickly sweet spice—elements of a powerful charm gone wrong. No one else seemed to notice the growing smell or the alarming emerald mist weaving its way through the tables. It obscured faces and covered bodies. Overwhelming dread coated her in sweat. She couldn't stop herself from yelling, "Run! Something terrible is coming!" And then it came. The ground trembled with fury, rattling the tables and chairs. Plates and trays crashed. Stu-

dents screamed and ducked under tables. Bookshelves in nearby classrooms smashed to the ground, and the lights extinguished.

Marigold shook her head to dislodge the memory of the earthquake and all the events that had tumbled down upon her alongside it. She forced a smile at Lauren. "Sure. I understand. But now that I'm back . . . maybe we can do something this weekend."

Lauren toyed with a lock of her hair, and the silence stretched between them. A grapefruit-sized lump lodged itself in Marigold's throat. Lauren was going to say no.

"Actually, we can't. We're going to Eastport for lunch on my uncle's boat and don't have enough space for another person. Sorry," Lauren said, a pitying droop to her mouth.

Kendall met Marigold's eyes. "Me too."

Their words stung Marigold all over like jellyfish. Last year Lauren would never have planned a trip to Eastport without inviting her.

Marigold blinked her eyes rapidly to hold back tears. "No problem. I forgot I have plans this weekend anyway."

"We should get to class," Lauren said. "We'll see you around, though, okay?"

"Definitely." Marigold dug her nails into her hands to stop herself from crying.

Marigold watched them leave. Lauren said something that made Kendall laugh, and their identical backpacks knocked together. Marigold closed her eyes. It was exactly as she'd feared. No one had forgotten the rumors—how she'd known the earthquake was coming, how Mama maybe had caused it, how the Lafleurs might be dangerous. Even though it had been five months, nothing had changed; no one wanted anything to do with Marigold Lafleur.

CHAPTER THREE

Plant rosemary to strengthen memories, but be wary of recollections best forgotten.

Marigold FaceTimed Daddy on Saturday morning; it had been their weekend ritual since he'd left Luna Island. Today she'd pulled on a cheerful pink shirt with a sequined heart in honor of the call. This was one of her favorite moments of the week. She got to hear about Daddy's recovery, to see for herself how much better he looked, and to forget he was so far away.

After a week of sitting by herself in class and at an empty table—except for Sam—at lunch, she needed to see Daddy's face. More than that, she needed to see his face in real life. She missed his terrible jokes and his daily routines. Unlike Mama, Daddy didn't wander around town in flannel shirts that were three sizes too big, or forget to pick up groceries for supper. Daddy went to work every day, cooked broccoli, and made friends with the Moon Market checkout girls. Marigold would eat broccoli for an eternity if only he'd come home.

Daddy's face appeared on the cell phone after two rings. "Marigold! It's great to see you." He was smiling, and the creases in his cheek almost covered up the scar down the side of his face.

"How's Asheville?" Marigold asked.

Daddy had moved there after the accident. He was living with his sister, Aunt Lynn. There was a rehabilitation center right by her house where he could continue his outpatient therapy. Mama said it was much better than any place in Eastport. Marigold didn't believe her.

"It's already cooling off here because of the mountains. I'm taking a lot of slow walks on the trails. I could maybe beat a turtle if I tried," Daddy joked. He was outside on Aunt Lynn's deck, and the tips of the leaves on the trees in her backyard were tinged a pale yellow.

"That's great," Marigold said, settling into the pillows behind her head. "I guess that means you're coming home soon?"

Daddy looked down for a moment. Even on a small phone screen, Marigold could see the discomfort on his face. Her heart plunged to the floor.

"Might still take a while. Doctors say I've got to increase the range of motion in my legs."

"It's been five months," Marigold said. "We miss you."

"I miss you too," Daddy said. "It's not the same without my girls, but you'll come up later this month to visit, right?"

Marigold and her sisters had only seen Daddy four times since he'd moved to Asheville. It wasn't nearly enough.

"Yes, but I don't understand why you can't get better from here now. You've already made a ton of progress. If you were on Luna Island, we could help take care of you. I'll cook for you every night," Marigold said.

"Oh, you will?" Daddy asked in a mocking tone. "I know I've been gone a while, but I don't remember you spending a lot of time in the kitchen."

"But I'm the best at delegation," Marigold said, teasing him back. "I'll have no trouble convincing Birdie to make all your favorites, and Lou has started cooking everything-but-the-kitchen-sink soup where she combines all our leftovers into one pot. Sometimes it even tastes okay. It drives Birdie crazy that she won't use a recipe."

Daddy laughed. "I'll need to taste this new soup."

"You can taste it tomorrow if you come home," Marigold

said. She gripped the phone tighter, wishing she could walk straight through it and into Daddy's arms. "Please."

"I wish I could. But I still need a bit more time here." The lines in Daddy's forehead deepened.

Marigold swallowed, remembering why Daddy was recovering in the first place. He and Mama had separated last year. He'd moved out of Lilac Cottage but had been living in a condo right down the road. That is, until he'd broken the news about the extended business trip. Marigold hadn't wanted him to leave the island. She'd mixed up a charm without telling Mama. Her sisters had agreed to help. It was only a protection charm, after all, until she'd added her intentions to keep Daddy on Luna Island forever. She hadn't considered what might happen.

Marigold's charm had stopped Daddy from leaving but had caused a minor earthquake in the process. It had damaged parts of the town and nearly killed Daddy. The town blamed Mama, but the vex was all Marigold's fault. Her pulse quickened as she relived seeing Daddy before the helicopter took him to the hospital. His face was white and still, as if he were already dead. Time and again Daddy had sworn that he forgave her, but she couldn't totally believe him. After that, she and her sisters had made a pact never to use aromagic again.

"I understand," Marigold said, trying to smile. "We'll be fine until you're back."

Marigold must not have looked too convincing, because a shadow crossed Daddy's face. He peered into Marigold's eyes, not blinking. "You're all okay, though, right? None of you girls have had any accidents or—or anything like that? You'd tell me, wouldn't you?" There was a sudden urgency to his voice.

Marigold frowned, taken aback at his seriousness. "I think I'd remember to tell you about an accident. Why would you even ask that?"

"No reason. I just . . . worry about you three." Daddy averted his eyes from her gaze, and then plastered on a goofy grin. "Your personal worry machine."

Marigold smiled at his dumb joke, yet she wanted to ask more about what he meant by "accidents." But he immediately turned the subject to school. He asked about her classes and friends and didn't seem to notice how her answers were all a little forced. Not wanting to upset him, she didn't mention how her old friends were ignoring her.

When they said goodbye, Marigold still had no idea as to when he was coming back to Luna Island. Throwing the phone down onto her bed, she flopped onto her stomach and buried her head in the pillow. This was all her fault. She only wished she could think of a way to get Daddy back home to Luna Island where he belonged.

• • •

Later that afternoon Marigold, Birdie, and Lou were on their hands and knees, weeding the flowers and plants, the same way they did every Saturday afternoon until it was too cold for anything to grow. Clouds layered the sky in puffs of white, and a soft breeze ruffled the flowers. Marigold tugged hard at one stubborn weed. Her thoughts were all mixed up since the call with Daddy, and the weeds weren't helping matters.

Weeds were not allowed in the gardens around Lilac Cottage. Mama used the flowers and plants for her charms, and the garden beds were her pride and joy. Lilac Cottage itself had been built in the 1800s by Marigold's ancestors Clemence and Elise Lafleur. The old house had belonged to her relatives for generations, same as their last name since the daughters of her family used the name *Lafleur* even though their fathers had different surnames.

Lilac Cottage hovered on the edge of the forest, though the sand dunes were visible from the corner of the yard, and the ocean peeked over their tops. The house was flanked by enormous lilac bushes. In the spring, purple clusters burst out of the leaves, and the heady fragrance reached all the way to Captain Scar Marina. Yet today the branches were bare and looked as tangled up as Marigold felt.

Lou's head popped up from behind a bush. "Why are you wearing that hat? It's not even sunny. You look ridiculous."

Marigold adjusted the wide-brimmed sun hat on her head that she'd found in the basement, pulling it down farther on one side until it hung at just the right jaunty angle. "If you'd watched any musical, you would know this is the sort of hat a girl wears flower picking. It's practically mandatory."

"We wouldn't want our heroine to look anything less than stage-ready at all times," Birdie said, efficiently pulling a row of barely sprouted grass from beside the lavender beds.

Marigold stuck out her tongue. "You should appreciate my attention to detail."

"As long as I don't have to wear it," Lou said.

"What do you think I'm getting you for your birthday?" Marigold asked.

Lou shook her head, and Birdie started laughing. Lou joined in a minute later.

Her sisters' laughter lingered and curled around Marigold. Somehow she'd find a way to get Daddy back to Luna Island, and everything could be the way it was before. They'd go back to grilling hamburgers on Sundays, watching movies together on Friday nights, and teasing Daddy about his off-key singing in the shower, which only made him sing louder the next day. The bright pink sedum blooms brushed against her calves, and the yellow faces of the pansies peeked at her from the edges of the worn brick where she sat weeding.

Marigold settled into her work, her sisters close and her mind finally still.

Out of nowhere a chill wound its way up her body and draped over her shoulders like a cold cloak. Marigold closed her eyes and drew in a deep breath. A strange scent clogged her nose. It was sickly sweet, like the water in a vase of dying flowers left out a day too long. Her neck prickled and she looked around, half expecting to find someone behind her, dumping out the dirty water into their garden beds, but the yard was empty except for her sisters.

"Do you smell that?" Marigold said.

"Smell what?" Birdie lifted her head from a row of dahlias.

Marigold stood and peered into the bushes, trying to identify the origin of the smell. It seemed to come from the sky and the ground and the trees all at the same time. There was something unnatural about its intensity. Her stomach turned sour right as the sky darkened overhead, growing thick with clouds.

Birdie stood, wiping at her shorts. "That's weird. I smell it now too."

Lou wrinkled her nose, joining them on the brick path. "It's like something died."

Marigold took a step toward her sisters, wanting to huddle close for protection. Why was she finding it hard to breathe?

Mama hurried down the path, waving her arms. "Girls, you can stop with the weeding and come inside now. It's about to rain."

Birdie crouched back down. "We're almost finished. We've got some time before the storm."

"Hey, if she wants us to stop weeding, we should stop weeding," Lou said, raising her eyebrows and gathering up her spade. Her meaning was clear—*No need to do extra work.*

Marigold shivered as the wind picked up and the smell grew stronger. Thunder rumbled overhead.

Mama wrapped her arms around her waist. "Come in the house. Now."

"Maybe we should listen to Mama," Marigold mumbled. The terrible smell spread through the garden. There was something wrong about it.

Birdie's hands went to her hips. "Both of you should be helping me finish our chores. If we don't weed today, there will only be more tomorrow. I'm not doing it all myself."

"No one asked you to," Lou said, an odd sharpness in her voice. "Why do you always assume we're going to leave you with the chores?"

"Because you usually do," Birdie snapped.

"And then you get to feel like you're better than us, so it's a win-win for everyone," Lou said, an ugly sneer on her face.

At times Birdie did act superior and Lou didn't help out. Yet neither usually seemed to mind this much—it had been this way for as long as Marigold could remember—but now there was a nasty bite to her sisters' voices. It reminded her of Mama and Daddy's fights before he left. Marigold looked from Lou to Birdie, swallowing down a rising panic.

"How about we all come back and weed more as soon as the storm is over?" Marigold said, trying to agree with both of them.

Before either sister could respond, Mama caught Marigold's hand and tugged her up the path. She flicked her head at Birdie and Lou. "Let's go."

The two girls startled at the firmness in her voice and followed behind, both frowning. Above them the clouds blackened even further. Fat drops of rain spattered on the ground. Thunder cracked, and the wind whooshed past them, tugging Marigold's hat from her head.

"My hat!" Marigold cried.

Birdie rushed after the hat that was circling in the air back toward the garden.

"Get back here, Birdie," Mama called. She gripped Marigold's arm tightly.

The hat touched down in the middle of a flower bed. Birdie plucked it up and held it aloft in triumph. She was jogging back toward them when a deafening boom shook the ground. Marigold gasped as a jagged bolt of lightning slammed into the dirt right where Birdie had been standing only seconds before.

Marigold blinked, momentarily blinded by the spark of white light. When her vision cleared, she saw the hole in the middle of their garden, the dirt tinged with soot. The air now smelled of rotten flowers and burning wires. Static shot up her arm, sending pinpricks into her skin. Without another word, all four of them spun around and sprinted the rest of the way into the house, slamming the door behind them.

"What just happened?" Birdie asked. She was breathing heavily, and tendrils of auburn hair curled around her flushed face. "I'm shaking."

Marigold's own hands were shaking too. Birdie had almost gotten struck by lightning. Lightning! Her insides quivered. The possibility was nearly too much to comprehend. She stepped closer to Birdie, studying her face and making sure she was really all in one piece.

"I'm okay," Birdie said, hearing Marigold's unspoken thoughts.

"Birdie, you were almost a french fry," Lou exclaimed. "That scared the—"

"We're all fine," Mama said firmly.

"I don't know about that." Lou peered out the window

of the kitchen door. "This is crazy. The thunder and lightening are gone. That was like some sort of micro superstorm."

Lou was right. That storm had tripled in strength and ferocity in mere seconds, and then suddenly stopped. Marigold shivered, not wanting to think about it any longer.

She grabbed the hat from Birdie's hand. "Well, this is clearly going into the trash."

Her sisters burst out laughing, their relief unmistakable. Their shoulders relaxed as the weight of fear and shock lifted.

Lou opened the refrigerator. "I'm starving. Is it weird to make pancakes after a near death experience?"

"It's only weird if we don't make enough," Marigold said.

Birdie added, "You're in luck. I picked up more maple syrup last week."

"Do you want any, Mama?" Marigold asked, expecting her to say no. She always said no.

"No, I . . . I'm not hungry right now." Mama had cracked the door again and was sniffing the air, oblivious to her daughters. A foul aroma wafted in through the opening. She pushed the door closed and hurried down the hall, her face troubled.

"Should I run over to Miss Eugenie's and borrow a few raspberries?" Lou asked, raising her eyebrows with a wicked smile. "Berry pancakes are way better than plain."

"No," Birdie said instantly. "Have you forgotten that last time she caught you *borrowing* a few blueberries and threatened to call Mr. Jackson?"

"I'm obviously not going to let her see me," Lou said.

"Berry pancakes are my favorite," Marigold wheedled.

"Can we really deprive our baby sister of her favorite pancakes?" Lou asked, and pouted her lips at Birdie.

Birdie let out a long stream of air. "Go through the back by the holly bushes." Lou and Marigold grinned as Birdie admitted what they all knew to be true, "Berry pancakes are better."

Lou jogged out the back door. Marigold made her way toward the stairs to change her clothes while Birdie made the batter. At the end of the hall, the front door cracked open and Marigold could see Mama standing outside, her back to the door, cradling her phone to her ear.

"The smell returned, Mother," Mama said.

Marigold stopped, instantly curious. She slid behind the door so Mama couldn't see her. So Mama had smelled the rotten flowers too, but why was she calling Gram about it? Marigold's grandmother lived in Eastport and never came to Luna Island. Gram and Mama had had a mysterious falling-out years ago and barely spoke.

"Birdie was nearly struck by lightning. It can't be a coincidence," she said.

Mama grew quiet, listening to whatever Gram was saying on the phone. When she spoke again, she was farther away, and Marigold could barely hear her.

". . . evil in the air . . . I'm afraid."

Evil? Afraid?

Marigold stepped back from the door, twisting her hands together. Her heart suddenly beat as fast as hummingbird wings. Mama was never scared. Their aromagic sometimes had unintended consequences, but it never brought about evil. What was Mama afraid of, and what did it have to do with the terrible smell outside?

CHAPTER FOUR

Spearmint will heal indigestion and a poor reputation.

S am and Marigold walked down the hallway at school on Monday morning. She hadn't been able to see Sam on Sunday, and she'd just finished telling him about the lightning, the terrible smell, and Mama's reaction to it.

"Maybe she was just scared about Birdie almost getting electrocuted," Sam said. "My mama freaks out if I'm caught in the rain. If I was almost struck by lightning, she'd never let me leave the house."

"Your mama also helps you study for math tests. Mine once told Birdie her straight-A report card was a sign of a boring mind. My mama doesn't usually worry like yours does." Marigold flexed her hand, remembering Mama's fierce grip on her arm and the fear in her voice. "Why would she talk about the smell and the lightning as if they were connected?"

Sam shrugged. "I don't know. Why don't you just ask her?"

Marigold sighed. The smell had been much fainter this morning when she'd left for school. "It's not like she'd tell me if I asked."

"I guess," Sam said. "But I still think—"

Marigold stopped and clutched Sam's arm as her eyes landed on the bulletin board. "Do you see that?"

"What am I looking at?" Sam asked.

"You're looking at a miracle, a wonderful, amazing miracle!" Marigold exclaimed, stepping closer to the bulletin board littered with flyers and school news. She jabbed a finger at the sign announcing the upcoming auditions for the fall musical. "This is exactly what I need to get my life back on track."

Luna Island Middle School put on a musical every fall, but auditions were only open to seventh and eighth graders. The performance took place in the large town auditorium. Everyone on Luna Island went to see it, the local paper did a write-up, and people talked about it for weeks. Volunteers from the community helped build the sets, make the costumes, and post flyers. This year she would finally be able to try out, and the opportunity couldn't have come at a more perfect time.

"I don't understand how the musical is going to get your life on track." Sam leaned against the wall.

"Don't you see? This will change everything. It's my chance to show everyone I'm not different. This is the town's biggest event of the fall. How could Lauren and Kendall not want to be friends if I get the lead? Everyone loves the star."

Sam wrinkled his forehead, looking skeptical. "I'm not sure that's how it works."

"Remember Agnes Montview?" Marigold said. "She had no friends until last year."

"I liked her fine."

Marigold raised her eyebrows. "You like everyone. The point is, she got the lead in the musical. After that, she had a bunch of new friends. She even started texting with Tyler Walters. She used the play to make herself cool. If she can do it, so can I."

"Or maybe Agnes just likes singing." Sam's fingers tapped the wall in a silent rhythm as if strumming an invisible guitar.

"Maybe," Marigold said, though she doubted it. "But

this is also the perfect opportunity to get back on the town's good side. I'll convince my sisters to help out too. They can volunteer to paint the sets or pass out programs. We'll be part of the community again, and people will forget about the earthquake."

"I think you should try out for the play because *you* think it's fun, not because you're trying to prove something. Why would you want to hang out with people who only like you because you're starring in a musical?" Sam looked pointedly across the hall at Lauren standing beside Julia Kim and Alison Saunders.

"You don't think I can get the lead," Marigold said in a small voice.

"I didn't say that," Sam protested. "You always got a good role in the elementary school plays. But this is bigger. It's a whole town event, and a lot more kids try out every year. I don't want you to get disappointed."

"I still have to try. You can't understand. You don't care what people think."

Sam didn't mind if someone made fun of his purple socks or tore down the *Drummer Wanted!* poster he'd taped to the student bulletin board last week. He'd started a band with Will and Charlie two weeks ago, and they'd already offered to play for a student pep rally. He didn't seem at all worried about people hating his music.

Marigold continued, "I'm tired of people thinking there's something wrong with my family. I only want them to see me the same way they used to, as fun and nice and normal."

"But you're not normal," Sam said. "You can make potions—"

"Charms," Marigold corrected.

"Whatever. Your family can mix up charms that are magical," Sam said. "*That's* cool."

Sam was the only one with whom Marigold could discuss her aromagic. Mama had always taught her that aromagic was a private matter. People knew about the family's gifts mostly through whispers. There were those who believed Mama could help them, and others who thought her magic was all nonsense. Yet since the earthquake, many now considered Mama dangerous, whether they'd believed in her before or not. Marigold wanted to make sure no one saw her in the same way. That meant keeping aromagic to herself.

"Charms can also make bad things happen. Remember Lorelai Warren?" Marigold asked.

"You can't blame your mama for that," Sam said in a reasonable voice.

"Mylie left the day after Mama made Beck Pritchard fall head over heels for Lorelai with that love charm. It wasn't natural. Mama changed fate, and when she did, Lorelai got

Beck and lost Mylie, her best friend. That's the way aromagic works. Changing one thing creates a vex that makes something bad happen."

"But not always," Sam said. "Your mama made a spray that healed me right up when I had pneumonia."

"Because you were always going to get better. Mama didn't alter your destiny. She made you heal a little faster. That's different," Marigold said.

"Maybe Mylie was gonna move anyway. My mama said she's got a great job in Charlotte," Sam said.

"It doesn't matter. I don't want anything to do with aromagic ever again." Yet Marigold's own hands twitched at her pronouncement. She remembered sprinkling bits of thyme over a bubbling glass cup that had smelled of gardenia and orange peel. The plumes of smoke had curled into the air, and a breeze had lifted her hair. Blinking, she shook out her hands as the memory dissolved into a busy hallway.

"What about your special smelling thing?" Sam leaned in and lowered his voice. "Did you forget you can literally smell secrets?"

"Not anymore," Marigold said briskly. "I'm learning how to ignore it."

Except, if she was being honest with herself, she had no idea if that would work. After a year of trying, Marigold wasn't getting any closer to controlling smelling secrets the way her sisters could control their abilities. Last fall Birdie had smelled when John Bradbury sprayed graffiti down the senior hallway, and had convinced him to confess. Yet Marigold couldn't just sniff out a secret when she wished, and she couldn't stop from smelling ones she would rather avoid. Birdie and Lou said she needed to block all outside smells from her mind and imagine herself pulling in or pushing away the particular scent of the secret. They made her sit in their room with her eyes closed and practice. But none of it made sense to her. Maybe Mama could have done better at teaching Marigold. Yet Mama seemed to look through her rather than actually talk to her since Daddy had left.

"If I can get the lead, I won't have time to think about anyone else's secrets," Marigold continued.

Anna Perez walked by, her large backpack engulfing her entire back. "See you in homeroom, Marigold." Her voice was quiet, and Marigold almost didn't hear her.

"Okay," Marigold said absently.

"See," Sam said.

"See what?" Marigold said.

"Anna likes you without any play. Not everyone cares about what happened last April. Will and Charlie think witch powers are pretty cool."

"I don't have witch powers," Marigold snapped.

Sam put his hands up. "Sorry."

Marigold looked across the hall again. Alison, Julia, and Lauren were all laughing. Lauren was probably telling them a hilarious story right now, which she'd turn into an inside joke they'd talk about for days.

"It's fine," Marigold said shortly. "I'll see you this afternoon."

Sam only nodded as Marigold hurried over to Lauren. The girls glanced at her, then immediately looked away. Marigold plastered a bright smile on her face anyway.

"Are y'all trying out for the musical?" Marigold asked.

Julia smiled back. "I signed up, though I'm totally nervous."

Alison angled her body toward Julia and Lauren, effectively blocking out Marigold. "What are we going to sing for auditions?"

"Maybe something from *Les Misérables?*" Marigold moved around Alison so she stood at Lauren's side. "We spent enough time rehearsing those songs. Remember how I always sang Éponine's parts?"

"And I would sing Cosette's." Lauren's face softened.

Marigold remembered her and Lauren singing at the top of their lungs in Lauren's room, parading around her carved white canopy bed. Mrs. Spelling had brought them cups of tea with honey to soothe their vocal cords. She'd gushed over Marigold's voice and made a joke about Lauren needing to practice more. When Mrs. Spelling had left, Lauren's eyes had welled with tears, which she'd quickly swiped away. Then she'd lifted one side of her mouth in a dejected, one-cornered smile, and said, "She always says that. Don't tell anyone."

"Is Kendall trying out?" Alison asked, shifting Lauren's focus back to her.

Lauren scoffed. "Kendall sings like a squalling cat even though she tries, poor thing."

"I think we'd all be happier if she didn't try," Marigold quipped without thinking.

"Exactly," Lauren said with a little laugh. "Marigold knows."

Marigold's stomach twisted, already regretting her mean comment. What if it got back to Kendall? It would hurt her feelings.

Marigold cleared her throat. "We should all rehearse our audition songs together."

"Maybe," Lauren said, and glanced down at her watch. "I need to talk to Mrs. Browning before class. She gave me a B on my essay for no reason." She whirled around and started down the hall, Alison and Julia trailing behind her. Not one of them waved goodbye to Marigold.

Marigold tore her gaze away from the back of Lauren's head and set her shoulders straight, tipping up her chin.

The musical was the answer to her problems. She would practice every day, audition with the best song, and memorize every line. Getting the lead was the only thing that mattered; she had to get her old life back.

Marigold headed to the ferry station the next day. She'd stayed late at school to practice for her audition on Saturday and planned to meet her sisters at the ferry so they could all walk home together.

The low, open-air, wooden structure housed the small ferry office and a covered wooden deck. Below was a large dock set over the water, with the ferry loading platform and rows of wooden benches. As soon as she walked up, Marigold knew something was wrong. The public safety golf carts were parked in front. Clusters of people had formed on the sidewalk. One woman was lying on the grass holding her arm, and another man was slumped on the ground moaning in pain. Dr. Scott knelt beside Abigail Monrow, the head of the town council, who had a bloody gash down one leg.

Strangely, the faint scent of decaying flower petals and wet leaves was back in the air again. Marigold craned her head around and spotted the large, white ferry boat with blue stripes down the side. The boat was tipped to one side and was halfway on top of the dock instead of beside it in the water. The wooden planks were cracked around the sharp point of the hull, and two benches were crushed beside it.

Marigold's heart rate sped up. A ferry accident? There were never ferry accidents. Were her sisters hurt? Her eyes swept the crowd, searching for Lou and Birdie. She spotted them off to one side and raced over.

"What happened?" Marigold asked at once. "Were you on the boat? Are you okay?"

"We're fine," Lou said, waving her off.

Birdie wrinkled her forehead. "It was the oddest thing. Instead of slowing down, the boat sped up as it got closer to shore, and slammed into the dock. A few people fell out of their seats and crashed onto the deck."

"I heard the porter say it was a mechanical error," Lou said.

The rotten flower scent seemed to hover around them, making Marigold think about Mama's words—"evil in the air." She suddenly remembered Daddy asking if they'd had any accidents, almost as if he'd known something like this might happen. But that didn't make sense. None of this did.

"I can smell that gross stench from our garden again," Marigold said. "Isn't it strange that the same smell is noticeable here just like with the lightning storm on Saturday? Do you think it's some kind of a bad omen?"

"Oooh . . . a scary smell!" Lou said in a fake scared voice. "I swear you live for drama, M. It's no big deal. Something is rotting on the island. That's normal; this place is full of foliage."

Marigold frowned. She hated when Lou treated her like she was too young to know anything. "I also heard Mama on the phone Saturday, talking about the smell."

"What did she say?" Lou asked.

Marigold hesitated. "I couldn't hear her because I was hiding behind the door, but she definitely sounded nervous."

Lou smirked, not impressed with Marigold's explanation.

Birdie pursed her lips. "It's not nice to eavesdrop."

Marigold bit back the urge to scream. They were missing the point entirely. She followed them onto the sidewalk, wishing they would actually listen to her for once instead of treating her like a five-year-old.

Bryan Cunningham and Gabe Jones slouched on a nearby bench, watching all the chaos. They were in eighth grade at Luna Island Middle School, on the football team, and were always pushing each other in the halls. Their sneakers scuffed the ground as they glared at Marigold and her sisters.

In a loud voice Bryan said, "No surprise the Lafleurs are here. Bad luck follows them everywhere."

Marigold flinched, speeding up to get past them. But Lou stopped. She turned around and faced the boys head-on. "We're bad luck, huh?"

Gabe shrank back, but Bryan sneered at her. "Hey, I'm just saying what everyone else is thinking. No one wants you here."

Birdie pulled on Lou's arm. "Let's go. These kids aren't worth it."

Lou winked at Marigold before turning back to Bryan. "I don't care what everyone else wants. What do *you* want?"

Bryan narrowed his eyes and crossed his arms. "I want you to leave."

Lou closed her eyes and breathed in deeply, her shoulders rising with the movement. When she blinked her eyes open, a cruel smile turned up her lips. "I think what you actually want is Birdie's phone number, but that's not going to happen in this lifetime or the next. And we're certainly not leaving anywhere because of jerks like you."

Marigold stared at Lou, aghast. She'd recognized the deep breath and concentration. Lou had used her gift on Bryan and smelled what he wanted.

Bryan gaped. "I—I do not want her phone number."

"Dude, let's get out of here," Gabe said, rising to his feet.

Bryan pointed at Lou. "You witch! I bet you caused the ferry accident just like your mom caused the earthquake! Stay away from me!"

Lou raised her eyebrows. "I do believe I struck a nerve."

The groups of people on the sidewalk weren't even

pretending not to listen anymore. They'd turned toward Lou, staring avidly. Fragments of whispered accusations swept through the crowd.

"... dark magic."

"... the Lafleurs are trouble."

Birdie tugged Lou in the opposite direction of the boys. Her mouth had firmed into a narrow line. When the girls were out of earshot of the ferry station, she hissed at Lou, "I can't believe you did that. We're not supposed to use aromagic. Everyone saw you. We're trying to stop gossip, not make it worse."

Lou waved a hand. "They don't know what I did, and he deserved it. Besides, he's too much of a coward to tell anyone I could actually smell what he wanted. Also, how gross that he wanted your phone number. He's, like, twelve." She wrinkled her nose.

"We made a pact, and you broke it," Birdie said, her voice rising. She planted her feet in the middle of the path, her hands balled into fists at her side.

Lou faced her and clenched her jaw, raising her own voice. "It was a one-time thing, Birdie. Calm down."

"One-time is too much!" Birdie shouted.

A memory of Mama and Daddy's awful yelling rang in Marigold's ears. *Calm down*, Mama would say. *You don't understand*, Daddy would reply. Marigold squeezed her eyes shut, wanting to push the shouting away. "Please! Stop yelling. I hate yelling."

When she opened her eyes, Birdie and Lou were both staring at her. The woods were quiet around them except for the distant cry of a seagull.

Birdie reached out a hand to Marigold's shoulder and squeezed it gently. "You're right, M. I shouldn't have yelled. I'm off today. I guess I didn't get enough sleep last night."

Lou cleared her throat. "Maybe neither of us did."

Marigold exhaled a shaky laugh. "Either that or you're a little tense from crashing into the dock."

Her sisters both smiled at her, and Marigold's knees relaxed.

"Speaking of crashes, if they can't get that boat fixed, we might have to miss school tomorrow," Lou said, grinning at Marigold and making a victory sign.

"I'm not missing school," Birdie said.

"Yeah, *you* probably shouldn't. You need to lock down your homecoming date," Lou said nonchalantly.

"Excuse me?" Birdie said.

"Forgot to tell you. I heard Ava Warrenton ask Brant if he had a date yet," Lou said.

"Oh, um, what did Brant say?" Birdie asked. Her shoulders bunched up.

"He said no, obviously. Everyone knows he's asking you," Lou said in mock exasperation.

Birdie flushed. "Everyone doesn't know that."

"Why would he take anyone else?" Marigold said, outraged.

"Exactly," Lou said. "And you should have seen Ava's face when she turned around and saw me standing there."

"What did you do?" Birdie asked, her eyes widening.

"I didn't *do* anything," Lou said. "But I might have *said* she sounded desperate."

"Lou! She's going to hate me," Birdie squealed. Yet try as she might to maintain a stern expression, her mouth curled up into a smile.

"If she hates anyone, it's me, and I don't really care," Lou said.

"Serves her right." Marigold nodded. "Brant likes Birdie."

"I don't know about that," Birdie said, shaking her head.

"He texts you all the time," Marigold said. Birdie looked at her in surprise. Marigold continued, "I see his name come up on your phone every day, and then you always smile when you're reading his texts, which means you like him back."

Birdie buried her face in her hands. "You need to mind your own business."

"Rule number one: Sisters do not mind their own business," Lou said. "I was thinking we should mix up all the worst scents Mama keeps downstairs into the grossest smell possible and pour it into Ava's locker."

"Absolutely not," Birdie said in horror. "We'd ruin all her books."

"Plus, no aromagic," Marigold reminded her.

"I know, I know," Lou said, holding up her hands. "I was kidding. Mostly."

They continued down the path, talking about Brant and Ava and homecoming. Lilac Cottage came into view. Marigold breathed in deeply. The rotten flower smell was a little stronger now, as if coming from their own yard. Her neck tingled, and Bryan's words echoed in her head. *You caused the ferry accident.*

Even if her sisters thought her theory—that the smell was connected to bad things happening—was dumb, Mama knew something about it. Marigold would have to talk to her and find out the truth, before another catastrophe occurred and the town began blaming the Lafleurs for more than just an earthquake.

CHAPTER FIVE

Daffodil amplifies the inner voice to discover important truths.

The following afternoon Marigold's shoulders bowed under the weight of her backpack. She barely noticed the star-shaped leaves spiraling down to the path below or the cotton-ball clouds meandering across the blue sky. Her own thoughts muffled the busy clanking of the grocery carts from Moon Market. Worries chased one another on a never-ending merry-go-round inside her head—the lightning, the ferry accident, Mama's voice on the phone, the dreadful smell, even Daddy's strange question on the phone. Though the smell was strongest around their house, she could detect a whiff of it here by the marina and halfway down the path to school. It seemed to grow a little stronger every day. Something wasn't right. Her only option was to talk to Mama, face-to-face, but that was easier said than done when Mama didn't say much about anything to Marigold.

If only Daddy were here, he'd have a solution. He was the one who would always answer her questions at the kitchen table, whether it was how to solve a word problem in math class or which bait to use for flounder. He'd talk to Mama about the smell and get the answers Marigold needed. But Daddy hadn't answered her call last night.

Scanning the deck beside Dream Pies Bakery, Marigold spotted Mama in her usual seat. Overlooking the far corner of the marina, the deck itself was covered with a smattering of iron tables and chairs. The cheery yellow-and-white-striped umbrellas shaded each table like a cluster of daisies. Mama sat at one of the tables. Her hair hung over her shoulders in two red braids, and she'd pulled a baseball cap low on her forehead as if to block out everyone around her.

Miss Iris and her brother, Jackson Spencer, were sitting at a table near the front. Mr. Jackson was the director of public safety on the island, which meant he was in charge of the fire department, the tiny one-room emergency center, and checking in on all the townspeople. He and Miss Iris were sitting on the opposite end of the deck from Mama. Though Miss Iris and Mama had once been friends, recently Miss Iris had been staying away from her, much like everyone else.

But as Marigold passed by, Miss Iris stopped her. "It's a beautiful day, isn't it?"

Marigold paused her steps. "It is."

"The kind of day where you can't imagine anything bad happening here on Luna Island," Miss Iris said.

"Let's hope not," Mr. Jackson said with a penetrating look at Marigold. "I'm looking forward to a quiet afternoon."

Marigold's face heated up. "Me too," she managed to say before fleeing from their table. She knew what the Spencers really meant. They were warning her not to cause any more trouble. They probably thought she, Birdie, and Lou had caused the ferry accident too. Marigold wished people didn't now assume the Lafleurs were out to mess up people's lives.

Marigold flung herself into the chair beside Mama, shrugging off her backpack.

"This is a surprise," Mama said. "I don't often see you out in public."

"That's not true," Marigold protested, yet guilt snaked through her stomach; she did avoid being seen with Mama outside of Lilac Cottage.

There had been a time when Marigold had adored Mama.

Mama knew the secret places where wild mint grew. She woke her daughters up at midnight to enchant peonies, and she had let Marigold wear fairy wings for a month straight in third grade. But that was before Marigold had realized that wearing fairy wings when it wasn't Halloween made people look at you funny. She was in middle school now and didn't understand why Mama insisted on acting weird all the time. Why wasn't she meeting people for lunch like Sam's mama, instead of always sitting alone? And did she really have to walk barefoot into the Dogwood Coffee Shop on Sunday morning when *everyone* was leaving church?

Jessica Willard swept out the back door of the bakery, carrying a battered tray and a pink notepad. Dark curls spiraled around her smiling face. "What can I get you, Marigold?"

"I'm not hungry today," Marigold said.

"Not even for a slice of chocolate pie? Folks come from all over North Carolina for my chocolate pie. You can hardly ignore that kind of popularity," Miss Jessica teased.

Marigold smiled up at Miss Jessica, remembering how she had dropped a chocolate pie off at their house after Daddy's accident. "I'll let you know if I change my mind."

"Suit yourself," Miss Jessica said, and moved on to the next table.

Mama took a bite of her pie and leaned back in her seat. "So why don't you tell me."

"Excuse me?"

"The reason why you're here," Mama said simply.

Marigold swallowed. "It's about that awful smell outside our house."

Mama suddenly became interested in a large boat pulling into the docks. "I'm not sure what you're talking about."

Though it wasn't too hot, the sun's relentless rays beat down on Marigold. "You must have smelled it. It's so strong. Birdie, Lou, and I searched all over the garden after dinner last night for whatever is causing it, and we still can't figure it out. I smelled it by the ferry yesterday too, right after the accident."

Mama took another bite of pie, and seemed to chew much longer than was necessary for the small piece. "It's likely a dead animal. The smell will fade with time. It's all part of the circle of life."

"This is not about the circle of life. The smell is strange. It gives me the creeps."

Mama stared off at the waves instead of responding. Marigold needed to stop being so cryptic; she didn't know how much longer she could hold Mama's attention.

"I heard you on the phone with Gram the other day," Marigold said.

Mama's eyes snapped back to Marigold. "That was a private conversation."

Marigold continued. "You said something about the smell and . . . and evil."

Mama breathed in deeply and squinted.

"Don't do that," Marigold said.

"Do what?" Mama asked innocently.

"Don't smell my fears." Marigold's eyes watered. She hated when Mama used her gift. Fears were private, and Mama didn't have the right to take them from her. "Please tell me the truth."

"There's nothing to tell," Mama said. "And no cause for concern."

"Really? That's all you have to say? Because it seems like the smell is related to dangerous things happening on Luna Island. I don't want anything else bad to happen!" Marigold raised her voice, remembering how Mama hadn't told her that Daddy was leaving either, until he'd walked out the door and it had been too late to stop him. "I deserve to know what's going on for once!"

Miss Eugenie and Miss Lizzie, who must have sat down while she and Mama were talking, looked over from another table. Their eyes widened, and they stared at Marigold in surprise. Marigold's cheeks flushed.

"I should go," Mama said. "It's late and I have some— some scents to mix up."

A weight settled into Marigold's chest. Why didn't

Mama understand what she needed to do to fit in? She should have been trying to show the people of Luna Island that she was a proud member of the community, not ignore everyone and let more awful things happen. Surely Mama didn't want that either, but . . . maybe she didn't care. Otherwise, wouldn't she gather the girls up and tell them what she'd told Gram? Whatever the reason for her silence, it had been silly to think Mama would confide in Marigold. She lived in her own world, one into which her daughters were not invited. If Marigold was going to get her life back to normal, she needed to figure out this thing on her own. Otherwise Sam was right; the play wasn't going to make any difference at all.

Mama gathered up her tote bag, the one with the faded fabric and fraying straps. It looked as if it were about to unravel at any moment. She stared down at Marigold. "I'm sure the smell will come to nothing. I really believe that. This is not the Great Hurricane. The call with your Gram was a lapse in judgment."

"But—"

Marigold didn't finish her next question, for Mama had already tossed some dollars onto the table and hurried off the deck. She'd left half her pie uneaten. Mama never left chocolate pie.

Marigold stared after Mama before dropping her chin

into her hand. Why could Mama not give her a straight answer to anything? This was the same as those times when Marigold asked when Daddy was coming back. Mama would only say he was doing better, without addressing her question.

Clouds covered the sun, dimming the light. The ferry horn sounded in the distance, low and sonorous. Marigold raised her head, feeling the noise all the way through her bones. Looking over the deck, she noticed Miss Eugenie and Miss Lizzie darting glances at her and almost certainly gossiping about Mama rushing off. They were such busybodies . . . which could work to her advantage.

Straightening up, the spark of an idea sent a zing through Marigold's veins. Mama had just mentioned the Great Hurricane, an event that had taken place ages ago, yet Marigold couldn't remember much more than that. She should have paid more attention to fourth-grade local history. But since Miss Eugenie and Miss Lizzie knew practically everything about anything that had ever happened on the island, she bet they could tell her more about it.

Marigold pasted a smile onto her face and walked over to their table. "Hello, Miss Eugenie, Miss Lizzie."

The two women looked up with surprise.

"Marigold, how nice to see you," Miss Lizzie said in a fake friendly voice.

"Everything all right with y'all? We couldn't help but notice your mama leave so abruptly." Miss Eugenie's white hair was a puff around her face.

"Everything's fine. Mama had to go to the store to get some . . . things." Marigold swallowed, not exactly sure where she was going with her words. "She, um . . . she wants to make sure we're prepared for hurricane season."

Miss Lizzie looked up at the clear sky. "I'm not sure that's much of a concern today."

"Oh, you know Mama. She really worries about what could happen in the future." Marigold nearly choked on the lie. Mama didn't worry about what could happen in an hour. "Sometimes she even talks about the Great Hurricane and how terrible it was."

Miss Eugenie's eyes widened in recognition. "My goodness, I should certainly hope we never have another tragedy like that."

"Me too," Marigold said, leaning forward. This was her chance. "Although, she's never told us many details about what actually happened."

"I'm not surprised," Miss Eugenie said, picking up her teacup. "Most people simply don't care about our history these days."

"That's not true at all. I care a lot," Marigold said with a bright smile. "I'd love to learn about it, and you're probably the only one who can tell me all that happened during the Great Hurricane. You know more about this island than anyone else." Below them, the water splashed against the bulkhead, pushing and pulling at the old wood.

"You do know quite a bit about the town, Eugenie," Miss Lizzie said loyally.

Miss Eugenie set her teacup down and smiled. "I guess it couldn't hurt to educate our youths. This story goes all the way back to your original ancestors, Clemence and Elise Lafleur."

The first Luna Island sisters had always fascinated Marigold; their powerful aromagic was legendary. Gram had once told her they'd created a charm that cured the Louisiana governor of cholera when Clemence was only nine years old and Elise was twelve. Clemence's own diary was full of recipes that Mama still used for her own aromagic.

Miss Eugenie continued, "The Great Hurricane hit Luna Island in 1811 and destroyed most of the town. No one was prepared for the flooding or winds. Elise died, as did many others."

"Awful," Miss Lizzie murmured.

"There was even talk afterward that there was something unnatural about the storm. It blew up out of nowhere," Miss Eugenie said, widening her eyes.

A *storm that blew up out of nowhere?* Marigold couldn't

help thinking of the lightning in their garden.

"Horrifying," Miss Lizzie said, and shivered.

Miss Eugenie lowered her voice. "My grandmama said there was a smell of rot coming from the woods for days after the hurricane. The whole island reeked of it, and then the smell mysteriously disappeared. Poof! Some of the townspeople were said to have practiced witchcraft back in those days. They believed the smell was a sign of black magic and a warning against its consequences. Isn't that spine-tingling?"

The hair on Marigold's arms rose as if a cold wind had blown right through her. *A smell of rot?* This was sounding all too familiar.

"Grandmama even said there were rumors that the same smell would come back every couple of decades, and when it did, something terrible always happened on the island," Miss Eugenie went on. "It was part of an old curse."

"What kind of terrible things?" Marigold asked, her voice quavering.

"I don't know," Miss Eugenie said. "Grandmama never would say. She was particular about the inappropriateness of frightening small children."

"Just so," Miss Lizzie said.

"You haven't smelled any strange smells around here lately, have you?" Marigold asked, trying to act casual and not let on how much the story had scared her.

"I did notice the garbage was more pungent than usual on Starline Way this week, and I've already complained to Mr. Jackson. But that has nothing to do with Grandmama's stories. The curse is merely an old superstition," Miss Eugenie said. "I only know of it because Grandmama was quite superstitious herself. Why, nothing odd has happened on this island since before I was born."

"Well, except for the earthquake." Miss Lizzie stopped and looked at Miss Eugenie. They both pressed their mouths closed.

Marigold stepped back. "I should get home."

The two ladies didn't try to stop her as Marigold hurried from the deck, lost in thought. Mama was afraid of the smell. It was written across her face. Daddy had asked about any recent accidents. Did he know about this curse?

According to Miss Eugenie, Marigold was right to be worried because the smell could mean something terrible would happen on Luna Island. Marigold's family, Sam, and many others could get hurt, even killed. That was bad enough without the additional fact that it wouldn't take long for the town to blame the Lafleurs.

Especially when they realized the smell was coming from their yard.

CHAPTER SIX

Lemon balm has a cleansing effect on the mind.

So yeah, that's about it," Marigold said, having filled Sam in on everything at lunch in the cafeteria the next day. "A curse is getting ready to descend over the island." She leaned forward in her seat and whispered in her best horror-movie voice, "We all could die at any moment."

Sam reared back. "Who said anything about dying?"

"Well, if you're cursed, you could die. Everyone knows that about curses."

"Miss Eugenie isn't the most reliable source. Remember when she started the rumor that Mr. Jackson was planning an eight o'clock curfew for everyone under twelve?"

"But this isn't a rumor. It's actual fact. The Great Hurricane happened. And now there's a rotten smell around my house that won't go away and it's spreading. Two terrible things occurred this past week that luckily didn't end up doing great harm, but who knows what might happen next!"

Sam bit his lip. "I'm not sure I believe it, but I see your point. I did notice the smell when I was over at your house. What do Birdie and Lou say about this?"

Marigold rested her elbows on the table. "They think I'm overreacting. Birdie said she'd talk to Mama, but I can tell she doesn't believe me."

The small windows beside the food line showed a steady, gray rain outside. The smell of tater tots and soggy green beans mingled with the scent of antiseptic cleaner from the linoleum floor. All around them, seventh and eighth graders were pressed next to one another, eating and talking. Yet their end of the table was deserted. Lauren sat across the room with Kendall. They were surrounded by a group of eighth-grade boys. Marigold sighed. When she'd tried to sit there during the first week of school, all the seats had been taken, and nothing had changed since.

Marigold kicked her heel against her chair. "I feel bad that you eat lunch with me every day. Don't you want to eat with Will and Charlie sometimes?" Her question lingered in the air, pungent and uncomfortable, like week-old garbage.

"No," Sam said. "I like this table. It's close to the tater tot line."

Marigold gestured to the empty seats around them. "But we're alone."

"You're the one who decided to sit at an empty table. Despite what you think, not everyone cares that you come from a long line of witches, or about what happened last year."

"Yes they do. I'm your pity friend," Marigold said pathetically.

"No, you're my best friend, who's also a mess right now."

"Tell me how you really feel," Marigold muttered.

Sam picked up his second ham sandwich and raised one eyebrow in a funny expression. "I always do, lucky for you."

Marigold cracked a smile despite her worries. It was impossible to stay annoyed with Sam.

"But maybe sometimes *both* of us could hang out with Will and Charlie at lunch. They might make you laugh too," Sam said. "You could hear about the band. We're getting better with every practice."

Marigold breathed in, and a sharp burning aroma flooded her nostrils. She squeezed her eyes shut tight. *Push it away.*

"But Will is terrible," Marigold blurted out. She buried her face in her hands. It was even harder to suppress her gift when she was upset or tired. "I'm sorry! I didn't mean to say that."

"It's okay. Plus—" Sam groaned. "It's true. Will's bass solo was so bad yesterday, my ears were bleeding. He'll get better, though. At least I hope so; otherwise we're going to bomb at the pep rally."

Marigold hung her head, mad at herself for intruding into Sam's private thoughts. "I don't know why I can't handle this better. I keep practicing in my room, breathing out and concentrating on getting rid of all smells so I can control this. It never works."

Sam sighed. "I know you don't want anything to do with aromagic—"

"I don't."

"Okay, but maybe your nose is trying to tell you something."

"Is it trying to tell me I'm a freak?" Marigold asked, and flopped her head onto the table.

Sam sighed. "It's trying to say you can't ignore this part of yourself. Your ability to control your gift has gotten worse since you stopped helping with your mama's potions. What if—" Sam hesitated. "What if your aromagic wants out?"

Marigold gulped. "No way. It's not getting out. I told you, aromagic is bad."

Sam frowned, not looking convinced.

"Blurting out people's secrets isn't even my biggest problem right now. What am I going to do about the curse?" Marigold moaned.

"Start with eating." Sam handed her half of his second sandwich. "I'm full anyway."

Marigold took it gratefully.

"So how do we figure out more about this supposed curse?" Sam asked, drumming his fingers along the table.

Marigold eyed Sam. This was what she'd wanted to bring up. "I can think of one person who might be able to help."

Sam squinted at her, then started shaking his head. "No. No way."

"I haven't even said anything," Marigold protested. "But if we did go see—"

"Marigold, she made my granny die," Sam said.

Sam could play his guitar in front of an entire music classroom. She'd seen him dive deep into a murky marsh to chase a striper. Sam never got scared, except around Gram.

"Gram did not make anyone die," Marigold said. "She smelled you going on a journey to Alabama, and that's where you went five days later."

"For my granny's funeral," Sam whispered.

"I have to go see her," Marigold said. "It's the only way

I can think of to get some real information. I know she's a little creepy—"

"A lot creepy," Sam said.

Okay, Gram was strange. She lived in the woods in Eastport, in a small house that smelled of spicy incense, and all the windows were covered with thick black curtains, so you had to strain your eyes to properly see. A battered pot was always heating up something on the stove, covered and mysterious, and green-tinted steam misted out of it like it was a real-life cauldron. Marigold hadn't seen Gram since Daddy had gone into the hospital last spring, and she absolutely didn't want to go see Gram alone.

Sam cradled his forehead. "You're gonna owe me big."

"Anything," Marigold said, her shoulders collapsing in relief.

"You have to come to our band practice and give me your honest opinion," Sam said.

"Definitely," Marigold promised. "We'll take the ferry over next week. Monday after school?"

Sam gulped. "All right. But if she starts sniffing me, I'm totally out of there."

After school on Friday, Marigold folded her legs beneath her on the couch and placed her hands on her knees. She was trying to focus on the single rose she'd placed on the coffee table. So far, it wasn't working. Birdie had suggested this as a way to learn to control or, better yet, contain her gift for smelling secrets. She closed her eyes and blew all her air out through her nose once again. She smelled chamomile from her tea and the lavender candle on the mantel and—and—

"Marigold." Mama called her name from the basement.

Marigold's eyes flew open. Mama had avoided Marigold since their talk at Dream Pies two days ago. *What could she want now?*

After cautiously making her way down the rickety steps to the basement, Marigold stepped onto the concrete floor. The high windows tucked beneath the ceiling let in the dimming afternoon sunlight and cast a pretty glow onto the large wooden table that dominated the center of the space. Clear glass vessels, funnels, and pipettes were lined up in careful rows on a counter beside a battered white sink. Jars of dried herbs, flower extracts, and exotic spices crowded onto thick wooden shelves along the walls.

Before the earthquake, Marigold and her sisters would work with Mama on her charms from time to time. Mama had always tried to help the people of Luna Island. Lou would use the mortar and pestle, and Birdie would lift Marigold up to reach the jars on the top shelves. Even Mama had been focused and relaxed then, humming as she'd mixed the ingredients together. Yet Mama didn't hum as she used to, and Marigold never came down here any-more if she could help it.

"I was hoping you'd gather some lemon balm leaves for me," Mama said. She plucked a dash of cardamom seeds from a jar and sprinkled them over the glass vessel in front of her. Marigold stopped herself from moving closer to see what else Mama might add. Would it be jasmine for love or eucalyptus for healing? A coral plume of smoke drifted from the glass, beckoning Marigold closer.

"Why do you need the leaves?" Marigold asked, mes-merized by the smoke.

Mama turned to the shelves behind her, her voice muffled. "A small purification charm."

Marigold's eyes snapped up. "For who?"

"Myra Picado is divorcing her husband. This will clear the house of negative energy."

"Did Myra ask you to make it?" Marigold asked, crossing her arms.

"If you're too busy, I'll gather it myself," Mama said, not meeting Marigold's gaze.

"Did Myra ask you to make the charm?" Marigold asked, insistent.

Mama wet her lips. "Not exactly. I smelled her fears when I passed her at the marina today. She needs this, and if I present it to her—"

"Mama, you can't meddle in people's lives," Marigold said sharply. "Especially now. What if that charm causes a vex and Myra forgets her husband ever existed?"

"That's ridiculous," Mama said. "Purification charms are harmless."

"We can't take the chance. Something strange is going on. You know it as well as I do."

"I already told you, the smell is nothing to worry yourself about," Mama said.

"But it won't go away, and other people are starting to notice. Sam overheard his mama's bridge club talking about it yesterday. They think the garbage collector is skipping streets or not bringing our bags to the right dumping site, but that's not it. There's something unnatural about the smell, and how do you explain the ferry accident?"

Sam had said that mechanics had examined the boat and hadn't found anything wrong with it, which was further evidence of this unexplainable island curse. The last thing the Lafleurs needed was Mama tampering with someone's fate, causing harm, and putting more blame on their family.

"The ferry accident has nothing to do with us. I wish you would remember. Aromagic is nothing to fear." Mama reached out a hand as if to touch Marigold's arm but dropped it before making contact.

Marigold stared at the space between them. She remembered how Mama used to tuck her in every night, pulling the covers all the way up to Marigold's chin and folding them around her arms until she was cocooned in blankets. When was the last time that had happened? It was before Daddy had moved out. Now Mama went straight to her room after supper most evenings, though Marigold could sometimes hear her pacing, the floorboards creaking late into the night.

"I'm home," Birdie called from above.

"You should go," Mama said, her head bent over a book.

Marigold wanted to say more but wasn't sure what words to use. Instead she clambered up the stairs and went into the kitchen.

Birdie was staring down at a piece of paper, her brows drawn together. Her eyes widened as she caught sight of Marigold. She quickly crumpled up the paper and shoved it into the garbage can.

"What was that?" Marigold asked.

Birdie turned to fuss with the kettle on the stovetop. "Nothing."

Birdie never could meet Marigold's eyes when she was lying. Marigold opened the lid on the garbage pail and plucked out the crumpled paper.

"Wait, that's just garbage, M," Birdie protested. "Don't read that."

Marigold scanned the words written in large, block letters: WE HATE WITCHES! LEAVE LUNA ISLAND! There were a few mean curse words below. A painful tightness seized Marigold's throat.

"It's probably that kid from the ferry," Birdie said, grabbing the note and tossing it back into the pail.

Marigold stared down until the old floorboards blurred. It was like last April all over again. Things weren't getting better like Birdie and Lou had said they would.

"Look, even if some silly people think we caused the ferry crash, they'll forget about it soon enough. This talk never lasts," Birdie said.

"Unless something worse happens. The smell outside isn't going away."

Birdie tipped up Marigold's chin. "I know you're worried about this old curse idea, but I'm sure there's nothing to it. There's no one around to curse anyone, except for us, and even Mama wouldn't do that."

Marigold didn't argue. She knew Birdie's mind was made up, and without more evidence, Birdie would only continue to say there was no problem.

"You have that audition tomorrow, right?" Birdie asked.

"You remembered," Marigold said, pleased.

"Of course I remembered. You've only mentioned it fifteen times or so in the last week." Birdie made a mock surprised face. "I also might have heard you practicing a monologue in your room. Do the lines require you to shout quite that loud?"

Marigold couldn't help smiling. "It's called intensity."

"I remember your intensity when you played Alice in Wonderland and got into a yelling match with the Queen of Hearts."

"I loved that scene." Marigold warmed at the memory. The crowd of parents had laughed at all her lines. "But this part is a much bigger deal. The whole town comes to the middle school play."

Birdie sank into a kitchen chair. "Do you need help with your audition song?"

"That would be great. And I have another tiny favor." Marigold clasped her hands into prayer like she was a prisoner in a movie begging for mercy. "Will you help with painting the sets? There's always tons of volunteers, so you won't have to do much. It could be fun?" She quickly glanced at the garbage pail with the crumpled-up note inside, its ugly words seared into her mind. She wanted to add, *I'm sure the town will appreciate our help,* but decided against it.

Birdie's face softened. "I've got a lot of schoolwork right now, but I'll think about it."

Marigold smiled. That meant Birdie would do it.

"Now, did you hear about Tara Ricketts?" Birdie asked.

"Turns out her husband, Ray, got some amazing job offer like Mama promised. Only problem is, the job is in Alaska, and Mrs. Ricketts hates the cold."

"Fate demands its price," Marigold said.

"This time it's demanding it in the middle of nowhere." Birdie cocked her head and stared out the window, her eyes far away. "Not that I would necessarily mind. I'd go anywhere to escape from here. There's so much else to see."

For an instant Marigold imagined a world without Birdie cooking supper, helping Marigold run lines, and checking on her at night. It was a world Marigold never wanted to live in.

"Do you really want to leave Luna Island that badly?" Marigold's voice quavered.

Birdie's eyes sharpened on Marigold. "Not anytime soon. Not until we're all ready to go."

"Good. Now if we can only get Daddy back too, everything would be perfect."

Birdie shifted away, her face cast down.

Marigold bit her lip, interpreting Birdie's silence as the blame she deserved. "I know it's my fault he's not here."

Birdie's head popped back up. "No, it's not. You didn't mean for any of this to happen. This is Mama's and Daddy's mess."

"Daddy couldn't help getting hurt," Marigold said.

"But he could have helped what happened before, his fighting with Mama and leaving in the first place," Birdie said fiercely.

"Well, the good news is that Daddy is getting better and he's coming home soon," Marigold said in a bright voice. "I know it. I'm absolutely positive. You have to expect the best, and it will happen."

"You're right." Birdie pulled Marigold to her in an abrupt, one-armed hug. "And you know what? I talked to him last night, and he's already planning for our visit next month."

Right then Birdie's phone dinged in her pocket. She pulled it out and scanned the new text. Her mouth tightened. "Are you kidding me?"

"What's the matter?" Marigold asked.

"It's Lou. She's skipping supper again. She was supposed to buy the chicken on her way home from practice. Typical. She's so thoughtless sometimes!" Birdie's jaw jutted out. "Sandwiches it is."

"Sandwiches are fine with me. I'm not upset."

"I am," Birdie spat, clenching her hands on the arms of the chair.

"Wait until you hear some of my lines from the end of the first act," Marigold said, trying to change the subject. "They're so funny, you won't be able to stay mad at anyone."

"Lines in a play won't make me feel better."

Marigold squinted at her sister. Was she really that upset? "Lou's skipped supper before. It's not a big deal."

The sky outside the kitchen window grew a bit darker, and the fading light traced Birdie's smooth cheeks. A tiny muscle twitched near her mouth as if she were holding in a torrent of words.

Birdie finally exhaled, relaxing her hands. "You're right. I'm just exhausted from everything—Lou not doing her chores, kids at school talking about college applications, Daddy not around to help out . . ." She swallowed and looked away. When she turned back to Marigold, she'd pasted a smile onto her face. "It's okay. Don't worry, M. Grilled cheeses for supper?"

"Sounds good to me!" Marigold said, also trying to smile.

Birdie went upstairs, but Marigold stayed still. She thought back to how angry Birdie and Lou had gotten with each other after the ferry accident, and the way Birdie had looked when she'd just received Lou's text. This wasn't her calm, even-keeled sister. Marigold couldn't help but wonder if the smell was affecting more than the town—if it was *infecting* the Lafleurs themselves.

CHAPTER SEVEN

Sunflower harnesses positive energy and bestows luck.

Auditions for *The Magical Town of Oz* were held in the town auditorium on Saturday afternoon. By the time Marigold arrived, there was a crowd already gathered in the first four rows. The heavy red velvet curtains framed Ms. Ballard standing center stage. She clapped her hands, and everyone quieted down. Marigold crept to the aisle and slipped into a seat toward the back. The plush forest-green seats sloped down to the stage. Above were two large chandeliers dripping with crystal, and a balcony with more seating. She imagined the auditorium full of Luna Island residents, all clapping for her as she took her final bow onstage in a few weeks' time. No one would be thinking about the earthquake.

"I'm glad to see all of you here today," Ms. Ballard said. "I recognize many of you from our production last year but see a bunch of new faces too. For today's auditions we'll hear you sing one stanza and one refrain from the song of your choice, as well as perform a short reading. Based on that, we'll make our decisions for the callback auditions."

Ms. Ballard was one of the youngest teachers at Luna Island Middle School and wore her black curls piled high on her head in a large bun. Her cheeks were tinted tulip pink against amber skin, and her eyes crinkled with her frequent smiles. Everyone who'd performed in one of the school plays talked about how Ms. Ballard bought pizzas for late rehearsals and wrote a personal note to every cast member before opening night. Marigold had been looking forward to performing for her for years, but instead of being excited, she was nervous. There was so much at stake.

Ms. Ballard smoothed down her denim dress and gestured to the last row. "And don't forget to ask your family and neighbors to help with our production. There are sign-up forms in the back."

Marigold had already signed Birdie and Lou up to help

with set painting. Birdie hadn't fully agreed, and Marigold hadn't talked to Lou about it yet, but she was sure they'd both help.

Ms. Ballard called Megan Gleeson up first. The opening bars of her song filtered through the air, but Marigold barely heard them. She was too busy going over the words to her song in her head. There was no room for error; she couldn't forget a single note. Rubbing her temple, she thought about how she would have felt a whole lot better if her sisters had helped her rehearse the night before.

Though their battered family piano was woefully out of tune, Birdie and Lou could both pluck out a simple melody. Marigold had counted on them to help with her audition song. But last night Birdie had holed up in her room to study, despite promising earlier to help. Lou had come home late with a headache and had collapsed on the couch. For the first time that Marigold could remember, there had been no sister to give her a pep talk or help her practice.

Anna slid into the seat beside Marigold as Megan finished up her song. "Are you nervous?" she whispered.

Marigold stared at her, wondering why Anna was speaking to her. They'd never had a real conversation before. Anna kept her head down in class and sat in the last row. She didn't seem to talk much with anyone. "A little," Marigold replied.

"I'm petrified," Anna confided. Her teeth flashed chalk-white in the dim light.

"I didn't know you liked theater," Marigold said.

"Oh, I don't really," Anna said. "But *The Wizard of Oz* is my favorite movie, and this play is based on that, so I thought it might be fun. I'm regretting my decision now. I don't have any experience like you. You were so funny in that Declaration of Independence skit last year."

A warmth spread through Marigold's chest as she remembered the audience laughing at her lines, and how wonderful it had felt when everyone had applauded at the end. That was before everything had gone wrong last spring. "Thanks. But I was nervous too."

Anna's mouth dropped open. "Really? You seemed so calm."

Marigold shook her head. "I was a wreck before."

"Maybe there's hope for me, then," Anna said with a small smile.

Marigold's shoulders relaxed. She did have experience. She'd always managed to secure a role in their class skits and annual elementary school plays, even as one of the youngest kids. Plus, she wanted this more than anyone else did. That must count for something.

"Anna Perez," Ms. Ballard called out. "You're up."

Anna stood, her face tense and worried.

"Break a leg," Marigold whispered.

Anna gave her a wobbly smile. She crept down the row, skittish and hesitant. Marigold hoped Anna didn't completely embarrass herself. She probably had one of those whispery singing voices you could hardly hear.

The voices in the auditorium silenced as the music began. Anna stood on the stage, twisting her hands together. Marigold was sure Anna was about to faint, until she started singing.

Anna's voice was high and pure, her tone as smooth as rich chocolate coated in cream. It easily reached every corner of the auditorium. She hit each note perfectly. When she finished, there was a burst of applause. Anna beamed as she stepped off the stage.

"Marigold Lafleur," Ms. Ballard called.

Marigold sank deeper into her seat. Her forehead broke out in beads of sweat. This was a total disaster! Of all the terrible luck in the world, she had to sing after Anna Perez, the secret singing star of the seventh grade. There was no way Marigold was getting the lead, not after that performance.

"Marigold," Ms. Ballard called again.

Marigold stood, her legs shaking. She brushed past Anna returning to her seat.

"Good luck," Anna said.

Marigold didn't respond. Her mouth wouldn't work. She trained her eyes forward as she forced her legs to walk to the stage.

After her audition Marigold went out into the hallway. She'd sounded fine, remembered all the words, and nailed the high note at the end. If Anna hadn't gone before her, she would have thought she at least had a shot at the lead role.

After slipping into the restroom, Marigold went into one of the stalls, closed the door, and leaned her head against the hard plastic of the door. The cool surface was comforting against her flushed cheeks. Why had Anna chosen this year to try out? This play was Marigold's best hope of reclaiming her life. This was her chance to get her friends back and make everyone forget about the earthquake, her weird mama, and her cafeteria meltdown. Now, though, she'd blown her chance by not being the best.

The bathroom door creaked open, and footsteps echoed across the floor.

"I'm not saying she was bad. She has a good voice. All I'm saying is, there's no way Ms. Ballard is going to give her the part."

Marigold peeked through the crevice between the door and its frame. Lauren, Alison, and Julia had walked into the bathroom. They stood in front of the sinks, pulling lip gloss out of their pockets and applying it in the mirror.

Lauren leaned in close to the mirror, examining her rose-tinted cheeks. "You're right. Ms. Ballard knows the entire island will flip if Marigold gets the lead."

They were talking about her. Heat swept across Marigold's chest. She stood absolutely still.

"I don't know. Her song was pretty," Julia said.

Lauren leaned against the sink. "Things have changed since the earthquake and her daddy. Do you really think it's a coincidence he was the only one hurt right as her parents were getting a divorce?" She lowered her voice. "And Marigold looked so embarrassing that day in the cafeteria when she was freaking out in front of the entire school. If her mama didn't cause the earthquake, how could Marigold have known it was coming? My mama says the whole family is down in that creepy basement of theirs every night brewing up potions that could make your skin break out in boils, and confuse you into forgetting your name."

"That's not true," Julia protested. She lifted her heavy curtain of straight black hair into a long ponytail. "Marigold isn't like that. She's nice."

"My mama said the Lafleurs are bizarre and always have been," Alison said. "Some people are even saying they're behind the ferry accident last week. All three of them were there. I'm not sure why you think Marigold is any different."

Marigold's entire body clenched. Tears pooled in the backs of her eyes. Is this what everyone thought about her and her family, that they were bizarre and made people's skin break out in boils? Yes, Libba Acker had developed a temporary rash when she'd used a beauty charm to darken her lips. And sure, Macon Corrigan had forgotten his name for twenty-four hours after Mama had given him a memory charm to find his lost wedding ring, but it had only happened one time!

"You're good friends with her, aren't you?" Julia pointed out to Lauren.

"We're not good friends," Lauren said, sniffing. "We were friends. I felt sorry for her, okay? I always knew she was strange. I almost never went over to her house, and the couple of times I did, her mama was never around. There were always these weird smells. It was terrible." She shuddered. "I never slept over. I was way too scared."

"I wish you had," Alison said. "You might have some cool stories for us."

"You're right," Lauren said, laughing. "I should invite myself over there to spy."

"Totally," Alison exclaimed.

Tears trickled from Marigold's eyes, leaving hot tracks down her face. All those times Lauren had invited Marigold over and confided about how her mama called her sister the smart one in the family and wouldn't let Lauren have chocolate because of her complexion. Marigold had believed Lauren trusted her with these secrets, had imagined they were close. It sure didn't sound that way right now. It didn't sound as though anyone on the entire island liked her. How could Marigold ever look at Lauren again? It was one thing to guess what people were saying about you. It was entirely different to hear it come out of their mouths. She wanted to curl into a ball on her bed and never leave her house again.

"We should get back," Julia said. "I'm up soon."

The girls exited the bathroom, chattering away as they pushed open the door and stepped into the hallway. Marigold's breaths came in short gasps, and she couldn't stop her eyes from welling up again. She needed to get out of there before anyone saw her.

Yet she stayed put, the girls' words imprinted on her brain. She was weird. Her house smelled terrible. No one wanted to be friends with her anymore.

Why wasn't there a charm to make her life normal? Marigold wished Mama got up in the mornings. She wished Daddy lived in their house again. She wished there were no worries about an earthquake or a curse. Most of all, she wished she didn't have an ounce of aromagic. Right then Marigold wished she could change every single thing about her life, including herself.

• • •

Lou was sitting on the front porch wrapping a bandage around her left ankle when Marigold plodded up to the house, her eyes still stinging with tears.

"What happened?" Marigold asked.

Lou clambered to her feet, putting a tentative bit of weight on her left foot. She winced and lowered herself back into the rocking chair. "I rolled my ankle in practice."

"Does it hurt?" Marigold asked, leaning down to examine the puffy ankle.

"Not too bad," Lou said. "It was worth it. I scored on Callie, and Coach is starting me for the next game. I'm the only sophomore to start on varsity."

"That's good, I guess." Marigold sat beside her in the other rocking chair, barely hearing Lou. She kept remembering Anna's audition and what Lauren had said in the bathroom.

"What's wrong with you?" Lou asked.

Marigold rocked back and forth, the movement soothing. "Unlike your practice, my audition didn't go so great. I'm never going to get the lead."

The wind whistled through the trees around their house, bringing with it the scent of brine and roses and the now familiar rot. Well, at least the awful smell suited her mood today. Her chin trembled. All her hopes for things getting back to normal seemed silly now. There was no chance, not with what everyone thought about her.

"But the lead isn't what you really want," Lou said quietly, a statement not a question.

Marigold whipped her head in Lou's direction. Was she smelling what Marigold wanted? "We promised we wouldn't use our powers."

"I can use my powers if I want." Lou pressed her mouth into a firm line.

"But Birdie says—"

"*Birdie* doesn't know everything," Lou said in an overly loud voice. She bared her teeth, reminding Marigold of a snarling wolf.

"I know that," Marigold said quietly, leaning away from the anger on Lou's face.

Lou relaxed her mouth, the sudden flash of anger gone as quickly as it had arisen. Yet Marigold couldn't help feeling as if Lou's anger were right under the surface, ready to raise its head and bite her if she said the wrong word. It was as if Birdie's name were the trigger for Lou's rage, but why would her sister's mere name make Lou so upset?

"Anyway, I didn't use aromagic on you. I wouldn't invade your space like that. I'm not the most sensitive Lafleur, but I don't have to use aromagic to guess that something else is going on with you." There was a hurt tone to Lou's voice.

She stood, putting weight on her uninjured foot and turning to go inside.

"Wait," Marigold said, grabbing Lou's arm to stop her. "You were right."

"You don't have to tell me," Lou said, shaking Marigold off.

"I want to. I—I thought if I got the lead role in the musical, I could make everyone like me again. I thought I could make them forget about the earthquake. But I overheard some girls saying I'd never get a good part. They're probably right."

Lou opened, then closed, her mouth. She sank back into her seat and stared at the wisteria vines creeping up the side of the porch.

"You think it's silly," Marigold mumbled.

"That's not true," Lou protested. She rapped her knuckles on the arm of the rocking chair. "I think it's ambitious. What's next—taking over the island? World domination?"

"I'm considering that for next year," Marigold said, her mouth turned up in a small smile.

"Good to know you're realistic," Lou said. "It wasn't a horrible plan, and it can still happen. They haven't decided on the roles yet. You have a chance."

"Not much of one," Marigold said, frowning. "There's another girl who's better than me."

Lou leaned toward Marigold, her face intent. "Then

don't let her be better. Use everything you can to get what you want. Sometimes you have to take a risk and break a few rules. It's not enough to sit back and let life happen to you." Her eyes gleamed aquamarine, and she swept her arm out toward the sea and the world beyond "We deserve more than this."

Marigold squinted at her sister, not understanding. "I don't know what kind of risks you're talking about, but I'm practicing really hard, if that's what you mean."

"That's part of it," Lou said encouragingly. "You should sing that song from *The Sound of Music*. The one you're always belting in the shower. You sound great on that."

"You really think so?" Marigold asked.

"I do. I've got a good feeling about this role, Marigold," Lou said, smiling.

Birdie sauntered up to the house, carrying a bag of groceries. She stared at Lou's bandaged ankle. "Are you okay?"

Lou waved her off. "Fine."

"I picked up chicken for supper. How was the audition?" Birdie asked Marigold.

Marigold looked at Lou, and Lou lifted her chin as if to encourage Marigold to lift hers as well. "I did okay."

"But?" Birdie asked, resting the grocery bag on her hip.

Marigold hesitated.

"Some of the other girls were jerks after the audition,

and Marigold is worried about getting a good role," Lou said, saving Marigold from having to go into it all over again.

"But Marigold is an amazing singer. She *should* get the best role. I swear, sometimes this town . . ." Birdie glared hard into the distance. "You know what? Forget chicken. Let's have popcorn and ice cream for supper, and Marigold can pick the musical."

The stinging in Marigold's eyes lessened for the first time since she'd overheard her ex-friends in the bathroom. "But it's Saturday night. Don't you both have plans?"

Birdie shrugged. "I can skip them."

"Makes sense. Brant will only like you more if you play hard to get," Lou teased.

Birdie turned red. "I was going out with a big group. I don't even know if Brant will be there. Not that I really care," she said hastily.

"Sure you don't," Lou said in a knowing voice. "Well, I can't do much tonight anyway because of my ankle. I'm up for a musical as long as Marigold promises not to sing every song."

"I'll settle for half," Marigold said, grinning.

Lou groaned.

It was Daddy who'd started the tradition of watching musicals with Marigold. They always made popcorn and had their own spots on the couch—Marigold on the left side and Daddy on the right. But last year, work had always seemed to come up on movie nights. Marigold had watched the musicals alone those first few times, trying not to look over at the empty space beside her. But then Birdie and Lou had begun slipping into the living room as the opening credits rolled. They'd watch the entire movie, even if Lou complained about the dance numbers and Birdie did her homework on the coffee table.

"I'll get *Annie* ready on the television," Marigold said happily now.

Birdie swept open the door, asking what kind of ice cream they wanted. Lou limped after her, wondering aloud why there weren't more horror musicals. Marigold lingered on the porch. Her sisters' words had soothed the roiling in her stomach. It wasn't going to be easy to get the lead, but her sisters were right; auditions weren't over yet and she was a good singer. She could prove she was more than one unfortunate event in the cafeteria, more than the rumors surrounding her family. She still had a chance. Her sisters had said so, and if there was anyone Marigold believed, it was Birdie and Lou.

CHAPTER EIGHT

Sage leaves promote wisdom.

It was Monday afternoon when Marigold and Sam hopped off their bikes and threw them into the tangle of bushes beside the dirt path. Gram's cottage lay directly ahead, nestled in the trees. Deep green vines crept up the sides of the house, twining into curlicued patterns along the dark gray shingles. Flowers spilled onto the front walk in a riot of roses and violets. It might have looked welcoming, if not for the large sign pinned to a tree trunk that proclaimed NO SOLICITORS in big orange letters. Marigold stared at the house, not knowing what to expect.

"You're sure she knows we're coming?" Sam asked.

"Positive," Marigold said. "Mostly positive."

"Mostly positive?" Sam's face tightened into an accusing frown. "You said you told her."

"I left a message. She didn't call me back, but I'm sure she's looking forward to our visit," Marigold said doubtfully.

"How long has it been since you last saw her?" Sam asked.

Marigold shifted back and forth, knowing Sam was not going to like this answer. "Um . . . maybe . . . around six months."

"Six months!" Sam yelped. "That's practically forever. What if she's mad you haven't visited in so long? This is a terrible idea. I say we go straight home and send her a super nice email asking how to break a curse."

"Gram doesn't have a computer. It'll be fine," Marigold said, dragging Sam forward by his arm. "If she slams the door in our face, we'll leave."

"I just hope she doesn't decide to curse us too," Sam mumbled, pulling on his purple hair.

"She won't." Marigold sounded confident, but her insides were quaking as she and Sam approached the door. Gram wasn't the friendliest under good circumstances, like when Daddy brought her hazelnut chocolates and charmed her into a pleasant mood. Showing up after six months of no contact probably didn't count as a good circumstance.

Marigold hopped up the two steps and rapped her knuckles on the door. The sound echoed in the quiet woods.

"Maybe she's not here," Sam said hopefully.

Marigold knocked on the door again and waited. Nothing. Her shoulders drooped as she considered the closed-up house.

The door was flung open. Startled, Marigold tripped backward off the step and into Sam, who also lost his balance and tumbled to the ground, pulling Marigold over in the process.

Marigold looked up. Gram glared down at them.

"What are you doing here?" Gram barked.

Marigold sprang to her feet, dusting off her jeans. "I came for a visit."

Sam popped up, his eyes wide. "She made me come."

Marigold tried a winning smile. "I hope you got my message."

"I didn't," Gram said.

"We can come back another time," Sam said, already backing up.

"We won't stay long," Marigold said, grabbing Sam's arm.

"Well, I suppose you can come in since you're already here." Gram moved to one side. She kept her silver hair coiled into a bun and had tawny-colored eyes with irides-cent green flecks, as if someone had sprinkled green glitter inside a bottle of amber perfume. Only, right now these eyes were annoyed.

Marigold kept smiling, praying she looked natural as she followed Gram inside. Sam quietly groaned behind her.

Gram led them past the kitchen, with dish towels hung side by side at the same precise angle. The familiar black pot bubbled on the stove, and wisps of smoke curled from the top. The whole house smelled of sage and lavender with a hint of ginger. Sage bestowed wisdom. Perhaps the smell was a good sign; Marigold needed some answers.

The sitting room overlooked a backyard crowded with trees. Four iron chairs circled a low, dark wooden table. The room itself was painted a deep eggplant. It was like stepping into a dark cave with no escape.

Gram sat down in a chair and gestured for them to fol-low. Sam perched on the edge of his seat, ready to bolt at any second. Marigold gave him a reassuring smile, though her throat was as dry as dust. What if Gram refused to tell them anything?

"How is your father?" Gram asked.

"Much better," Marigold said.

Gram eyed Marigold carefully. "When did you last see him?"

"A month ago," Marigold said. "He's almost ready to come home."

"Mmmm," was all Gram said, as if she didn't believe a word of it.

"He misses us," Marigold added.

Marigold didn't mention that she couldn't understand why Daddy wasn't home already, especially because she needed him. They'd missed their Saturday FaceTime call because of her audition, and when she'd called to tell him about the curse after talking to Miss Eugenie, he'd been on his way to physical therapy. He'd promised to call later that evening. That was five days ago, and she hadn't heard from him yet. Of course, he was busy getting better, but he still should have called back by now.

"I doubt you're here to inquire about my health, and I've never been one for pleasantries. So we might as well get on with it. I know why you've come," Gram said.

"Did you read our minds?" Sam whispered, his eyes widening.

Gram curled up her lip. "Don't be ridiculous, Samuel. I spoke with Evelyn last week, and she told me the peculiar smell has returned."

"Yes, exactly. Mama won't tell me what it means, but I know it's something bad." Marigold's mind flashed back to when Birdie had been a hair away from that bolt of lightning, the townspeople lying on the dock after the ferryboat crash, and her sisters getting into an argument every time they spoke to each other. "I heard rumors about a curse. But I know it probably isn't real and there's a reasonable explanation—"

"The curse certainly is real. It's been real for over two centuries," Gram interrupted.

Marigold froze. "Are you saying people on Luna Island were hurt by this curse before?"

"The curse has hurt many islanders but only because they were in the wrong place at the wrong time. It isn't Luna Island itself that's cursed. It's us." Gram leaned forward and stared into Marigold's eyes. "The *Lafleurs* are the ones who are cursed."

Marigold gasped. Her body deflated like someone had taken a pin to the balloon in her chest. Deep down she'd known there was something wrong. She'd hoped Gram would brush off her concerns. Or tell her how to quickly get rid of the curse. She should have known it wouldn't be that easy to remove whatever was hovering around their family. But Gram was confirming her deepest fears—her family, maybe even the island too, was in serious trouble.

Gram continued to speak. "I'm not going to hide this from you. I told Evelyn time and again to be careful, but did she listen to me? No. She never worries about consequences."

"Why now? Please, what is the curse?" Marigold asked.

Gram cleared her throat and recited, "'Bound by blood and born as friends. The rot foretells the bitter ends. Misfortune and hate tear apart. Dark magic stole a sister's heart.' The curse started with our ancestors Clemence and Elise. Clemence's daughter found that poem amongst her mother's papers after her death." She gave them a pointed look. "Clemence left a warning."

"What kind of warning?" Marigold whispered.

"Whenever the Lafleurs have two or more daughters, an older sister leaves the family before adulthood. From what I know, one Lafleur died during a flu epidemic, another ran away, and another burned in a fire that swept the island. My own aunt feuded with my mother and left Luna Island, never to contact her again. And it goes all the way back to the founding of Luna Island. As you may know, Elise perished in the Great Hurricane. Sometimes the curse causes a natural disaster on Luna Island such as the Great Hurricane of 1811 or the fire of 1876, and sometimes it merely causes a rift between sisters that can't be mended. But each time, a rotting smell was prevalent on the island and someone in the family was gone within a matter of weeks."

Sam and Marigold exchanged a look. The horror on his face mirrored her own.

Marigold counted backward to when she'd noticed the smell. "But it's already been nine days."

"Yes," Gram said solemnly. "You haven't got much time."

"Maybe those things in the past were all a coincidence," Marigold said in a desperate voice. "A lot of bad stuff happened in olden times."

"There are some in our family who have shared your point of view. They believe these unfortunate events are mere accidents. Yet I've studied our family history. This is the reason why my mother and I each had only one daughter. We were afraid of the curse repeating itself." Gram's eyes were pitying. "I'm sorry to tell you this, Marigold. The Lafleurs are cursed to lose a sister."

Marigold's vision went dark. *A curse that might hurt Birdie or Lou?* But—but Mama was barely around, and Daddy was on the other side of the state. Without her sisters, she had no one, except Sam. Her hands were shaking like leaves in a windstorm. "Birdie and Lou . . . they're everything to me. I can't lose them f-forever," she practically yelled, trying to hold back the anger and fear building inside her.

"We have to fix this!" Sam burst out.

"There's no simple fix. A curse is different from a vex, which is a consequence of you changing your own fate. A curse is misfortune wished upon you by another. It's outside our control," Gram said.

"Why didn't Mama or Daddy warn us about this?" Marigold asked.

"Evelyn doesn't believe in it, and she convinced your father it wasn't real. She only called me the other night because she got spooked. The other day, when I called to check in on you, she was back to saying it's all superstition," Gram said.

"But you believe," Marigold said. "You think the curse has started again."

Gram folded her hands in her lap and stayed silent, not denying the statement.

Marigold stared hard out the window, her eyes stinging like blazes, her lungs squeezed tight. She spotted the large oak tree outside and remembered when she'd hidden beneath it during a game of hide-and-seek and had fallen fast asleep. Lou had woken her with a crushing hug before shaking her soundly. Birdie had scolded Marigold in a raspy voice as if she'd been crying. Afterward, Lou had given her a piggyback ride into the kitchen, and Birdie had given her the last cherry Popsicle. As the youngest, Marigold had usually had to make do with lime, the flavor no one really wanted.

"Okay," Marigold whispered. She forced herself take a slow, steady breath, then spoke more loudly. "So how do we end this thing? How do we break the curse?"

Gram sighed and looked away. The silence between them was thicker than wet sand. "That's a difficult question to answer. Many of your ancestors have tried."

"There must be something," Marigold said. "It's like at the end of every movie when the lead finally solves the problem by trying one more thing. There's always something you can do to make things better. Everyone knows that. It can't be—it's not—" A hiccup cracked her voice. Marigold closed her mouth around a sob and buried her face in her hands.

"I didn't say it was impossible," Gram said.

Marigold looked up, tears pooling in her eyes.

"Highly improbable, yes. But not impossible," Gram continued.

A faint glimmer of hope stirred inside Marigold. "Whatever it is, we'll do it." Marigold turned to Sam, and he nodded agreement, his face full of determination.

"The first thing you must understand is that the curse spans generations, which means it's not an ordinary hex tied to one person. It's tied to something else—a malediction," Gram said.

"A male-what?" Sam asked.

"Ma-le-dic-tion," Gram repeated, emphasizing the syllables and glaring at Sam. "It's a physical object to which the curse is bound. To break the curse, you must find the malediction and destroy it."

"What does it look like?" Marigold asked.

Gram lifted one narrow shoulder and dropped it back

down. "I don't know. A malediction can be nearly anything. But for the curse to have survived this long, it's still intact."

"What if it's a rock?" Sam asked.

"Did I say it could be a rock?" Gram asked. "No, I did not. It must be something of great significance to the wielder of the curse. A rock. How preposterous."

"How do we destroy it?" Marigold asked.

"Melt it down, break it into pieces, crush it. You must physically destroy the object. At least, that's what I've been told," Gram said.

Marigold rubbed her temple. A headache was forming behind her eyes. The impossible reality of this task was beginning to set in. How could she find and destroy a two-hundred-year-old object when she didn't even know what to look for?

The wind blew cold and bitter on the ferry, and the water frothed around the sides of the ship, splashing against the window as the ship cut through the ocean on its way back to Luna Island. Marigold and Sam had taken seats at one of the booths inside the passenger cabin and were huddled over the papers Gram had loaned them.

Before they'd left, Gram had given them a shoebox filled with old letters from various Lafleur women over the years. Many of the pages were spotted with water, wrinkled from folding and unfolding, and yellowed with age. Gram had said these might provide some clues about the malediction. She hadn't looked particularly confident about their chances, but it was all she could do by way of helping them.

Sam's face was bright with excitement. He sifted through the letters as if they were made of gold instead of paper. He loved research, especially if it was about something out of the ordinary and not well known. He'd spent one entire summer researching dog allergies when his dog, Major, had a bee sting reaction.

"Now, this is interesting." Sam pointed to the page in front of him. "This is a letter from Millicent Lafleur to her mother in 1892. She apparently studied magical histories, and it's her belief that the curse imprints onto the original spell location. If the malediction is moved from that location, the curse loses all power."

"Why does that matter?" Marigold asked. The closer she got to home, the more she wanted to believe the curse didn't exist and the terrible things that had happened to her ancestors were only bad luck. Yet try as she might, she couldn't dismiss that the two bizarre events, the lightning storm and the ferry accident, had both happened when her sisters had been around. She couldn't forget the smell that clogged her nose every time she left the house, or the strange animosity growing between her sisters.

"It matters because this means the malediction is still on Luna Island. Millicent says the curse wouldn't have lasted this long if it had been moved." Sam grinned. "Don't you see? This is great news. Now we know to look on the island."

"I guess. But we don't know what we're looking *for*." Marigold dropped her head to her forearms and moaned. "Face it, Sam. We're never going to find it. Maybe the curse will take me instead of my sisters."

Sam flicked the top of her head. "Stop whining and think. We have to narrow down the possibilities of what the malediction could be."

Marigold raised her head at Sam's words. An idea began to form. "Wait a minute. Gram said this all started with Clemence and Elise. They were the first ones cursed. So, if we want to narrow down the possibilities, we have to figure out who held a grudge against them."

Sam slapped a hand onto the table. "You're right! Once we figure that out, we can look for an object that belonged to that person."

"A member of the five founding families must have wielded the curse," Marigold said. "They all had some magic in them."

Gram had told her about the founding families before. According to legend, the Willards baked feelings into their food, and the Spencers spotted patterns in the water to predict when a storm might occur or an unwelcome visitor might arrive. The Allertons healed fellow islanders with their touch, and the Foxes heard what someone didn't want to say out loud.

"We can keep looking through the letters and read up on Luna Island history," Sam said.

"I can search through Clemence's diary, too. Maybe that will give us a clue about who hated her. Once I tell Birdie and Lou what I learned, they'll want to help; I'm sure of it."

"And hey, maybe you can even mix up one of your charms to help us find the malediction," Sam said.

Marigold frowned. "I can't make a finder charm without knowing what I'm trying to find. Anyway, even this won't get me to brew a charm. I won't do aromagic anymore, Sam. I'll make something awful happen if I try." The image of a falling tree hurtled into her vision. She blinked it away.

"It was just an idea," Sam said, backing down at whatever he saw on Marigold's face. "We'll rely on our investigative skills. No problem."

"Exactly. No problem," Marigold repeated, trying to sound as positive as her best friend.

Yet as Marigold stared out the ferry window and the island came closer into view, fatigue settled into her body. Though she wanted to remain hopeful, it was impossible to ignore the fact that for hundreds of years no Lafleur had managed to find and destroy the malediction.

CHAPTER NINE

Plumeria is most powerful at night when used to alleviate family discord.

T he note was nailed to the front door, the words in large black letters like a scar upon the splintered wood. *LEAVE THIS ISLAND BEFORE WE MAKE YOU!*

Marigold froze. On the porch, below the note, was a dead seagull. It's feathers were waterlogged and bedraggled, and its eyes were blank and staring right at her. It must have washed up along the beach. She was glad Sam hadn't walked her home. If he'd seen this, he would have insisted on starting another investigation into whoever had left this for her to find. But she only wanted it to stop.

Tearing down the note, Marigold crumpled up the paper and crammed it into her backpack. She nudged the bird out of the way. The rotten smell flooded her nose. She'd stopped in the Moon Market on her way home and heard the checkout girls gossiping about the stench; they'd said Mr. Jackson was checking the dumpster behind the store after getting complaints. What would happen when everyone realized the smell was much stronger in her yard? Even worse, what if people like Miss Eugenie remembered the stories from Luna Island's history and tied the smell to the town's misfortunes? If she and her sisters couldn't break the curse, something else was bound to happen. The town already wanted them gone; another tragedy would run them off the island for good.

Marigold burst into the house, ready to spill everything she'd learned from Gram, but she heard shouts ricocheting off every corner of the living room. Lou stood in front of the fireplace, her fists clenched by her side. Birdie's face was mottled red like the skin of an apple.

"I know you used aromagic," Birdie said in a loud voice. "I can smell it. Stop denying it!"

Lou threw her hands up, her own voice sharp. "Fine. You're right. I used aromagic. Not that it's any of your business, but all I did was improve my shots at the goal line."

Marigold sucked in a breath, unable to believe what she'd heard. Why would Lou do something so dangerous?

"Of all the stupid things to do. You're always out for yourself," Birdie yelled. "You could have hurt someone! We made a pact!"

"You made the pact and demanded we go along with it," Lou yelled back. "You're such a control freak!"

Marigold swayed on her feet as she considered how to fix what was going on in front of her. This wasn't ordinary fighting. Yes, Birdie and Lou sometimes snapped at the other, but they didn't hurl insults and scream. They didn't narrow their eyes and curl their fists. This was the curse already working, driving them apart like Gram's poem had predicted.

Marigold took a tentative step forward. "I know what's going on here—"

"It's not fair to expect me to ignore aromagic forever," Lou interrupted, not even glancing at Marigold. "You don't get to tell me what to do. You're not my parent." Her face was pale, and her foot tapped the ground. This jittery Lou looked all wrong.

"Our parents are basically nonexistent right now," Birdie said.

"That's not true," Marigold shouted, trying again to get their attention.

Lou turned, her gaze finally fixed on Marigold. "Do you really need to get involved?"

Marigold bit her lip, frowning at Lou's rude tone.

"There's nothing you can do here, M," Birdie said dismissively.

"All I was going to say is that Daddy *will* come home soon," Marigold said.

"Doubt it," Lou muttered.

Marigold's chest itched. "I know you're both upset, but I have to talk to you. I just came from Gram's house."

"Why would you go there?" Lou asked, wrinkling her nose.

"Mama's keeping a terrible secret from all of us, and we have to do something about it." Marigold stared into their eyes, making sure she had their full attention. "We're suffering from a family curse."

"I'm sorry, what?" Birdie said, her brows raising like winged arches.

Lou started laughing.

Marigold huffed out a breath. "I'm not kidding. Gram told me everything. The Lafleurs are cursed. One of you is going to leave or get hurt!"

"I hope monsters aren't coming to get us." Lou had stopped laughing, though a half smile still lurked around the corners of her mouth.

"I've never heard this before," Birdie said, frowning. "Why wouldn't Mama have said something about a curse?"

Marigold hesitated. "She doesn't believe it's real."

"Well, it's probably some silly superstition of Gram's and means nothing," Birdie said, brushing off Marigold's concerns.

"It's not like that. Gram told me about our family history, about all the accidents and feuds between lines of Lafleur sisters, and it's true," Marigold said, her voice rising. Her hands were shaking now. Saying everything out loud suddenly made it all the more real.

"You know Gram. She's always got a story to spin," Lou said. "Besides, who's going to curse us? There aren't any other families that still practice magic on Luna Island."

"Not anymore, but there was all kinds of magic here once," Marigold said.

"This is ridiculous. I have things to do, and besides," Lou said, and glared at Birdie, "as you can tell, we're all still stuck here together."

"What's that supposed to mean?" Birdie shot back. "You wouldn't survive without us taking care of you."

Lou tried to move around Marigold, but Marigold wouldn't budge.

"What about the awful smell?" Marigold said. "That's the first sign of the curse."

"It's been abnormally warm," Lou said. "Things smell worse in the heat. So what?"

"It's not a normal garden smell, and you know it," Marigold said. "And I think the lightning storm, the ferry accident, and all your fighting is because of the curse."

Birdie looked troubled. "Maybe Marigold has a point. I'm not saying there's a curse." She brushed her fingertip along the windowsill and frowned down at the dust clinging to her skin. "But something doesn't feel right either. You're both making me crazy, and it's not as though either of you are much different than normal. Lou, you're still acting selfish all the time, and, Marigold, you're still acting immature, so I'm not sure why it's annoying me so much."

Marigold's jaw dropped. "I'm not immature."

Lou leaned against the mantel, pale but still furious. "I couldn't care less what you think."

"Only a selfish person says she's not worried about people thinking she's selfish," Birdie said smugly. "I'm right, as usual."

"You certainly think so, as usual," Lou said, and edged around Marigold.

"Wait!" Marigold said, tugging on Lou's arm. "We need to talk about this and figure it out. I need your help. We have to work together to break the curse."

"You always overreact, Marigold," Lou yelled, shaking

off her hand. "Life isn't a movie with you as the star. We're not all going on an epic quest to break a nonexistent curse."

Marigold swallowed, her eyes pricking with tears. "I know that. But—"

"I'm going to lie down. Don't bother me," Lou added, and left.

Birdie edged toward the door, not meeting Marigold's eyes. "Sorry, M. I don't know what's going on, but I can't bring myself to care about it right now. Not with Lou being the way she is at the moment. I need to get started on my homework." Without a backward glance, Birdie strode out of the room.

Marigold gazed outside at the darkening sky as it spit out drops of rain. She knew something was wrong at Lilac Cottage. Her sisters didn't act like this. After everything they'd gone through in the past year with their parents separating, Daddy moving out, the accident . . . the three of them were all one another had. Her sisters were all she had.

Sweat broke out on Marigold's forehead and her heart galloped inside her chest. She couldn't lose her sisters, yet there was no possible way she could break the curse on her own. She was only twelve years old. A wave of dizziness knocked her over, and she collapsed onto the couch, trying to catch her breath.

Several long moments passed, and Marigold's heart rate

steadied. The spots faded from her vision. She focused on the incense by the door, the smell of faded mint tea leaves still in the mugs from that morning, gardenia from Birdie's perfume, vanilla from Lou's lotion. She curled onto the couch.

From across the hall the basement door beckoned. Mama kept Clemence's diary in the basement. Marigold sat up, remembering her earlier plan to search the diary for clues. She could at least do that.

After hurrying across the hall, Marigold crept down the stairs and flicked on the iron pendant lights suspended from the ceiling. She wasn't sure when Mama was coming home and didn't want to be caught snooping around in her stuff. Marigold crossed to the mahogany wardrobe along the far wall. Tugging on the thick metal handle, she opened the center doors and peered inside. She spotted Clemence's diary in the back and pulled it out. Leaves and flowers embossed the worn leather cover, and the thick paper was yellowed. Though she hadn't seen it for months, the deep and mysterious smell of vetiver seeped off the pages, the same as always.

Marigold slid down to the floor, turned the book over carefully in her hand, and opened it. The pages were covered in faded black cursive writing. She flipped through Clemence's entries until she found the months leading up to the Great Hurricane, before Elise's death.

Scanning the pages, Marigold read about how Clemence and Elise had concocted charms to bring luck to a friend while fishing, and to ward a neighbor's home against evil. Elise was eighteen years old and Clemence only fifteen, but they'd already left their home—a small town in Louisiana—and settled on a wild island. Though, it certainly wasn't easy. On June 1, 1811, Clemence wrote:

> *Some days I think I might die without my sister.*
> *She's the only one who understands me. It is so hot*
> *here on this island, as if we are living on the sun.*
> *Yet Elise's laughter is a cool breeze, her pleasant*
> *moods the only respite from my own dark thoughts.*

Clemence and Elise might have been sisters, but from reading the diary it was clear they were the best of friends too. They lived together, worked together, enchanted together. Marigold sighed, longing for her own sisters. Though they were only upstairs, they seemed an ocean away tonight.

Marigold continued reading. She knew about Clemence's unique talent because Mama had told Marigold stories. Clemence could smell when someone suffered from a broken heart, and it seems she didn't always want her talent, the same as Marigold. On June 8, she wrote:

Jacob Spencer smelled of rotten eggs today. His
fiancée fled Luna Island months ago. I fear his
heart is hurt forever. This gift of mine feels wrong.

Marigold kept flipping through the diary, searching for anything useful. Peering down a few pages later, she stopped at an entry on July 6:

Everything has gone wrong. May Fox blames
me for her daughter's death. She mourns at her
daughter's grave, day and night, clutching her
beloved locket. I should have refused like Elise
warned. Yet I could smell May hurting, and she
pleaded . . .

There were several scratched-out words Marigold couldn't decipher. She raised her head, suddenly scared to continue. This had all taken place over two hundred years before, but in the dim quiet of the basement, Clemence's predicament was as urgent as the curse hanging over Marigold's own head. Dread rose inside her like the crashing tide on the beach as she peered back down.

Elise believes the Foxes will retaliate. The family
heads have called a meeting at the insistence of the

Shadow Lady. She's tried to run us off this island before, and her influence is considerable. Now the Foxes, our only allies, have turned against us as well. I'm scared for what will come.

Marigold went cold as she reread the words. Turning the page, she could see the binding was ragged and tufted with bits of paper. Someone had torn out a page from the diary, and the next entry began months later, after the hurricane and Elise's death. Marigold didn't know what had happened at the meeting or who the Shadow Lady was. Yet any further answers were long gone. She had to make the most of what she did know.

There had been a rift between the Lafleurs and the Foxes over the death of May's daughter. The diary also mentioned May holding a *beloved locket*. Maybe May had cursed the Lafleurs, and the locket was the malediction? That was a possibility. It was at least something. But if that was the case . . .

Goose bumps chased themselves up Marigold's arms. There was only one Fox descendant left on Luna Island, and he lived deep in the Whispering Woods. Legend said if you listened hard enough in those woods, there were echoes of unsaid whispers in the trees. That was creepy enough on its own without the other problem of Curtis Fox himself.

Mr. Fox didn't associate with anyone and hardly left the woods. There was a rumor that he kept several poisonous snakes on his property to ward off visitors. One time he'd yelled at Marigold when she'd accidentally stumbled into him at Dream Pies. She'd never forgotten the spark of anger in his eyes.

Closing the diary, Marigold held the book in her lap. The realization of what she must do next plunged through her as if she'd jumped into the depths of the ocean in midwinter.

Marigold had to brave the Whispering Woods. She had to talk with Mr. Fox.

CHAPTER TEN

Magnolia purifies the surrounding environment to grant longed-for wishes.

The following day after school, Marigold slumped in her seat in the town auditorium, waiting for her callback audition. She was trying to stay positive for even making callbacks, but her heart wasn't in it. Usually she ate breakfast with her sisters every morning, but Birdie had left before Marigold had woken up today, and Lou had pointedly ignored her while sipping her coffee. The curse was working its horrible magic, and it seemed to grow stronger by the minute.

To make things worse, the callback auditions had her skin fizzing with nerves. There were so many people watching, and not just students. Along the back row were several townspeople. Miss Eugenie and Miss Lizzie were chatting away as usual, along with Miss Abigail; Mr. Corning, owner of the Moon Market; and Mr. Keith, editor of the local newspaper, the *Luna Island Ledger*. Mr. Wilmer, who ran the Go Fish Supplies and Hardware Store, always built the sets and kept bustling onto the stage between auditions to take measurements. The rumor was that this year's set design would be the most elaborate one yet, with an actual Emerald City built out of wood.

Though everyone knew Ms. Ballard had the final say on casting, the other townspeople donated time and money to the play for costumes, the auditorium rental, and publicity. There was an unspoken understanding that they weighed in on who was cast too.

Anna had already sung and, if possible, had sounded even better than during her first audition. Lauren, Julia, and Alison lounged in the front row, acting as if they were the judges rather than Ms. Ballard. Marigold dreaded standing onstage today, after what she'd heard them say in the bathroom. If she got the lead, maybe it wouldn't make Lauren her best friend again, but it might temporarily take Marigold's mind off everything at home and get at least some of the town back on her family's side. If everyone got to know her better, they'd stop being afraid of her. They'd remember that her family was a part of Luna Island, just like everyone else.

Anna took the seat beside Marigold.

"You sounded amazing," Marigold said, a tinge of sadness in the words. She was happy for Anna but wished it were her sounding that good, assured of the lead.

Anna shrugged. "To be honest, I can't tell. I couldn't even find a place to practice last night because my brothers took over the family room and the basement. Two were watching baseball and one was watching football."

"They won't let you rehearse?" Marigold asked, curious. She'd never heard Anna talk about her three older brothers.

"Oh, sure they will. But not if it interferes with their sports. I swear it's the only thing they care about." Anna chuckled and didn't seem actually mad about it. "I keep trying to make a deal with them where I'll sit through an entire football game if they'll watch My Fair Lady with me. It's my favorite musical."

"I love musicals, especially My Fair Lady," Marigold exclaimed. A pang of longing rose in her chest as she thought of watching the musical with Daddy two years before. She still hadn't talked to him since last week and needed to call him tonight.

"It has the best costumes, like the black-and-white dress with the big hat," Anna said.

"That's the most beautiful one," Marigold agreed.

"We should watch it together sometime," Anna said, ducking her head.

Marigold nodded, surprised at the offer but happy to get it. "That would be fun."

Anna looked up and smiled. But when she glanced over Marigold's shoulder, her brow furrowed. "I think your sister is here."

"Th-that's impossible," Marigold spluttered. She peered into the darkness. Lou's fiery red hair was unmistakable in the thin light seeping through the crack in the doors. She stood at the edge of the last row and lifted a hand to wave at Marigold.

Marigold fumbled with the pages of her sheet music. "What's she doing?"

"She's here to support you. You're lucky," Anna said.

"Marigold Lafleur, you're up next," Ms. Ballard called.

Marigold stood, clutching the pages to her chest.

"Good luck," Anna said cheerfully.

Marigold walked slowly up the aisle. Lou hadn't even spoken to her that morning. Was she here to support Marigold, or yell at her like she had last night? A sick churning began in Marigold's stomach. Lou might say something terrible in front of half the town.

The heavy red curtains framing the stage smelled of old

sweaters that someone had packed away all summer. Her shoes made echoing thuds as she crossed the wooden floorboards to hand her sheet music over to Mr. Ford at the piano. The spotlight in the center reflected off her eyes, and gold halos clouded her vision. The figures in the audience looked hazy, but she could see Lou sneaking down the side aisle.

The piano began playing the first tinkling notes. Marigold's legs wobbled, but she steadied herself. She sucked in a breath and started singing, barely hearing her own voice. Her eyes locked on Lou, who was reaching into her pocket.

Lou pulled out an object and held it aloft. Light glinted off the small glass bottle—the kind Mama used for her charms—with a gold atomizer at the top. Dread coated Marigold's entire body in a cold sweat. *Put it away,* Marigold urged Lou in her head. *Don't ruin my audition.* Yet to Marigold's horror and utter shock, Lou raised her hand and sprayed into the air above her.

Suddenly the most delicious scent filled the cavernous room. It was balsam wood and magnolia and a hint of exotic musk. It was relaxation and happiness, Marigold's favorite memories. A collective sigh rose from the audience.

Each person in the auditorium tilted their head and leaned closer to the stage. Their attention was glued to Marigold, who was singing better than she ever had in her life. The music came from deep in her chest, a place she hadn't even known existed. She hit every note. Her voice became more powerful; the high notes soared into the rafters. Marigold was the best singer she'd ever heard!

Marigold's thoughts sprinted through her mind as she kept singing. The mist was obviously enchanted, and Marigold might pay the consequences. She should stop right now and end this entire audition. *And yet* . . .

Marigold saw Ms. Ballard beam her widest smile at the stage. Lauren's mouth hung halfway open. The door in the back flew open, and all the students still in the lobby streamed into the auditorium, crowding behind the townspeople in the last rows. There was an intake of breath from at least fifty people when Marigold hit a high note.

Despite knowing that Lou's charm was helping her, Marigold grinned. She simply couldn't stop. When the song wrapped up, the entire auditorium sprang to their feet, clapping wildly.

Lou bowed her head to Marigold before slinking up the stairs and out the door. Marigold froze under the spotlight, not sure what to do next. Her gut squirmed as if the worms in Mama's garden were digging holes inside her. Lou had rigged the competition. It didn't seem fair. . . . Except Marigold needed this role right now, probably more than anyone else. Didn't she deserve something good after everything awful that had happened?

Ms. Ballard flew up to the stage, still clapping. "Well, I think we've found our lead actress. Marigold, you were a revelation!"

Marigold ducked her head, unsure what to say. Guilt warred with excitement. She'd gotten exactly what she wanted . . . but at what price? But maybe there was no price. She could have gotten the lead on her own, and she would have at least made the play. Her singing was good without aromagic. Lou had given her the extra push she'd needed but hadn't actually changed fate.

As Marigold climbed down the steps, Julia stopped her. "You were incredible."

"I thought you sounded like a professional," Lauren said from behind them. "Are you going to Dogwood Coffee Shop later?"

"You should join us," Julia urged.

Marigold hadn't set foot in Dogwood Coffee Shop since last spring. All the middle schoolers hung out there after school, grabbing decaf coffee milkshakes. But she hadn't wanted to walk in alone and suffer the embarrassment of standing in line by herself while everyone stared at her, whispering behind their frozen drinks.

"We'll meet you there after the auditions," Lauren said, as if Marigold had already agreed to her plan. "Friends help each other celebrate. You're the lead!"

They were friends now? But what about the things Lauren had said behind Marigold's back last weekend?

"I don't know," Marigold said, looking away, a hollowness expanding in her chest. Why did she still feel so unhappy? This was what she wanted, wasn't it?

"Oh, come on. After all those times we practiced singing in my room and dreamed of starring in the musical, and now you've done it. My mama always said you had the best voice," Lauren said.

Lauren's face settled into that slightly sad, one-cornered smile Marigold remembered. Maybe Marigold had misunderstood Lauren in the bathroom. Maybe Lauren had only said those things because she was scared of Marigold after Daddy's accident and the earthquake, the same way a lot of people were. What if now Lauren realized Marigold wasn't terrifying and wanted their friendship back?

"I'll try to be there," Marigold said to Lauren, smiling.

As she moved up the aisle, several other kids reached out their hands to high-five her. They were saying things like "amazing," "the best song I've ever heard," and the sweetest word of all, "congratulations." Marigold's face lit up.

Miss Abigail stopped her in the aisle. "I'm committing some additional town funds for the sets. We've got to make sure the scenery lives up to our star's talent."

Miss Iris beamed. "I'm proud of you, Marigold. Great job!

I guess all those performances in your living room paid off."

"I guess they did." Marigold used to insist on singing a song for Miss Iris when she was over visiting Mama. It had been at least a year since that had happened, but Marigold was touched that Miss Iris remembered.

"Ask your mama if she's interested in joining the planning committee," Miss Eugenie said. "We spearhead this entire production and oversee all the volunteers. It's a *very* select group."

"Very," Miss Lizzie echoed.

Marigold nodded and smiled, her heart as light as air. Her getting the lead, Mama joining the planning committee . . . it was only a matter of time before they were a welcomed part of the community again. It was everything she'd hoped for.

Anna's eyes were soft and wide when Marigold took her seat. "You were wonderful. I don't blame Ms. Ballard for giving you the lead on the spot. I'm really happy for you."

"Thanks," Marigold said, sinking down. Another twinge of guilt reverberated inside her like the pluck of a guitar string. "I'm sure you'll get a good role too."

"I probably would get horrible stage fright if I had to stand up in front of a full audience anyway. You're the one who deserves it."

Did she? Marigold wasn't sure.

Ms. Ballard called Tom Lee to the stage. He liked to play the comedic roles and was always pretending to trip or was twisting his mouth into these crazy faces at school.

"Come on, Tom." Ms. Ballard beckoned to him. "We don't have all day."

Even from her seat near the back, Marigold could see Tom frozen by the stairs. The din in the audience hushed as everyone realized something wasn't right.

"Are you okay?" Ms. Ballard asked, moving to the edge of the stage.

"N-no," Tom said. "I can't go onstage. I'm scared." He turned on his toe, raced up the aisle, and stumbled on his way out the door.

After a long moment of total silence, some uncomfortable whispers and giggles filtered through the auditorium. Tom was obviously playing one of his pranks, Marigold thought. Except, when he'd run by her, his face had looked absolutely terrified.

Genevieve Brolin was next. When she began singing, every note was flat or sharp or completely wrong. Clapping a hand over her mouth midsong, she went silent.

"I don't know what's wrong," Genevieve burst out, and hurried off the stage.

"She sounded good in the last audition," Anna whispered. "Do you think she has a cold?"

Marigold shook her head, unable to come up with an explanation for why Genevieve suddenly couldn't sing a note.

"Nico Jones?" Ms. Ballard said, a hint of concern lacing her voice.

Nico bounded up to the stage, a broad smile across his face. On the last step he tripped and fell flat on the ground with a resounding boom. A collective gasp rose from the audience. When he lifted his head, the gasp turned into groans. Blood streamed from his nose. Ms. Ballard raced back up to the stage and helped him to his feet.

"I'm sorry, everyone, but we're going to have to end the auditions here. I believe I've heard enough to assign parts. I'm taking Nico to the emergency room. Thank you all for coming today." Ms. Ballard's voice was calm, but under the lights her face looked worried as she escorted Nico out.

"What a weird ending to the callbacks," Anna whispered.

Marigold couldn't speak because she knew this wasn't normal sickness or fear or nerves or accidents. This was something else entirely. This was the result of aromagic. Fate had demanded its price for Marigold's audition, and the price might be a musical disaster.

CHAPTER ELEVEN

Sweet pea can banish negative energy and put an end to gossip.

Marigold skipped the Dogwood Coffee Shop and headed straight home. The closer she got to the house, the stronger the sickly-sweet smell became. She ignored it, flung open the front door, and stomped into the living room, where Lou was lying still, her feet kicked up on the couch. The floors creaked under the heavy tread of Marigold's shoes, echoing her anger. Late afternoon shadows shrouded the room, making the space look darker and gloomier.

"This is all your fault," Marigold said in an accusing voice.

Lou opened her eyelids and frowned. There were gray smudges under her eyes, and she looked even paler than she had that morning. "What are you talking about?"

"The auditions today. You used aromagic."

"Yeah, I know," Lou said. "You're welcome, by the way."

"Thanks for nothing. You gave the rest of the cast stage fright and bad luck! Someone might have broken their nose," Marigold half shouted, her breath coming fast and hard. "Ms. Ballard had to cancel the callbacks."

"So what?" Lou rolled her eyes. "I don't see why you're upset. You got what you wanted."

Marigold's phone chimed three times in a row with incoming texts. She pulled it out of her pocket and checked the screen.

Julia: missed u at dogwood!!!

Kendall: congrats on the lead!!!

Lauren: u were the best today! find me at lunch tmrw!

"Who's texting you?" Lou asked.

"Just . . . friends," Marigold said, shoving the phone back into her pocket. Her phone chimed twice more.

"Seems like your grand plan worked," Lou said, smirking.

Marigold crossed her arms. "I didn't want to cheat."

Lou sat up, her legs dropping to the ground. "Oh really? You could have stopped singing at any time. You saw me spray the charm. But you didn't stop, did you?"

"I thought about it," Marigold said, her eyes sliding to the side.

"And you decided to keep going because you wanted the lead. I don't blame you," Lou said. "If a few people couldn't audition after that, well, bad luck happens sometimes."

"But it happened because of me." Marigold sank onto the couch, the fight draining out of her. "I feel awful about it."

"I'm sure it's only temporary," Lou said.

Marigold clasped her head. "What if it's not?"

Lou only shrugged, not looking concerned.

"This isn't like you," Marigold said. "You've always cared about what happens to other people."

"I care most about what happens to me," Lou said matter-of-factly. "I won't apologize for that. You should feel the same way. And part of that means not ignoring our aromagic anymore. We deserve to use our gifts."

"We should tell Birdie about this." Marigold shifted uncomfortably.

Lou stiffened. "Birdie won't help with aromagic. If you had heard what she said to me last night . . ." She stood up and clenched her fist as if the very thought made her want to punch something.

"Whatever it was, I'm sure she didn't mean it. What if we all discuss it together over hot chocolates?" Marigold had to convince Birdie and Lou to start speaking to each other again. She couldn't let her sisters' entire friendship disintegrate right in front of her eyes.

"I'm done talking to her," Lou said, and started to make her way out of the room.

"This is the curse, Lou," Marigold said, her voice a plea. "If you help me break it, you won't feel so mad at Birdie anymore."

Lou curled her lip in a sneer. "There's nothing supernatural about the fact that Birdie and I disagree about everything. I'm tired of listening to her tell me I'm wrong all the time. Now I'd like some quiet before she comes home and ruins the rest of my night."

For the first time Marigold registered that Lou shouldn't even have been home yet. She usually had a field hockey game on Tuesdays. "Didn't you have a game?"

"I skipped it today," Lou said, looking too tired to make her way upstairs and lying back down on the couch.

Marigold stared at her. "But you love field hockey. You'd never skip a game."

Lou was holding something back, but Marigold didn't know what. She could usually read her sisters like lines on a script. Not now, though. She had no idea what Lou was thinking.

"Did something happen?" Marigold prodded again.

"I have a headache," Lou said.

Marigold noticed the beads of sweat on Lou's brow. "Do you need me to get you something?"

"That's okay. If I rest, it will go away." Lou winced.

"I'm worried about you," Marigold said.

Lou sighed. "It's nothing. I used a charm for some help with a geometry test this morning. I've had a headache ever since."

Marigold bit her lip. When had Lou forgotten that aromagic was dangerous? What about the promise Lou had made to her and Birdie not to practice anymore? Her fighting with Birdie was causing Lou to act recklessly. She would never have done this if she'd still trusted her sisters' guidance.

"Stop looking at me like that," Lou growled.

Mama wandered into the room, holding a large basket filled with blooms and a brown paper bag from the Moon Market. The riot of pale pink and white sweet peas peeked over the side of the wicker. She fussed with the flowers, not looking at her daughters. "Everything okay?"

"Fine," Lou said shortly.

Lou eyed Marigold, the warning on her face clear. *Don't say anything.* Marigold cast her eyes down. She might not have liked what Lou was doing, but she kept her sisters' secrets always.

"What's in the bag?" Marigold asked as a distraction.

"Frozen burritos for supper," Mama said, looking pleased with herself.

"Frozen burritos taste like frozen manure," Lou said, pushing herself to standing.

Normally Marigold would have laughed at the joke, but Lou's words weren't teasing and light. They were flat and mean.

"You could say 'thank you.'" Mama raised her eyebrows.

Lou clapped her hands in a slow, deliberate slap. "Thanks for making such a big effort to fix an impressive supper of frozen burritos. It's only been a few months since you bothered or cared that we've eaten. Mother of the year award, for sure."

Mama stared at her. "What's wrong? Something smells off."

"What's wrong is everyone in this house." Lou left the room, stormed up the stairs, and slammed her door. The little cottage shook with the reverberation.

"What did I walk in on?" Mama asked.

Marigold blinked back the tears in her eyes. Lou had skipped field hockey and hated Birdie and was harming herself with aromagic. Nothing was as it should have been. This was the curse, the awful, hopeless curse. She had to figure out how to break it.

"I never know what's going on in your heads," Mama said quietly.

If Mama didn't know what was going on, it was because she never wanted to know. She was too busy sleeping in till late morning and staying up all night with her charms. She no longer asked how Marigold's day was or sent her off to sleep with one of their famous family stories. It was as if when Daddy had left, Mama had too.

Weariness settled over Marigold. She didn't know what she could say to make Mama understand. Mama was part of this problem. She hadn't believed in the curse or tried to find the malediction herself before having three daughters. If she had, maybe Marigold wouldn't have been on the verge of losing everything she cared about.

"I don't want to talk about it," Marigold said.

"Is this because I haven't cooked in a while?"

"A *while?*" Marigold laughed bitterly. "You haven't cooked in months. But no, the problems in this house have nothing to do with your cooking. The problem is the curse."

Mama shook her head. "I don't know what you're talking about—"

"You do. And if you can't see that it's real, you don't understand anything."

Marigold fled up the stairs to her room. She flopped onto her narrow bed. The sky was darkening outside, and shadows loomed in the corners. She wanted to pull the covers over herself and disappear until Birdie and Lou came to their senses and fixed this problem between them. They could end the curse if they tried. Or at least help Marigold figure out what to do.

Marigold reached for her cell phone with shaking fingers. She needed to hear Daddy's voice right away.

Daddy picked up on the third ring. "Marigold, how are you?" His face came into view on the screen. Green eyes twinkled at her.

"Not that great," Marigold said. She then registered the voices in the background, loud and happy. Music blared through the phone.

Daddy shook his head. "Sorry, couldn't hear you. Can you speak up?"

"Why is it so loud?" Marigold asked.

Daddy used the phone to pan around him. Beside rows of books was a long dark wood bar along one wall. Tables and chairs filled with people surrounded him. Daddy was sitting at his own table with a bearded man in a flannel shirt and a tall woman with a mane of black hair. At the front of the room was a small band with a banjo player, a drummer, and a fiddle player.

A smile lit up Daddy's face. "Our local coffee shop is having a concert tonight. One of my physical therapists is playing in the band."

"Richard, who's that?" a high feminine voice called.

"It's my daughter," Daddy said, smiling at the woman across the table from him.

"I thought you needed rest," Marigold said stiffly.

Daddy shrugged. "I'm trying to get out now and then."

"Looks like you're too busy to talk," Marigold said.

Daddy rose to a half crouch. "I can take this outside if you need me."

Marigold wanted to scream, *Yes, I need you. I'm your daughter and I have no one*. But how could she say that when he didn't want to even come home to her?

Swallowing, she said, "That's all right. I need to go anyway."

"Are you sure?" Daddy glanced off to one side and spoke to the person out of range of the phone screen. He wasn't even giving her his full attention.

The music was growing in volume at the coffee shop. Daddy looked to the stage, smiling. That was a smile she hadn't seen in a long time, and it wasn't meant for her.

She disconnected the call without saying goodbye.

CHAPTER TWELVE

Iris and sassafras are a deadly combination signaling danger. They must never be combined.

Vines climbed up Curtis Fox's shack. A few red paint flecks still clung to the old metal door, and one black shutter swung from a single hinge like the flapping wing of a bird. The front yard was overgrown with knee-high grass and a tangled mess of weeds; huge trees created a dark canopy overhead. It did not look like the sort of house you wanted to visit.

All was silent in the Whispering Woods on Wednesday afternoon. Staring down, Marigold scanned the ground for snakes. This would have been a lot less scary with Sam, but he had a dentist appointment, and she couldn't wait any longer for this trip. Her sisters hadn't spoken to each other for almost two full days. Besides, she could handle this alone. She had to.

From out of nowhere, a wind rose, tugging at strands of her hair.

Beware.

The voice came from behind her, so faint that she barely heard it. Marigold's head whipped around, but there was no one. A nervous laugh escaped her. Nothing to worry about. No one was talking to her. The legendary whispers of Whispering Woods weren't real. She only needed to focus and—

Beware.

Marigold startled. There it was again, that one word weaving into her ears. Was it a warning in her head, or was something in the woods speaking to her? Her hands trembled. She sniffed the wind—iris and sassafras, jealousy and peril. This was not a safe place. But she already knew that. She only had to ask Mr. Fox a question and get out of there as quickly as possible.

"What are you doing on my land?"

Marigold froze before slowly turning around. Curtis Fox loomed, having snuck up behind her. He was a tall man with wide shoulders. He wore a stained gray sweatshirt and baggy brown pants. His face was dotted with gray stubble; he ran a hand over his head where a few stray white hairs clung stubbornly to the top.

Marigold tried to deliver her signature smile, the one she'd imagined using on the red carpet someday. "Hi there. I'm Marigold Lafleur."

"I know who you are," Mr. Fox said through clenched teeth. "What I don't know is why you're trespassing. You best leave before I get real angry."

Marigold didn't want to stick around to find out what real angry looked like to Mr. Fox. Honestly, regular angry was scary enough. Yet she couldn't leave. Her sisters' future was at stake.

"I—I'm doing a presentation for my history class on the original founders of the island, and I was hoping you could tell me more about your relative May Fox. It was so interesting how she, um, helped build this house and . . ." Marigold's voice faltered as Mr. Fox glared at her.

Marigold had practiced these lines in the mirror at home. It was part of her plan. After she got him talking about May, she'd casually ask about the locket, convince him to let her borrow it for her fake presentation, and then destroy it somehow. She hadn't worked that part out yet. It had seemed like . . . well, if not the best plan, at least an okay plan. Normally grown-ups loved to help kids with school projects, but she was beginning to suspect that Mr. Fox wasn't that kind of grown-up.

Mr. Fox's eyes narrowed. "What do you know about May?"

Marigold racked her brain for a good answer. "I know she was friends with my ancestor Clemence Lafleur."

To her surprise, Mr. Fox chuckled, though it wasn't a particularly pleasant sound. His piggish brown eyes narrowed even more until they were nearly slits in his sun-worn face. "What makes you think May and Clemence were friends?"

"It was in Clemence's diary, although I did read that they may have had a small disagreement." Marigold's voice wobbled with uncertainty. The way Mr. Fox looked at her, as if he might chew her up and spit her out in two seconds, made her second-guess every syllable.

"It was more than a disagreement," Mr. Fox sneered. "Clemence killed May's daughter."

Marigold swallowed. "That can't be true."

"Oh, it's true, all right. My granddaddy told me the story when I was only knee-high. Clemence said she'd help May's boy who'd gotten sick. But whatever she did killed May's baby daughter instead." Mr. Fox's face darkened. "My granddaddy told me to stay away from your kind."

Marigold's stomach twisted. The aromagic had saved one child and taken another.

"I—I'm sorry for what happened," Marigold said.

A leaf, yellowed and torn along its side, dropped from a tree overhead and landed at her feet. Marigold and Mr. Fox both stared at it, neither of them speaking.

"I'm not like Clemence," Marigold said finally.

Mr. Fox pointed a bony finger at her. "I hear things. 'Bout your mama. What she's doing on this island is wrong. That magic is evil."

"I don't use any magic. And I really am sorry about May and her baby. It's awful." Marigold hesitated, biting the inside of her cheek. It was clear her school project idea wasn't going to work, and she still had to find a way to convince him to give her the locket if he even had it. "The truth is, I'm here because something is hurting my sisters. I know May had a locket, which was really important to her. I think the locket is cursed, and I have to find it. If you'll only let me borrow—"

"No," Mr. Fox said flatly.

Marigold sucked in a breath. He wasn't even listening to her. "Sir, this is a matter of life or death."

"I've got a painting of May wearing that locket. My granddaddy said she never took it off. Was her good-luck charm. I'd never give it to a Lafleur even if I did have it."

"So you don't have it?" Marigold said, a hitch in her voice.

Mr. Fox crossed his arms and smirked. "Sure don't. May

Fox was buried with that locket round her neck."

The ground dropped out from under Marigold. The malediction was buried in a coffin?

A burning sensation filled Marigold's nose. Breathing out, she squeezed her eyes shut and tried to focus on the smell of the damp earth and leaves at her feet. Yet the stinging wouldn't go away. Her vision flooded with the image of Mr. Fox out in his dinghy at night, snatching crab pots along the back creek.

"You're the one stealing all the crab pots," Marigold said, her eyes flying open. The thefts had started over the summer. The whole island was trying to find the culprit. People had blamed the Lafleurs. They'd seem to blame her family for every problem since the earthquake. But now she knew who was really responsible.

Mr. Fox's mouth gaped. He stumbled backward. "You stay away from me. Get out of here!"

At once Marigold realized her mistake. She'd smelled his secret. She'd scared him, and now she was never going to get him to tell her anything else. "I'm sorry," she rushed.

"You talk of Clemence and May being friends, but you know nothing." Mr. Fox's face twisted into something dark and threatening. "The Lafleurs had no friends among the original families. The Lafleurs are dangerous."

Marigold's pulse sped up. "We're not dangerous. *I'm* not

dangerous." Did Mr. Fox see something terrible in her? All she wanted was her life and her sisters back.

Mr. Fox stalked to his ramshackle house. "Your family deserves anything it gets." His door slammed shut, the sound echoing through the quiet.

Beware or else.

That sinister whisper again. The rising smell of iris and sassafras enveloped her.

Marigold's chest squeezed. She could feel the blood pump through her veins as she jogged through the trees, out of the forest. If she hadn't been convinced before, she was now. May Fox had hated Clemence after losing her daughter. *That* was motivation for a curse. The only problem was that the source of the curse was somewhere deep inside the earth, along with a dead body.

Marigold was nearly home when she heard raised voices up ahead. As she turned the corner, she saw a crowd gathered on the sidewalk in front of the Moonside Villas. The public safety golf cart in its distinctive shade of cobalt blue blocked off the road. Even from a distance, she spotted Birdie's auburn hair. Birdie held a white rag to her temple. The rag had a huge red blotch on it. Alarm bells rang inside Marigold's head. She stiffened. That blotch was *blood*. She took off running.

"You've got to come down to the emergency room," Mr. Jackson said.

Miss Abigail nodded in agreement. She was wearing the signature navy-blue blazer that she always wore when she was on duty. "He's right, dear."

Marigold skidded to a stop beside Birdie. She took in Birdie's grimy face, her bleeding knees, and the blood seeping onto the cloth pressed to her hairline. A haphazard pile of roof shingles was scattered around the sidewalk nearby. The lingering rotten smell from the direction of their house mixed with the sickening metallic scent of blood.

"Are you okay?" Marigold asked.

Birdie flicked a glance at her. "I'm fine. Or I will be if I can go home and clean up." She readjusted her hand holding the rag and winced.

A group of women stood off to one side, clucking and shaking their heads. Marigold recognized Miss Eugenie; Miss Iris; and Miss Linda, Sam's mama. Standing beside Mr. Jackson and Miss Abigail was Mr. Wilmer, and another lady with frizzy hair.

"This isn't my fault," Mr. Wilmer said. "Those shingles were secure."

"Really?" Birdie said in an irritated voice. "Then why did a ton of them fall off the roof and onto my head?"

Marigold's breathing went shallow. She looked up to

the roof of the Moonside Villas and back down to the shingles piled on the sidewalk. Shingles had fallen off a roof and onto her sister! How was that even possible? It was a beautiful day with not even a slight breeze in the air. But Marigold knew the answer. This was no accident. This was more of the curse at work.

Birdie continued. "All I did was walk past *your* building." She nodded to the frizzy-haired lady, who Marigold now remembered was Becca Shanahan. She ran the Moonside Villas.

Mrs. Shanahan crossed her arms. "I'd say unlucky timing was to blame, but I suspect it was more than that. I saw Evelyn Lafleur hanging around Myra's condo earlier today. It's no coincidence this happened soon after. We all know what really caused the earthquake last April. If Evelyn keeps up her behavior, we're going to have an even bigger problem around here."

The ladies, who were listening to every word of the conversation, gasped in unison. Marigold bit her lip. Mama had made another mess dropping off her unwanted purification charm for Myra Picado.

"Are you seriously blaming my mama for your worker's mistake?" Birdie asked, narrowing her eyes. A drop of blood trailed down her cheek like a spot of paint on a white canvas.

"There was no mistake," Mr. Wilmer huffed.

"No, there wasn't," Mrs. Shanahan said in a snippy voice.

Birdie's face darkened. She breathed in deeply, her shoulders rising as she closed her eyes. Slowly her eyes opened. "Are you sure you have a permit for the roof work?"

At once Marigold realized that Birdie had used her power. But if there was ever a time to ignore their pact to not use aromagic, this was it.

"I don't have to listen to this," Mr. Wilmer blustered, turning red.

Miss Abigail frowned. "Come to think of it, I don't recall seeing a permit application."

"Neither do I," Mr. Jackson said.

Mrs. Shanahan stretched her thin face into a fake smile. "I'm sure we can work this out. The more important thing is to get this girl some medical attention immediately."

"We're in agreement on that." Mr. Jackson gave Mr. Wilmer and Mrs. Shanahan a stern look. "Clean up those shingles and vacate the work site until further notice. We need to evaluate this permit business."

Mr. Wilmer and Mrs. Shanahan stalked back to their golf carts, silent and fuming.

Mr. Jackson's phone chirped, and he pulled it out to read an incoming text. "Dr. Scott can see you now."

"We're going to have to insist, Birdie," Miss Abigail said.

Birdie groaned. "Fine. Let's get this over with." She limped off toward the public safety cart.

"I'm coming too," Marigold said, hustling to her side.

"No, go home," Birdie instructed firmly. "Mr. Jackson tried calling Mama but can't reach her. You can tell her where I am." In a lower voice she added, "If she even cares."

Marigold swallowed and stepped back to the sidewalk, watching as Mr. Jackson shuffled Birdie into the cart. She looked exhausted as they pulled away.

Miss Eugenie and Miss Iris offered to bring Marigold supper, though she suspected they only wanted to get inside her house and make up stories about what they saw. They asked where Mama had gone. Of course, Marigold had no idea. Mama was probably off buying some exotic spice in Eastport and had forgotten her cell phone. Still, Marigold pretended like Mama was on her way home. She couldn't let anyone get too close to Lilac Cottage or they might figure out that the smell drifting over the island was strongest in their yard.

The house was eerily quiet when Marigold finally made her way back to Lilac Cottage. There were no footfalls, no breathing, no voices anywhere around.

Birdie and Lou should have been teasing each other in the kitchen and asking Marigold if she would chop up the onion for supper, since it made Birdie's eyes tear up and Lou hated the smell. Lou should have been covered in dirt from practice and threatening to sit on Birdie's bedspread. Birdie should have been asking Marigold if she'd finished her homework. Instead Birdie was on her way to the island's emergency room, and Lou hadn't even bothered to come home.

She wandered upstairs to Birdie and Lou's room. It looked the same as it always did. Lou's bed was unmade, magazines strewn across her side of the floor, while the covers on Birdie's bed were pulled up tight to her headboard without a wrinkle.

Marigold clambered down into the space between the two beds. Grabbing Lou's pillow and Birdie's blanket, she lay down on the cold floor. The blanket barely covered her toes, and the pillow was musty-smelling.

A faint memory of gardenia mixed with vanilla wafted past her; the scent of her sisters. Breathing in deeply, Marigold closed her eyes for a long moment. Right then, in the quiet of the room, all she wanted was Birdie and Lou on either side of her.

Today wasn't a near miss like the lightning or the ferry. No, today Birdie had gotten hurt. She could have been killed. And the growing silence between her sisters would only make things worse. The curse was becoming more dangerous, more divisive. Soon there would be nothing left of the sisters she knew.

Breathing in again, she realized that the gardenia and vanilla were now gone, if they'd ever been there in the first place. All she could smell was dust and dirt. Marigold sat up straight, alarm shooting through her. If she wasn't careful, Birdie and Lou would disappear from her life exactly the way a scent fades, slowly at first, before it vanishes completely. They would disappear exactly the way her parents' relationship had. She couldn't allow that.

She wouldn't allow that.

Birdie and Lou were not swooping in to save her. Daddy was too busy with his own life to worry about them. Mama didn't believe her. All Marigold had were her own guts and determination, and Sam. It would have to be enough. If this were a play, this would be the defining scene where the lead actress takes a stand and prepares to fight. Marigold lifted her chin. This was her stand. She *would* destroy the malediction and break the curse.

It was time for Marigold to stop wallowing and save her family.

CHAPTER THIRTEEN

*Black pepper invokes fearlessness and courage when
carried in your pocket.*

Marigold was picking at a bowl of bran cereal
the next morning. It was the only kind left in
the pantry. Lou and Birdie hadn't gone to the
grocery store this past week. Their house felt like a shell of
a home, but she was going to fix that.

Marigold's phone chimed with a text from Lauren: dont
forget bracelet u will look soooooo cute!

Marigold smiled at the text and adjusted the turquoise
bracelet on her wrist. It *was* cute. Since the callback audition

two days ago, Kendall had saved a seat for her in English class. Julia had insisted she join them at lunch, and Lauren had loaned her a turquoise bracelet to match Lauren's yellow one.

Mama wandered into the kitchen. "I need you in the basement."

"Can it wait until later? I have school," Marigold said.

Mama shook her head. "I think you'll want to see this. It won't take long."

Marigold wanted nothing to do with whatever Mama was cooking up in the basement, but . . . she was curious. What was so important that Mama had gotten up before school?

The stairs creaked and groaned as Marigold followed Mama downstairs. Somehow the basement never leaked when it rained. Marigold had always wondered if Clemence and Elise had sprayed some protection charm around the outside that still lingered two hundred years later.

Mama bustled around the room, grabbing a clear bottle filled with a pale pink liquid, a jar of black pepper, and another of green speckled herbs. She opened Clemence's diary and scrolled through the tattered pages until she stopped at a particular one.

"Your daddy was trying to call you," Mama murmured, not looking up.

"I've been busy," Marigold said, running her hand along the table where the rough wood caught at her skin. She had three missed calls from him on her phone.

"He misses you," Mama said.

Marigold couldn't help herself. "Then why isn't he here?"

"He can't—that's not—" Mama stopped and looked up at the low ceiling for several seconds. "Marigold, he's still recovering, and there are other reasons why—"

"I don't want to talk about this," Marigold said. If Mama felt guilty for her part in driving Daddy away, she never let on. Marigold didn't want to hear what she had to say now. Too much time had passed.

"Maybe we should," Mama said simply. "We haven't discussed his leaving. It's my fault for not bringing it up sooner, but perhaps we can remedy that today."

Mama sounded so calm, unlike when she used to speak to Daddy. He would say one thing, and she would say another, and before anyone knew what was happening, their voices would grow loud and harsh. It always seemed to start about something silly, like Mama forgetting to pick up the milk or refusing to let Daddy paint the front door even though it was chipping like crazy. That's when Marigold would creep into Birdie and Lou's room and tuck herself into the space between their beds. Sometimes Lou would turn up the radio and pretend to be a rock star to make Marigold laugh. Other times Birdie would read from their old copy of fairy tales, her voice smoothing out the jagged edges downstairs. Marigold blinked away the memories, turning back to Mama.

"Can we get this over with?" Marigold asked, gesturing to the table.

"If you want to talk, I'm always here," Mama said.

"I don't."

Mama looked as if she wanted to say more but settled with a nod. "Prepare the candles."

Marigold focused on gathering the tall, cream pillar candles Mama favored and placed them on the table in the four corners. She spied a book of matches on the nearby chest and lit each candle until all the wicks glowed orange.

"For this particular charm, black pepper for courage, thyme for protection, and bluebells for happiness," Mama said.

Mama measured clear alcohol into the flask and added in drops from the bottles of fragrance and bits from the jars of herbs. Lifting the flask, she swirled it around and held it to her nose. She closed her eyes and furrowed her brow, listening as much as smelling.

The flask was now on the table in front of them. As Marigold stared at it, she felt the air itself change. It grew both heavier and lighter at the same time and glimmered with sparkling specks of light. A breeze came from out of nowhere and ruffled their hair, causing the liquid in the flask to bubble.

"Now picture intentions," Mama said softly, reminding herself as she always did.

Marigold wondered what she was picturing. Was it someone falling in love, which would end in heartache for someone else? Was it someone needing to heal, which would then make another person sick? Was it someone wanting wealth, who would sacrifice another's happiness?

The candle flames leapt. The scent from the flask intensified—spicy pepper, fresh bluebells, earthy thyme— and wafted across the room as if Marigold were bathing in it. The charm bubbled faster, and plumes of fragrant smoke rose from its depths in alarming colors of violet and fuchsia and jade.

Marigold wished she hated it, that she could smash the flask and race upstairs. Yet she found herself mesmerized by the smells and colors and the wondrous possibilities. She remained still, relaxing as the aromagic swirled around her. The worries that had plagued her—the curse, the play, Daddy—drifted away, and her shoulders loosened. This was where she belonged.

The smoke twisted around their heads in a rainbow-colored funnel. Mama drew in a deep breath and held it, concentrating on a pinpoint within the flask, then blew onto the liquid. All at once the bubbling stopped, the smoke dissipated. Everything went utterly still.

She picked up the flask and smelled. Her lips turned up. "Perfect."

Mama busied herself pouring the liquid into a small glass bottle. She capped it with a gold top, the spray feature hidden beneath the cap. Holding it out, she presented it to Marigold.

"Do you—need me to deliver it?" Marigold asked.

"No. I want you to have it."

Marigold backed away, shaking her head. Watching aromagic was one thing. Using it herself was quite another. "I don't want anything to do with your charms."

Mama sighed. "This is your heritage, Marigold. We are aromages. Our family has practiced for hundreds of years. There's nothing inherently wrong with the aromagic itself; the only fault is how it's used by others."

"I don't want to practice," Marigold said, but her voice wobbled at the edges, holding back her true uncertainty.

"It's a luck charm," Mama said, ignoring Marigold's protests.

"I don't need luck," Marigold said.

"It's not for you. At least, not exactly. It's for the other students in your play." Mama eyed Marigold knowingly.

Marigold blanched. "What do you know about the other students?"

"I know the school play was suddenly plagued by problems at the second round of auditions—illness, stage fright, injuries. I overheard some of the moms talking at the Moon Market. People are saying Ms. Ballard puts too much pressure on the kids."

"That's not true at all," Marigold exclaimed. "Ms. Ballard is kind to everyone. This wasn't her fault."

"I figured that," Mama said. "I doubt any teacher could cause cast members to suffer such poor luck. I'm not sure what happened—"

"Nothing," Marigold said, unable to tell Mama what Lou had done without revealing her unauthorized use of aromagic.

Mama gave her a skeptical look and continued. "So, I thought the cast could use a luck charm. It's not the kind of thing that will hurt anyone, if that's what you're worried about. This will generally make everyone a little bit braver, healthier, and luckier. It only encourages outcomes that are already probable. It's a good way to pay the debt to fate."

Mama had talked of paying the debt to fate before, when aromagic went awry and someone was unhappy with the consequences. Marigold never paid much attention because the idea of paying back fate seemed impossible. No one, not even Mama, knew what action might actually fix a vex. Fate wasn't easily controlled.

"It never works," Marigold said.

Mama stared straight at Marigold. "I wouldn't say that's true, and it's certainly worth a try. For example, if someone used aromagic to change their fate, and the consequence is poor performances by the rest of the cast, this could help."

"That's—"

Mama continued, speaking over Marigold. "If that same person made everyone more susceptible to fortuitous opportunities, that intention might be a way of balancing things. Balance is required in aromagic." Mama held the small glass bottle up to the light. "Even in this little bottle, the sweetness of the flower tempers the harshness of the black pepper. It makes the charm stronger, more powerful. Everything requires balance to work properly."

Marigold swallowed. Why had she ever thought that Mama wouldn't find out about the audition? She always knew when aromagic was at work.

"But what if the luck charm isn't enough? What if there isn't a way to pay the debt?" Marigold asked.

"There's always a way, but at times it's not a sacrifice people are willing to make."

"Doesn't that make you not want to practice aromagic at all? So many things can go wrong."

Mama set the bottle down and studied the contents of the table for a moment. "I won't deny my own gift. That doesn't help anyone. This is who I am, and I let people make their own decisions about what they are willing to risk." Bending her head back down to the diary, Mama spoke without looking up. "Take the charm. Use it or not. It's your choice."

But there was no choice, not really. Marigold had to fix what she and Lou had done. She reached for the mist. Mama might tell people the risks, but they couldn't really understand. Not until they lost something important and realized how dangerous aromagic truly was.

Marigold paced the lobby outside the auditorium later that day. During school she'd spent each period covertly spraying Mama's charm in the general direction of every *Magical Town of Oz* cast member she'd seen. *It must have worked*, she reassured herself. Mama was very good at her magic, even if things didn't always end well for those who used her charms.

Sam slumped against the wall near her. "If you don't stop pacing, I'm going to tackle you. You're making me dizzy."

Marigold huffed. "I'm nervous, okay? People will suspect something strange is going on once they realize that everyone in the cast except me is having a problem performing.

And just like everything else, they might start to blame the Lafleur lead for cursing the play, and then everything I've done to get this part is for nothing!"

"Calm down and maybe focus more on fixing your mistake instead of how bad it is for you," Sam said matter-of-factly.

"It wasn't totally my fault," Marigold hissed. "Lou did most of it."

Sam shrugged, and she knew he didn't agree with her. She could have stopped singing after Lou sprayed the charm, but the awe on everyone's faces had been impossible to resist. This was just as much her fault.

"Are we still on for meeting at the graveyard after this?" Sam asked.

Marigold nodded. Last night she had filled Sam in on her meeting with Curtis Fox. They'd made plans to search for May Fox's grave after rehearsal.

Ms. Ballard opened the auditorium door. "Let's go, kiddos."

The thin crowd shuffled into the auditorium.

"Oh and, Marigold?" Ms. Ballard said. "Your sisters haven't responded yet about volunteering. I know they're busy with school, but would you make sure they're getting my emails? Our first painting shift is this Saturday, and we could really use them."

"They probably didn't get the emails," Marigold said in a strained voice. "But I know they're excited to help. I'll talk to them."

"*Are* they excited to help?" Sam whispered as Ms. Ballard hurried off.

"How should I know?" Marigold burst out. "They're barely speaking to me."

Marigold twisted her hands into knots. How was she going to convince her sisters to volunteer? Neither of them had actually said yes, but Marigold had already promised they would. If everyone thought they'd backed out at the last minute, it would only make her family look worse.

"I don't know if I can do this," Marigold whispered nervously to Sam. "What if the play is ruined because of me? What if my sisters won't volunteer? What if this makes the town hate us even more? What if—"

"Marigold." Sam grabbed her elbows and made her stand still. "You're spiraling."

"I—I am. You're right. Okay." Marigold breathed in. There was the lingering jasmine of Ms. Ballard's perfume, the fresh paint for the sets, and the lemony wood polish of the seats; the smells of the town auditorium. She unclenched her hands. "It's going to be fine."

"It's going to be fine," Sam repeated. "And if not, we'll try something else. I could give tips on managing stage fright. I like to picture the audience in superhero costumes."

"I thought you were supposed to picture the audience in their underwear."

"Well, yeah, that's what unoriginal people do. But I've researched all the different superhero costumes from old comics, and I'm telling you, some of those getups are crazy funny. Imagining Lauren Spelling in a green goblin mask is enough to make anyone less self-conscious."

Marigold grinned. "Let's hope it doesn't come down to the green goblin."

Sam winked. "Text me after."

Marigold nodded and slipped into the theater. Anna sat in her usual spot in one of the last rows. She waved, her face open and bright in a smile. She moved her backpack from the seat beside her, making space for Marigold.

Marigold waved back but kept moving down the aisle. She tried not to notice Anna's smile fade when she didn't stop. It wasn't that she didn't like Anna. Anna was great. But Lauren and the others were finally speaking to her again. She was sure they'd only said those things in the bathroom because they'd been scared of her family gift, but now she'd succeeded in reminding them that she was just like them, that the earthquake should be forgotten. She was back where she belonged. Marigold touched the bracelet borrowed from Lauren, reassuring herself of its presence.

Marigold slid into the front row seat saved for her.

Lauren squeezed her arm. "First official day of rehearsal. Are you ready to be the star?"

Just hearing the word—"star"—dampened some of Marigold's fears. She was ready to prove to all of Luna Island that she had a regular talent, not a supernatural one.

"I'm ready," Marigold admitted. She craned her head around and noticed Anna still sitting alone. "We should ask Anna to sit with us."

"Why?" Lauren asked, wrinkling her nose.

"Why not? She's nice," Marigold said.

"She's not really our kind of friend, though. She never talks and is always reading by herself." Lauren made a face. "I mean, Anna's fine but just . . . different."

Marigold looked down at her lap, her face flushed. She opened her mouth to disagree, to say something in Anna's defense, but the words remained inside as if glued to her throat.

Lauren leaned in close. "I'm having a party before it gets too cold. Let's work on the guest list after rehearsal. You're the first one invited, but don't tell anyone yet because I haven't decided who else I'll invite."

Marigold smiled, her foot bouncing on the floor. Her concern about the charm slid away. Lauren had a heated pool at her house, and they could pull out all the different floats and make smoothies outside. It was always fun. Every girl in their class wanted an invite to Lauren's parties, and Marigold was the first one included at this one.

Ms. Ballard strode to the center of the stage, her face weary. "I guess there's some sort of stomach virus going around. I had planned to block the yellow brick road scene with all the Munchkins, but since we're missing half the cast, we can't do that today."

For the first time Marigold noticed the large number of empty seats. Her chin dropped. This was not a good sign.

"The play isn't off to a great start," Lauren whispered.

Marigold's heart sped up, but she forced herself to calm down. Maybe there really was a stomach virus going through the school. She certainly felt pretty sick right then.

"So we're going to work on the big song at the end of the first act," Ms. Ballard said. "All of you are in that number, and we can at least begin learning the music today."

There was a rustling around the room as everyone pulled out their scripts and flipped through the pages to the main song of the entire musical, "Mystical, Marvelous, Magical Oz."

Mr. Ford began to play the piano. Marigold sang the first few lines loud and clear, then stopped at the awful noise around her. She stared left and right. Half the cast wasn't singing at all but was staring down at their scripts looking terrified. The other half was singing all the wrong notes. They sounded horrible.

"Stop, stop," Ms. Ballard said, peering into the audience. "Are we all on the same page? We're starting on page twenty-five. Everyone got it?"

Heads nodded.

"All right, let's try that again, then." Ms. Ballard was smiling but there was a tightness to her voice.

Mr. Ford launched back into the accompaniment music. Marigold took a deep breath and sang the first line. Next to her, Lauren sounded like she was singing a separate melody. Julia was singing in an entirely different key, and the boys behind them were completely flat. If possible, it was even worse than the first try.

Ms. Ballard held out her hands, and the auditorium quieted. "What's going on? Have you all listened to the music like I asked?"

Alison raised her hand. "Ms. Ballard, I'm sorry but my voice is killing me. I think I should go home."

Ms. Ballard sighed. "Okay, Alison, you're excused."

Leila Jones raised her hand. "Um, I feel like there's something caught in my throat. May I go get some water?"

"Fine," Ms. Ballard said shortly.

"Me too," Patrick Myerson said.

Ms. Ballard choked out a half laugh. "Anyone else have something wrong with them right now?"

Most of the auditorium raised their hands.

Ms. Ballard turned to face the back of the stage, putting her hands on top of her head. She spun in a slow circle. Her entire back was stiff. "Let's take the afternoon off. We'll start fresh on Saturday, and maybe the rest of the cast will have recovered by then."

There was a chorus of students thanking Ms. Ballard and rising to their feet. Lauren stood beside Marigold, complaining. "My throat is scratchy today."

Julia was agreeing with her. "Me too."

Marigold's head was spinning. She'd have bet anything that there was no stomach bug, no one needed water, and no one had forgotten how to sing.

The entire cast had been vexed! Mama's charm hadn't worked. The Lafleur aromagic had ruined the musical, the same way it ruined everything else.

CHAPTER FOURTEEN

Sandalwood strengthens intuition and answers persistent questions.

Sam ran up to Marigold in the hall after fifth period the next day. Even though it was Friday, Marigold couldn't muster up any excitement about the upcoming weekend, not when her sisters were still barely speaking to each other.

"I might have found something about May's grave," Sam whispered.

Marigold and Sam had explored the tiny graveyard behind the church after the disastrous rehearsal the day before. There were several old gravestones but none from as far back as the early 1800s, when May Fox had lived on Luna Island. Marigold was worried she'd never find May's grave. Two weeks had now passed since the rotten smell had arrived in their garden. According to Gram, the curse took an older sister within weeks after the smell began. Either of her sisters could get hurt or leave at any moment.

Marigold pulled Sam into the small alcove beside the art room, clear of the crush of bodies in the hallway. "What did you find?"

"So, I was reading *The History of Luna Island* in study hall, and I found a reference to a graveyard used by the founders for their . . ." Sam's voice tapered off.

For their dead bodies. That's what Sam had been going to say. Marigold shivered.

"How do we find it? Can we go today?" Marigold asked eagerly. "And how weird that we've never noticed another graveyard before on the island."

Sam shifted back on his feet. "Yeah, there's a reason for that. The graveyard is somewhere we've never been. It's on top of the Wynding Cliffs."

Marigold's vision narrowed to the tiny crack in the wall behind Sam's head. The sounds of the hallway snuffed out. This was bad news. This was very bad news. The Wynding Cliffs rose above the ocean in a crumbling wall of rocks and dirt. There had once been a road that ran along the cliffs, but it had fallen into the water, along with one side of the cliffs, years before. Now the cliffs were deserted, and a ravine separated them from the main part of the island. There were several avalanches every year where the ground shifted, and the ocean reclaimed more and more of the land as if desperate to pull it back down into the rush of waves where it belonged.

"You don't have to go," Marigold said. "This is my search."

"I'm not letting you go alone, and you know it." Sam frowned. "But, Marigold, what's your plan if we do find May Fox's grave? We can't dig her up."

"I know that. Once we find the grave, I'll tell Gram everything we've discovered. I'm hoping she can come up with a way to get the locket."

But if Gram couldn't help, Marigold *would* dredge up the locket herself. Daddy's brand-new shovel was still at the house. She thought back to last year when he'd promised to dig out an old ligustrum bush for Mama. He'd gotten caught up in watching a football game. When Mama had realized he'd forgotten to do it, she hadn't spoken to him for an entire day. Lou had cracked joke after joke at the supper table to cover up the silence between their parents.

"Want to go this afternoon?" Sam interrupted her memory.

"Sure, okay," Marigold said absently before remembering the date. "Wait. Don't you have band practice?"

Sam shrugged. "I can skip it. This is important."

Marigold's feet tapped on the ground, as if already walking the path to the Wynding Cliffs. She flashed Sam a grin. "Today it is."

The way to the Wynding Cliffs broke off from the main road past the Whispering Woods. There wasn't a path anymore, and leaves lashed at Marigold's face as she and Sam ducked under branches and climbed over fallen logs. There was a faint milky scent of sandalwood lingering in the trees, a good sign for finding answers. They moved through the woods, and the ground sloped upward. They passed several NO TRESPASSING signs in the process. No one was allowed up here because of the potential for avalanches. The thought was not comforting.

The trees abruptly ended. There was a small stretch of bare land before the ground plunged down into a dizzying drop. The ravine itself was at least fifteen feet across. At the bottom was a trickle of water that looked awfully far away. The sides were ragged with rocks and scraggly underbrush. On the other side were more trees blocking the vast expanse of ocean beyond the Wynding Cliffs.

"How are we supposed to get over to the other side?" Marigold asked. She'd assumed the ravine was narrow enough to hop across. But it wasn't, not even close.

Sam looked right and left, then pointed. "Look! There's a bridge down there."

They picked their way along the ravine, careful to not get too close to the edge. When they reached the bridge, Marigold's heart sank deeper than the rift itself. The bridge was made of crooked wooden boards on the bottom and a frayed, waist-high rope along the sides. The wood was black and rotted in places, and there were huge gaps where boards were missing.

"This looks really unsafe," Marigold said.

Sam placed a tentative foot on the bridge. A few rocks broke off from the edge of the ravine and skittered down the steep side. Marigold peered over the edge. It was a long way down.

"I think we should turn back," Marigold said. "We can't walk over this thing. We could literally die." If Birdie and Lou had been there, they'd never have let Marigold cross the bridge. They'd have come up with some plan to cross safely and find the malediction themselves while she waited behind.

"How are we going to find May's grave, then?" Sam asked.

Marigold closed her eyes, kneading her temples. She breathed in the salty ocean air and earthy moss. The now always-present rot ruined the aroma. This was hopeless. "I don't know."

At the scrabble of sound, Marigold's eyes flew open.

Sam was halfway across the bridge, hopping from board to board. Seconds later he was on the other side.

Marigold yelped. "What did you do?"

Sam grinned at her, close but so far away. "Someone had to go first. Come on. It's sturdier than it looks."

Was Sam kidding? This bridge *looked* like a death trap. Marigold's hands went clammy, and sweat trickled down her back. She hated heights. They made her sick. Yet Sam was right; she couldn't turn back now. Her sisters weren't here to help, and she had to find the malediction.

Imagining she was on a movie set filming a big stunt, Marigold moved one foot to the first wooden board of the bridge. The bridge swayed slightly under her weight, and her stomach jolted. She took another step forward until all her weight was on the bridge, and then another and another. She gripped the rope, and its fraying threads dug into her skin. Just a few more steps. It wasn't until she was past the middle of the bridge that she made the mistake of looking down. She froze, suddenly dizzy and shaking. Her body wobbled.

All at once Marigold's foot slipped between two boards. She lost her balance, careening to one side. Her hand tugged at the rope, and her other foot scrabbled to find her footing. Her waist bent over the side of the rope. She screamed and stared down at the narrow stream and jagged rocks.

"You've got it. Pull yourself up. You can do it. Marigold! Pull yourself up now!" Sam's voice was loud and insistent.

Sam's words cleared the fog from her brain. Marigold blinked and pulled herself upright. Her foot was back on the bridge. Her other foot moved her body forward. Even though her hands were shaking, she didn't release the rope. Three big steps, and she was on the other side.

Marigold collapsed onto the dirt, her breath rasping. "That was . . . I could have . . ."

"You did it," Sam said, grabbing her hand and tugging her to her feet.

"I almost fell," Marigold whispered.

"But you didn't," Sam said.

"No." A hint of a smile crept across Marigold's face. Her breathing evened out. She had done it all on her own. Well, mostly. Sam had helped too.

Marigold and Sam split up and took different sides of the forest. The air was still, and though she could hear the distant roar of the ocean, it was muffled by the leaves and overcrowded tree branches. Marigold headed deeper into the middle of the woods. This patch of forest was bordered by the ocean on one side and the ravine on the other. Yet somewhere in the thicket of trees and brambles was the key to breaking the Lafleur family curse.

Marigold stumbled across the first gravestone. It leaned

to one side and had turned a weathered gray, half-hidden by moss and dirt. She rubbed at her shin that had banged into the limestone. The overgrowth of ivy and bushes climbed up the side of dark pitted stone. Several other gravestones were scattered around in what appeared to have once been a clearing but had since been taken over by the forest. She lifted a hand to her mouth, her pulse racing once again.

"Sam," Marigold called. "It's over here."

There was movement through the trees, and he was at her side. Sam sucked in a breath as he took in the scene— the graves dusted with fallen leaves and half-swallowed by the ground. "Whoa. This is eerie."

"It's sad. No one even remembers that these graves exist." Marigold bent down beside the first gravestone she'd tripped over and read the inscription. "*Amy Allerton. Born 1769, died 1831. Blessed to heal many, she rests at last.*" She looked up at Sam, her stomach fluttering. "Amy was one of the founders of Luna Island."

Sam and Marigold hurried from gravestone to gravestone examining the inscriptions of long-dead Luna Island residents. Marigold saw May's name on the fourth gravestone she found. She sat back hard on her heels. Bending closer once again, she reread the words etched beneath dark green and black moss: *May Fox, born May 5, 1791, died July 7, 1811. Beloved wife and mother.*

Sam knelt down and traced the words on the gravestone. "You really found it."

Marigold rose to her feet, stretching her arms overhead. There was a lightness to her limbs now. She'd climbed the Wynding Cliffs, crossed a perilous bridge, and ventured into the woods, and the malediction was right under their feet. Everything would be okay.

"Uh-oh," Sam said under his breath.

Marigold's arms dropped. "Uh-oh, what?"

Sam bit his lip. "It's just . . . well . . . it looks like May Fox died in 1811. Isn't that the same year as the Great Hurricane and the start of the curse?"

"So what?" Marigold said. "She must have died after she cursed Clemence and Elise on the night of the hurricane."

"Except, look, she died a month before the hurricane."

Marigold slumped, her body caving in as if something had sucked all the breath out of her. "Are you—are you sure?"

Sam nodded. "I read more about the Great Hurricane last night. It occurred on August 8, 1811. I remember because August eighth is my dad's birthday. May Fox died in July 1811."

"If May died a month before the hurricane, she couldn't have cursed the Lafleurs," Marigold said in a small voice.

Sam met her eyes. "I know."

Marigold stared down at the ground, the leaves and vines

blurring together until they resembled a mush of greens and browns. "I'm never going to figure this out." She'd been so sure May Fox was the one who'd cursed her family. Now she was back at the beginning and no closer to finding the malediction.

Sam had risen and was peering down at the other graves, one by one. Marigold sank to the ground, smelling wild mint mixed with the faint decay of flower petals. She rested her chin on her knees. She had no idea where to go next.

After several minutes Sam brushed the dirt off a grave and knelt down beside it. "Maybe there's something else here."

"There's nothing. It's no use," Marigold mumbled.

"Not with that attitude," Sam said, raising his eyebrows. He continued to stare at the grave in front of him. "You mentioned a Shadow Lady, right?"

Marigold frowned. "I read about her in Clemence's diary. She tried to run the Lafleurs off the island, but there was nothing else about her. I don't know who she was."

Sam motioned Marigold over. "Maybe I do."

Marigold's eyes widened. She ran over to where Sam was kneeling and bent to read the words on the gravestone. *Martha Willard, B. 1775, D. 1854. Our shadow lady enchanted in darkness, but her spirit was light itself.*

"The Shadow Lady," Marigold whispered. Hope washed

over her in a great wave. If an audience had been watching this scene, they'd have already broken into applause.

Sam had brought his backpack along and pulled out *The History of Luna Island*. "I thought we might want this for reference. I remember reading something about Martha Willard." He flipped through the pages and held the open book out to her. "Here it is."

Marigold scanned the page. One of the original founders of Luna Island, Martha Willard was known for baking but preferred to bake only at night. Perhaps that explained her Shadow Lady title. According to the book, the other founders believed she could bake feelings into food and considered her a leader with significant influence over the other islanders. Between the gravestone and the description in Sam's book, the connection was clear. Martha Willard was the Shadow Lady of Clemence's diary.

"Sam, do you know what this means?" Marigold clasped her hands together. "Clemence said the Shadow Lady wanted them gone from Luna Island. She was influential *and* magical. She could have cursed Elise." She noticed that a ray of sunlight had broken through the leaves, and she smiled as the golden beam sparkled on a bright green leaf. "We've got a new lead. Just as soon as we get back over that bridge."

CHAPTER FIFTEEN

*Calendula may strengthen familial relationships when
fidelity is uncertain.*

On Saturday morning Marigold awoke to the terrible clash of banging drawers. The sound was horribly familiar. For an instant she flashed back to last year when Daddy had stormed out of the house and slammed the front door after Mama had forgotten to pay their water bill. Marigold had chased after him, but he'd ridden off in the golf cart alone.

A muttered curse sounded from her sisters' room. Marigold popped out of bed and rushed next door. Lou was still buried under the covers, but Birdie was whirling around, searching under books and a pile of stray T-shirts beside the closet.

"What are you doing?" Marigold asked, rubbing the sleep from her eyes.

"I'm looking for something important." Birdie tossed one of Lou's cleats across the room and glared at the lump under her covers. "If someone wouldn't let their room turn into a total disaster, I could actually find my stuff."

Lou groaned and burrowed deeper beneath her blanket.

"Maybe I can help," Marigold said.

Birdie plucked a gym bag from the floor and exhaled, snatching a folder underneath. "Here it is."

Marigold squinted. "What's that?"

"College brochures."

"For online college?" Marigold asked, noting the thickness of the folder. How many online colleges were there? Her stomach was sinking before Birdie answered.

"These are for regular college," Birdie said. "My counselor pulled them for me."

"I don't understand. I thought you were going to start college classes online so you could stay here with us," Marigold said, her voice cracking on the last word.

Birdie gripped the folder tightly as if she couldn't bear to let it go. The bandage from her injury the other day looked all wrong on her face. "I know. But, M, I've been thinking about it more . . . and I . . . I think I should go to college off this island."

Marigold blinked hard. "Away from me?"

"Away from everything." Birdie sat down on her bed. "I always planned to leave eventually but I was willing to put it off for our family. But Lou and I keep getting on each other's nerves, Mama is more concerned with aromagic than anything else, and Daddy . . ." Her voice trailed off, and she sighed. "I'm sorry. I know things aren't great around here right now. Maybe we all need a reset."

"And you think leaving will make it better?" Marigold squeezed out a tear and let it dry on her cheek, hoping it might soften Birdie. If she tried, she could muster up a few more. All good actresses could cry on demand. She'd do anything to stop Birdie from leaving.

But Birdie wasn't looking at Marigold. She was staring down at her folder. "I can't help how I'm feeling. I'm mad all the time, about everything. Lou and I have barely spoken." She glared at Lou's motionless form. "Even this—this mess of a room didn't use to make me so angry, but now I can barely stand it. I'm tired. I can't always be the one cleaning things up."

"You don't have to," Marigold said. "I'll do more to help with the dishes and the laundry."

"It's a lot more than the dishes," Birdie said quietly.

Lou pushed the covers back from her face and opened one eye. "Can you keep it down? My head is killing me."

Birdie expelled a short humorless laugh and stood. "Typical. All about you."

Lou struggled up to her elbows, already glaring at Birdie.

"Don't you see?" Marigold said. "This is the curse. That's what's making you both feel this way. If you help me break it, we can go back to the way we were."

Birdie hesitated in the doorway. The darkness of the hallway cast shadows on her cheeks, and her ponytail drooped over one shoulder. "Maybe you're right. Or maybe things just change and you have to adapt or move on, M. You can't fix people when they're only being themselves." She glanced pointedly at Lou.

"But that's where you're wrong. You and Lou aren't yourselves right now," Marigold said.

Lou shook her head, fully awake now. "Cut it out, Marigold. This is not some big, bad curse. This is much simpler. It's about me not following Birdie's ridiculous rules anymore. She can't handle it, so she wants to leave."

"Not true." Birdie crossed her arms.

Marigold moved to the center of the room, between her sisters. "This isn't like us. We don't stay mad at each other. Lou, you never want to follow Birdie's rules, and, Birdie, you never want Lou to do anything crazy. But we always listen to one another, and sometimes we do what Lou wants, and sometimes we do what Birdie wants, and sometimes we do what I want. In the end, it all works out and we're happy doing it together. *That's* how we do things." She turned from one to the other. "Sam and I have a plan. If you help us, we can break the curse. I'm sure of it!"

Birdie gave Marigold a look of pity. In that moment it was clear; neither of them believed Marigold, or they didn't care enough to try. No matter what she said, she was only their silly little sister.

"I can't help with that right now. I'm off to the library," Birdie said.

"But you're supposed to paint the set today for the play," Marigold said desperately. "Both of you are. I promised Ms. Ballard."

"You shouldn't have done that." Birdie frowned. "I'm too busy."

"I never said I'd help with that dumb play," Lou mumbled.

Marigold's lip trembled. What else could possibly go wrong today?

"I have to get these college applications done and turned in on time," Birdie said.

"So you can move away," Marigold said.

"So I can start my life," Birdie corrected.

"Your life is here with us," Marigold said, reaching out for her sister.

Yet Birdie slid away before Marigold made contact. Marigold followed her out the bedroom door. Birdie stopped at the top of the stairs, her shoulders facing forward as if her body were already pulling toward the outside world. "I know you don't want to admit that things are changing. But they are. We're all moving in different directions. That's what happens. You're older now. You don't need me to do everything for you anymore. You can take care of yourself."

"No, that's not true. I'll always need you. You promised you wouldn't leave," Marigold said. Her voice was shaking, and the tears came all on their own this time.

"I shouldn't have said that." Birdie started down the stairs.

Marigold's insides twisted. How could she change Birdie's mind? She breathed in and closed her eyes, expelling all other scents and focusing only on Birdie. She felt guilty trying to smell Birdie's secrets, but she needed something to convince Birdie to stay. Yet, she smelled nothing at all. When she opened her eyes, Birdie was already at the bottom of the stairs, walking out the door.

"Are you going to do something?" Marigold asked, turning back to Lou.

Lou's lip trembled for a split second. "There's nothing to do. The sooner you understand that, the better."

Marigold fled, slipping out the back door in the kitchen and heading straight to the beach.

She collapsed in the sand, and stared at the ocean for what felt like hours as her eyes kept filling up, tears steadily streaming down her face. For a moment she wished she could call Daddy for their regular Saturday call, but she didn't know what to say to him. He was busy with his new life that didn't include her. The rotten smell pulsed all around her, and the dark gray-blue waves crashed in and back out, a futile journey that never went anywhere. The clouds hung low in the sky, the deep purplish gray of a fresh bruise. The earth seemed as sad as she was.

Birdie always kept her promises. That was as much a part of her personality as her straight-A report card and her perfect ponytail. Now she was breaking the most important promise of all with no real explanation or guilt. And Lou was no better, acting as if she didn't care. Marigold couldn't even convince them to help with something as easy as the play, and her plan to show the town they were all one normal family was failing badly.

Marigold's breaths were shallow. She pictured Daddy packing his bags, and Mama frozen at the top of the stairs. It was happening again. She thought of Clemence's poem—

Misfortune and hate tear apart. Dark magic stole a sister's heart.
It was true. She didn't have much time to break the curse,
to help Birdie and Lou fix whatever was going on between
them, to stop Birdie from leaving, and to keep Lou from causing any more destruction. There was even a chance Lou might
up and leave her too. The pit at the bottom of Marigold's
stomach hardened. What if finding the malediction solved
nothing and another disaster was on its way to Luna Island
at this very moment? Maybe there was no way to protect her
home and keep her sisters close and safe.

Marigold pulled her knees up to her chest and rested her
chin on top, working to make herself as small as the grains
of sand around her. Slowly, everyone she loved left Luna
Island, or maybe . . . everyone only left her.

Play practice was a complete disaster. It started off with Ms.
Ballard asking if Lou and Birdie were on their way to help.
Unable to look Ms. Ballard in the eye, Marigold lied and
said they were both sick. During the rehearsal no one could
learn any of the dance steps without tripping, and Mr. Ford
came down with a sudden case of indigestion. Marigold
tried not to outshine her cast mates, worried someone might
notice how her performance never seemed to change. She
hoped Mama's charm was just taking some time and would
balance out Lou's charm soon.

After practice Lauren asked Marigold to go to Scoops for ice cream with Alison, Julia, and Kendall. She accepted at once. At least with her friends she could pretend her life wasn't a disaster, instead of worrying about how to locate the malediction later that night.

Walking into Scoops was like diving into a bowl of rainbow sherbet. The walls were bubble-gum pink, the stools were orange, and the floors were sky blue. Miss Eugenie and Miss Iris sat at a table by the door and waved to Marigold.

"It's nice to see you out with your friends," Miss Iris said. "I hope rehearsals are going well. The whole town can't wait to see the show. There's already lots of buzz about your performance."

Marigold swallowed down her panic. At this rate there wouldn't be a performance unless the vex faded. Fast. "We've got a ways to go."

"Your mama still has not called me about the planning committee." Miss Eugenie peered down her nose with a disapproving look. "You did discuss it with her?"

Marigold swallowed. "She's been . . . very busy. But I mentioned it, and I know she wants to help."

Lies, lies, lies. Marigold still hadn't figured out a way to ask Mama about the planning committee. She was afraid Mama would say no, but she couldn't say no. They needed to do things like join committees in order to return to normal. She needed Mama to say yes, especially since Marigold already had to figure out how to cover for Lou and Birdie refusing to help with the sets after Marigold had promised they would. The family hadn't gotten another threatening note tacked to their front door in days, and Marigold was staying hopeful. But the town would go back to blaming the Lafleurs the second the next disaster struck if they couldn't prove they belonged like everyone else.

"I'll talk to her. I'm sure she'll call you tomorrow. I should catch up with my friends." Marigold hurried away before Miss Eugenie said another word. Her stomach was churning when she reached Lauren and the others.

They all paid for their ice cream except for Marigold. Mr. Goodman wouldn't accept her money, and insisted her sundae was a congratulatory gift for earning the starring role in the musical. He'd done the same thing last spring. For a whole month after Daddy's accident, he'd refused to let Marigold pay for anything. She was glad this time it was a free dessert for something she was happy about.

They headed outside to sit on the deck overlooking Captain Scar Marina, and settled into seats, with Lauren insisting Marigold take the one to her left.

Lauren wrinkled her nose. "Do y'all smell that? That disgusting odor won't go away. I swear it's getting stronger.

My mama thinks Miss Jessica is throwing out expired ingredients and stinking up the entire marina."

"She wouldn't do that," Marigold said weakly.

"Well, my nana said the smell is a sign of bad luck. But she also uses crystals to heal her backaches, so none of us listen to her," Alison said, laughing.

Lauren and Kendall giggled, and Marigold managed a tight smile. How much longer before everyone on Luna Island discovered that the smell was coming right from her backyard and realized Alison's nana was onto something?

Kendall took a scoop of her strawberry ice cream, and several rings glinted on her fingers in shades of ice blue, creamy pearl, and pale pink sparkles.

"Cool rings," Marigold said, changing the subject.

Kendall smiled. "My granny gave them to me. She wore them all the time, but then her fingers got too swollen."

"I told her that wearing one at a time would have more of an impact, but she insists on clumping them all together at once. It's tacky but cute." Lauren's smile seemed sweet, but her words stung.

"I like them all together," Kendall muttered.

Marigold did too but decided it was best to keep her mouth shut.

Lauren leaned over the table, her green eyes wide. "Okay. Let's play secret circle. Who's your crush?"

Marigold nearly groaned. She was not in the mood to play this game where they all traded secrets. The last time she'd told Lauren about her crush on Ben Lorrington during secret circle, Lauren had insisted on texting Ben and informing him that she knew someone who liked him. Lauren had reasoned that in return he would tell her who he liked. He hadn't, and Marigold had been terrified for weeks that he'd figure out she'd started the whole thing.

Lauren looked expectantly at Julia to her right. "Well."

Julia stared down at the metal bars on the table. "I don't know."

Lauren narrowed her eyes. "That's not an answer."

"You have to say someone," Alison added.

"I really don't know," Julia mumbled. Her cheeks turned cherry red.

Lauren would not drop this—she never let things go—and poor Julia looked as if she wanted to sink into the ocean. Marigold knew how awful it was when everyone was staring at you, expecting something, even if they were your friends. She looked around the deck, trying to come up with some way to change the subject.

"How can you not know?" Lauren demanded. "Unless you're afraid to tell us."

Julia gripped her spoon. "I—I'm not. It's just—"

From out of nowhere, a jangle of jarring notes and weird

banging noises traveled from the other side of the Dogwood Coffee Shop. The perfect distraction!

"We should go see what that is," Marigold said, hopping up before anyone could protest. Kendall and Julia both rose too.

"We're right in the middle of secret circle," Lauren said, annoyed.

"But who can think with that noise? Come on," Marigold coaxed.

Lauren stood slowly. "Okay, I guess."

The five girls followed the sound of the music, which was not improving as the song went on. Marigold could pick out a guitar melody, but the other guitar kept missing notes, and the banging was really odd. She soon found out why.

Sam's band had set up on the sidewalk. Charlie had turned over several buckets and was playing them with his hands like a makeshift drum set. Will truly was as bad as Sam had said and hit every wrong note. Underneath it all, Sam's guitar riffs sounded good, but Marigold could barely hear them because of the buckets and the awful bass. Meanwhile, Charlie and Will were singing a duet that had the small crowd wincing.

Sam noticed her standing in the crowd and nodded, smiling wide. Marigold's face went hot. The perfect distraction had turned into utter mortification. Why did he have to play right in front of everyone? She forced a half-hearted smile back.

Julia turned to Marigold. "I didn't know Sam was in a band."

"It's a new thing. I think they're still getting the hang of it," Marigold said.

Lauren barked out a laugh. "They have a lot to learn."

"They're worse than the first graders on their recorders," Alison said.

"Way worse," Lauren agreed. "Plus they look bizarre."

Lauren was right. They did look bizarre. For some reason they were all wearing matching cowboy hats and jean shorts.

"They aren't that bad," Julia said.

"Are you kidding? You can hear, right?" Lauren said in a snide tone.

Julia shrugged, looking down. Marigold bit her lip. She'd forgotten how mean Lauren could be sometimes.

The band stopped in an awful blaring sound. The small crowd of ten people clapped and quickly moved on, not wanting to get stuck listening to another song. Marigold knew she should go over and congratulate Sam on his first public gig. But what would Lauren think if Marigold talked to him now after he'd embarrassed himself in front of all her other friends?

"We left our ice cream on the table," Marigold said, shuffling in the direction of Scoops and avoiding Sam's eyes. "We should get back."

"Marigold, I can't believe you don't want to stay. Sam acts like y'all are BFFs. Shouldn't you cheer him on? Maybe put on a cowboy hat for support," Lauren teased.

Marigold's blush deepened as they all stared at her. "I'm more of a fan of real music."

"Good one," Lauren said, laughing.

Julia cleared her throat, her eyes snagged on something behind Marigold.

Marigold turned and saw Sam standing behind her, holding his cowboy hat in his hands and twisting it from side to side. Her breath stopped. Had he heard her? The corners of his eyes dipped down, and his chin strained forward like it did when he was upset. He'd definitely heard her.

"Let's go," Lauren said, and started back to Scoops, the other girls except for Marigold trailing behind.

The words barely registered. Marigold was too busy watching Sam's face go from pale to pink to gray. Goose bumps covered her body, little tingles prodding her legs and arms. She wished the water of the marina would swallow her whole.

"Sam, I—"

Sam held up his hand, stopping her. "Don't tell me you were only kidding."

"I was," Marigold protested.

"Well, it wasn't funny. It was mean." Sam turned on his heel and headed in the opposite direction.

Shame engulfed Marigold. She wanted to take back what she'd said about Sam's band. Her life was a total wreck, and she'd just messed things up with the only best friend she had.

CHAPTER SIXTEEN

Freesia can help locate a beloved object.

Jessica Willard's house hunched on top of the bluff overlooking the ocean. Low to the ground with windows that popped out of the roof, it reminded Marigold of a little gray snail. Miss Jessica's golf cart was nowhere in sight, and Marigold knew why: she was working at Dream Pies. Saturday was the only night of the week when the bakery stayed open until nine o'clock.

Even under the cover of darkness, with no other houses within spitting distance, Marigold crept up to the house, looking left and right. The front light illuminated the small porch swing and lone rocking chair. Flanking the door were flowerpots that spilled bright yellow mums like a splash of sunshine on the porch.

At the door Marigold's hands trembled. Tucking them by her sides, she looked down. She'd dressed the part, wearing all black and even borrowing a black stocking cap from Lou. When she'd left the house, she'd commended herself on looking like a real cat burglar in an old-time movie. That seemed ridiculous now that she was faced with committing an actual crime.

A golf cart turned the corner, and lights swept across the porch. Marigold hit the ground and lay absolutely still, her heart racing. If she got caught, she might go to a juvenile detention center. The school would find out and she'd lose her part in the play. The entire island would look at her even worse than they already did; they'd see a criminal, a villain, a crook!

The golf cart sped past, not slowing down. Marigold exhaled and lifted her head. Clambering to her feet, she brushed the dirt from her knees. She might get caught, but she didn't have a choice. Miss Jessica was the only descendant of Martha Willard on the island. During the Founders' Day Celebration last year, Miss Jessica had donated several objects belonging to her ancestors for display during the party. Marigold remembered the worn blackened pots and battered wooden spoons because they'd reminded her of Gram's. According to Sam's book, Martha's magic had come from baking. Marigold hoped this meant that the malediction was connected with Martha's old baking tools, which just so happened to belong to Miss Jessica.

Staring at the doorknob, Marigold prayed it was unlocked. Many townspeople never locked their doors. She hoped Miss Jessica was one of them. If the door was locked, she'd have to find another way in. If only Sam had been there, he'd have had an idea of what to do next, but he hadn't responded to any of her texts after their run-in outside Scoops.

Marigold cringed when she thought of Sam's face after he'd heard her talking about his band. He'd looked so hurt. Sam was the one person she'd been able to count on these past few weeks, and now she didn't even have him. She didn't have time to keep messing everything up.

Shaking her head, Marigold rolled out her shoulders. She had to find a way to make it up to Sam. But first she needed to get through the next half hour on her own.

Reaching out her hand, Marigold turned the doorknob, an inch at a time, and pushed forward. The door swung in, and she exhaled. Step one accomplished. Now all she had to do was find the malediction and get out of there before Miss Jessica came home.

The inside was dark, lit only by a small lamp beside the front door. Marigold scurried through the foyer. She pulled the flashlight out of her backpack and the small bottle of mist.

It was Sam who'd given her the idea. He'd asked why she couldn't use a charm to locate the malediction. Of course, all aromages knew that finder charms couldn't locate something without a general idea of the location and knowing exactly what the charm was supposed to find. But now that Marigold suspected the malediction was somewhere in Miss Jessica's house, and that it was one of her family heirlooms, she was hoping the finder charm would work. Though Mama had mixed up the charm of freesia for memory, saffron for success, and orange for physical energy, she'd allowed Marigold to infuse it with her own intention—*Find the Willards' cursed object.*

Marigold thought back to last night, when she and Mama had brewed the charm, how the warmth had suffused her hands as she'd held them over the glass bottle. She'd blown gently over the bubbling charm, and her chest had lightened. Now a laugh tickled her throat, despite the fight with Sam and the conflict with her sisters. But, Marigold reminded herself, it was a onetime charm. Birdie wouldn't like her doing aromagic. They'd made a pact, and she'd only broken it because the situation was dire.

Holding up the bottle, Marigold depressed the atomizer with her finger. A fine translucent mist sparkled in the darkness. The dominant base of freesia with its hints of strawberries and honey filled her nose. Tendrils of gold smoke stretched down the hall, leading Marigold forward. Her heart rose. She followed the mist as it curled past the living room and kitchen and turned into a bedroom.

The bed was centered in the room, flanked by two bedside tables. An object on one of the bedside tables was encircled in the golden mist. Marigold clicked on the flashlight and directed its beam at the object. It was a ceramic vase that had cracked in a few places and chipped at the top. Best of all, it looked old; old enough to have survived over two hundred years. The charm had worked.

Marigold dropped the vase into her backpack just as the bedroom lights flicked on. Screaming, she leapt backward. She yanked the stocking cap over her face and froze. *Oh my stars, I am so dead.*

"What's going on here?" Miss Jessica asked. Her face was a blur through the black fabric.

Marigold stared frantically around the room. Could she run past Miss Jessica and escape out the front door? Miss Jessica hadn't seen her face, or if she had, it was only for a split second. That wasn't enough for a conviction. Marigold could come up with an alibi for where she was all night. It was her word against Miss Jessica's. There was no proof!

Miss Jessica stood a few feet away from Marigold. "Marigold, I know it's you. You'd better take the hat off now."

Marigold hesitated, then pulled the cap off her head.

"Why are you in my house?" Miss Jessica asked, looking not exactly angry but not exactly friendly.

"I—I . . ." Marigold stuttered out a bunch of nothing.

Miss Jessica's eyebrows drew together. Definitely less friendly now. "Are you here to steal something?"

"No," Marigold said, shaking her head. "This is all a big misunderstanding."

"This isn't a joke, Marigold. I saw you put something into your backpack."

Marigold bit her lip. "Oh that. Well, that . . . was . . . Yes, I suppose I could see how you might think I'd taken that, but it was an accident, really."

Miss Jessica held out her hand, her mouth in a firm line. Marigold didn't even try to protest. She reached into her backpack, pulled out the vase, and handed it to Miss Jessica.

"Do you have anything else in there?" Miss Jessica asked, setting the vase on her bedside table.

Marigold shook her head. Miss Jessica continued to hold out her hand, and Marigold handed the bag over. She reached inside before dropping it to the ground, satisfied it was empty.

Miss Jessica reached for the vase once again and cradled it in her palms as if it were a baby bird. "Why would you take this? It's not worth anything."

"I don't know," Marigold said, bowing her head. Miss Jessica was going to call Mr. Jackson, and he'd haul her down to the police station in Eastport. Who knew if her mama and sisters would even pick up their phones? She'd have to spend the night in jail, all by herself.

"Hey," Miss Jessica said, bending down to look Marigold in the face. "You're a good kid and I'm pretty sure you're not in the habit of breaking into people's houses. What's going on, Marigold? I deserve an explanation."

Marigold coughed out a half laugh. "You wouldn't believe me if I told you."

"Try me," Miss Jessica said.

Marigold shrugged and sank onto the bed. What was the point of holding anything back? So Marigold took a deep breath and told Miss Jessica about the curse, the smell, the lightning, Birdie's accident, Lou's weird behavior, and the endless, horrible fighting. She explained about how Martha Willard might have cursed her family.

Miss Jessica sat down beside her. "That sounds awful."

"Do you believe me?" Marigold asked, staring at her in disbelief.

"I believe that you believe in it," Miss Jessica said gently.

Marigold gestured to the vase in Miss Jessica's hand. "I thought the vase was cursed."

Miss Jessica smiled down at the vase, turning it over in

her hands. "My brother, Cole, gave me this vase, and I guess it is cursed in a way. You see, Cole died in a car accident, and this vase was wrapped beside him in the passenger seat. He was on his way to my birthday dinner, and was late as usual because he'd gone to pick up this vase as a gift. It used to annoy me how he was always late, but I barely think about that now. It's easy to forget those unimportant things after someone is gone." Her chin trembled for a second before she righted it.

"I'm sorry," Marigold whispered.

Miss Jessica put the vase back on the nightstand, turning it until it sat in just the right spot on her bedside table where she must see it first thing every morning. "I know what it's like to miss a sibling. I'd do anything to get mine back. But you should have asked me for help before breaking into my house. You can't go around doing things like that."

"You're right. Are you going to call Mr. Jackson?" Marigold asked, holding her breath for the answer.

Miss Jessica sat still, letting the silence gather between them like a thick fog. After several beats she sighed. "No, but I am going to call your mama."

Marigold closed her eyes, imagining Mama's face when she heard the news. She couldn't picture her reaction. Would she discuss this with Marigold, or ignore the whole thing entirely? Marigold honestly didn't know.

Miss Jessica tapped her fingers against her chin. "I don't

have any family antiques here anymore. I let the visitor's center keep them all after the Founders' Day Celebration last year. But I do recall that there's an old bowl on display over there that supposedly belonged to Martha Willard. My granddaddy used to tell me stories about it being her favorite one to mix up her magical concoctions."

"I didn't know that," Marigold said slowly. Had the malediction been right in front of her all along, hiding in plain sight at the visitor's center?

After Miss Jessica called Mama, she sent Marigold on her way home. The lights from the harbor glinted on the water like stars in an ever-changing sky. It was a short walk back to her house, but her mind never stopped swirling. How could she possibly destroy Martha Willard's bowl kept locked up tight in the visitor's center? And what should she say to Mama about what had happened tonight?

Pushing open the front door, Marigold tripped over a large pile. She stumbled and snapped on the hall light. At her feet was a lumpy trash bag with Lou's field hockey sticks poking out the top. She opened the bag. There were balls, Lou's jersey, cleats, and shin guards.

In the kitchen Lou was sitting at the table, her hand cradling her chin. There was a bowl in front of her but she wasn't eating. The single light from the hallway barely lit the room, and Lou's face was all shadows and dark patches.

"Why is all your field hockey stuff in a trash bag?" Marigold asked.

Lou shrugged. "I'm throwing it away. I don't need it anymore. I'm off the team."

Marigold sank into another chair, unable to believe Lou's words. "What happened?"

Lou picked up her phone and stared down at it, though, as far as Marigold could tell, it was a blank screen. "It's not a big deal. I had a misunderstanding with Coach Bradley. I got into a fight with a girl on the team after the game today."

"A *fight?*"

"Yeah, Callie accused me of cheating, which was a lie, so I hit her."

"You started a fight on school grounds," Marigold said in disbelief.

"Callie started the fight when she said I cheated. She deserved it," Lou said in a fierce voice.

Marigold stood up and flicked on the kitchen light. The iron chandelier above the table flared to life. She gasped.

Lou had a large yellowing bruise on one cheek, an angry red scratch down the other, and a blackened eye. Her eyes were bloodshot and sunken in, and her mouth was twisted into an ugly snarl. Even the fiery red of her hair seemed dull. A smell of dirt and unwashed clothes clung to her skin. It was as if something—something evil—were eating her from the inside out.

"You look terrible," Marigold said.

"I feel fine," Lou said, raising a hand to her cheek and wincing at the movement. "More than fine, actually. I was ready to quit field hockey anyway. It's a waste of time and the girls on my team are losers."

"But I thought they were your friends," Marigold said.

"Are you siding with them?" Lou asked. Her face darkened with anger.

"No, I—I'm not." Marigold shrank back, wanting to put more space between herself and her sister. A sudden suspicion crept over her like a snake slithering up her arm. "You didn't use aromagic, did you?"

Lou glared. "What if I did?"

"Lou, you can't keep doing this," Marigold said urgently. "Don't you see? Aromagic is hurting you. You're getting sick and into fights, and now you're off the field hockey team."

Lou banged a fist on the table, and Marigold jumped to her feet, skittering backward.

"I'm getting what I want," Lou hissed. "And I like it."

This had to be the work of the curse. It was too much of a coincidence that Lou was turning into the worst version of herself right at this time. Whether it was the fighting with Birdie or the curse itself that was pushing Lou to misuse aromagic, Marigold had an awful feeling that something worse would happen if she couldn't destroy the malediction.

Mama appeared in the doorway and frowned at Marigold. "I can't believe you broke into Miss Jessica's home. Do I need to punish both my daughters in one night?"

"I already told you I'm not grounded." Lou sprang up, her entire body rigid. "You can't make me stay in this house."

Mama lifted her chin. "If you leave, I'll cut off cell service to your phone."

Lou flung her bowl across the room. It smashed onto the floor, breaking into a hundred pieces. "I hate you!" Lou yelled at Mama, and stormed out.

Mama glanced at the bowl and gathered the broom from the pantry closet, her movements slow. There was a suspicious brightness in her eyes despite the dim light.

"Did you really ground Lou?" Marigold asked. She couldn't remember Mama grounding any of them ever.

"I didn't have much of a choice," Mama said, sweeping the fragments of the bowl into a dustpan. "She got suspended from school for three days."

Not just kicked off the team but suspended as well. Lou was coming apart, and Marigold still hadn't managed to destroy the malediction.

"We should talk about Miss Jessica," Mama said, sitting down beside Marigold. "She told me you're afraid of a curse. She thinks you're unstable."

"You know that's not true," Marigold said.

"I know you're upset about Birdie's and Lou's behavior, as am I, but you must stop acting so recklessly."

"Fine. Whatever." Marigold wasn't stopping until the curse was broken.

"And can you explain why Miss Eugenie left me a message asking if I could attend the next meeting of the planning committee?" Mama asked, her eyes crinkling in confusion.

Marigold's chest tightened. She had forgotten about the show. "They want you to help volunteer for the play. It's an important job."

"I'm sure it is, but there's too much going on in this house at the moment. I'll help with the flower arrangements," Mama said as if the matter were settled.

Why couldn't Mama understand that the planning committee was a big deal? Did she even care that she would offend people and make Marigold look bad?

"Now, I've had a few ideas for how to resolve the conflict with your sisters." Mama reached into her pocket and pulled out a small glass bottle. The liquid inside was the pale green of a new plant shoot. "A touch of mint, rosemary, and plumeria. It's a protection charm. I blended it to rid a house of discord. This should help."

Marigold stared across the kitchen at the neat row of

potted herbs lined up on the window. They were perfectly green, preserved, and fragrant against the chipped paint and worn windowsill. Mama ignored the need for paint; she ignored the cracked countertops and scuffed floors. She didn't worry about what anyone thought of her, even if her not-worrying made things harder for Marigold. Mama cared about her plants and flowers and her dumb charms. She didn't bother with anything else, including her daughters.

"A protection charm? Are you kidding me?" Marigold said in disbelief.

"Why are you upset?" Mama asked.

"I'm upset because this is your fault. You won't admit what you've done. You cursed us!" Marigold said, almost yelling now.

"I did no such thing," Mama said in a quiet voice.

"You ignored the Lafleur curse. Gram warned you, but you didn't believe it because that would have meant you'd have to think about something else besides what you wanted, and I guess you wanted more than one child, though I can't figure out why since you barely spend any time with us. But you knew—you *knew*—there was a chance you would lose one or more of your daughters someday and that we could lose each other, but you didn't care." Marigold's voice shook. "You use aromagic, and you don't care that there are consequences to what you're doing!"

Mama's throat worked. "I always tell people about the possibility of a vex—"

"They're desperate, Mama. By the time they come see you, they don't care that fate demands a price. Shouldn't you stop people from doing something they'll regret forever?" Tears streamed down Marigold's face. She swiped them away, not wanting Mama to think she was sad. She wasn't sad. She was angry.

Mama stood and backed away. "Marigold, please calm down. You're worked up, and this isn't helping anything."

"I wish you would admit there's a curse and you didn't try to break it before we were born."

Mama stood, pacing the floor, not looking at Marigold. Each footfall sounded hollow and ominous. When she stopped, the lines around her mouth had deepened, making her look old.

"You're right, but I didn't . . . I don't believe in it," Mama said.

Marigold brushed past Mama. There was nothing else to say. She might have been furious with Mama, but she would still do everything in her power to fix her broken family. And she was headed straight to the visitor's center when it opened on Monday.

CHAPTER SEVENTEEN

Carnation alleviates depression and promotes healing of the heart.

Before Marigold opened her eyes the following morning, she felt the weight on the end of her bed, and there was the smell: orange and fir and wet grass. Her pulse quickened. She knew that smell. Her eyes flew open.

Daddy sat at the end of the bed, smiling down at her. "I was wondering when you were going to wake up."

Without thinking, Marigold shot up and flung herself across the bed, wrapping Daddy in a huge hug and letting the weight of everything that had happened these past three weeks release. He patted her back and whispered soft words. She wasn't sure what he said. It didn't matter. He was back at Lilac Cottage.

After several long moments Marigold pulled away. She rubbed her eyes, the wetness from her tears coating her knuckles. "What are you doing here?"

"I came to see you. You've stopped returning my calls. I was getting worried." Daddy's eyes were the same, a deep green like velvety moss. His face had the familiar small indentation between his bushy eyebrows. Yet there were differences too, even since the last time she'd seen him in person, just a month ago. His dark hair was mixed with more white, his shoulders were smaller than she remembered, and there was the scar down the right side of his cheek. It was fainter but still visible; a line drawn in the sand of his face that would never wash away.

"I thought you couldn't leave Asheville because of your treatment," Marigold said.

"I convinced the doctors to give me a reprieve, and your aunt Lynn wanted to visit some friends in Eastport," Daddy said. "Your mama also called me."

Marigold swallowed and stared at her hands, realizing they had curled into balls along her side. "Oh."

"She's worried about you," Daddy said. "She told me what happened at Miss Jessica's."

Marigold said nothing. There was so much to explain and no good way to do it.

"I picked up some chocolate chip cookies from Dream Pies on my way over here. I was thinking we could take them down to the beach. What do you say?" Daddy asked.

Marigold nodded. "I'd like that."

They left the house, holding their noses against the rotting smell. Marigold stayed quiet while Daddy told her about his physical therapy. He limped only a little on his right side as they walked.

The sun sparkled along the water, creating a golden path out to the horizon. They took off their shoes, and the sand was cool and yielding under their feet. The empty beach stretched out endlessly on either side of them.

Daddy sat down at the base of the dunes and opened the white paper bag, handing one of the cookies to Marigold. She took a bite, and the chocolate melted on her tongue. Sand dusted her feet. Daddy's arm leaned next to hers, barely touching but still warm. It would have felt so perfect if not for everything else going on.

Daddy cleared his throat. "You've been avoiding my phone calls."

Marigold remained silent.

"Would you like to talk about what's been happening around here?" Daddy asked.

"I don't know where to begin," Marigold said.

And right then she wanted to tell him all of it: how hard things had been since his accident, about how much she missed her sisters—her real sisters and not the people they'd recently become, about how scared she was. But he hadn't been there for months. As happy as she was to see him, there were things she couldn't tell him, that she needed to keep inside. She thought about how he kept prolonging his stay in Asheville, how he wasn't coming home to recover. He wouldn't understand the way he used to. He'd changed, she'd changed. So much was different.

"Why don't you begin at the beginning," Daddy said.

Marigold smiled a little. Daddy had always said this to her when she needed help solving a problem. Maybe the beginning was exactly where they needed to be.

"I suppose it started in 1811 when the curse was placed on our family."

Marigold told him about Birdie and Lou arguing, the accidents, and Lou misusing aromagic. At the end Daddy stared straight out at the ocean, not saying a word.

"Well?" Marigold asked.

"Well," Daddy said, and turned to face her. "I'm sorry, Marigold. I'm sorry I wasn't here, and you felt like you were on your own. Your mama had told me about the possibility of the curse long ago, but I trusted her when she said it wasn't real."

Marigold's eyes filled with tears. "It is real, and I've made a terrible mess of things."

"No, you haven't. Things were already a mess. You're just trying to fix them."

"I wish everything could go back to the way it was before, not just before the curse." Marigold ran sand through her fingers, watching it fall from her hands in a yellow landslide, unable to look at Daddy. "Before you left."

Daddy flinched. "I wish I had talked to you more and been honest about why I was leaving."

"I understand why. Who would want to live with someone who can smell their secrets and blurt them out for everyone to hear?"

"Are you talking about the night before the accident?" Daddy asked, his face puzzled.

Marigold bit her lip. "If I hadn't said anything, you and Mama might have stopped fighting. Maybe you wouldn't have wanted to take an extended business trip. I made it all worse. I don't blame you for wanting to get away from me."

On that awful night, Daddy and Mama had been arguing again, their voices sharpening like razors in her ears. She'd tried to block out the sound by burying her head under her covers, but it hadn't worked. Finally she'd crept downstairs, hoping her presence would quiet them. But as soon as she'd gotten halfway down the steps, the smell had risen, acrid and awful. She'd blurted out Daddy's secret all at once—*He hates it here*. At first Mama had looked shocked; then her face had closed up tight. Daddy's eyes had widened, then shut to slits. The following morning Daddy had announced his business trip, but Marigold had known he was leaving because of her.

"Oh, honey, your stating the truth about what I was feeling had nothing to do with me leaving. It is not your fault. I didn't want to get away from you. I'm getting old, and I want to see more of the world. And your mama and I . . . we needed time apart. But I still care about her, and the three of you girls, very much," Daddy said. There were tears in his eyes.

Marigold swallowed hard against the lump in her throat.

Daddy continued, "Things have changed. Heck, they're going to keep changing. But that doesn't mean I won't always find a way to see you and your sisters. I should have told you that months ago, but I was scared too."

Daddy put his arm around Marigold, and she leaned into him. None of this was fair. Even sitting with Daddy now, she knew it wasn't. He wouldn't return home anytime soon. Maybe he'd never live on Luna Island again. But now at least she understood and believed him when he said it wasn't her fault. She'd still see him, he still loved her, and she knew she could learn to live with all of that. What she couldn't live with was losing her sisters.

Marigold stared ahead at the ghosts of her, Birdie and Lou on the beach. She pictured the two of them in front of her, racing through the sand. Lou would throw sand onto Birdie's head, and Birdie would tackle Marigold to the ground in a hug, the three of them breathless with laughter. This was what she missed most, the happiness that only came from being with the two people who knew her the very best in the world, who had shared her heartaches and triumphs in equal measure. They'd taken care of her when she was little, and still did, in different ways now that she was almost a teenager. They knew every corner of her heart, all her drama, selfishness, and goodness. They understood the real her and never thought she should change a bit of who she was. Until the curse.

"I still don't know what to do about Birdie and Lou," Marigold said, her voice muffled against Daddy's arm. "If only they would help me. Birdie always knows how to fix a problem, and Lou can protect us against anything. I'm hopeless on my own."

Daddy straightened her up. "I'd hardly say that. You have a lot of talents too. You see things Birdie and Lou miss. You can tell when someone is sad or angry even if they haven't said it. You use that insight to cheer us all up, to stop unnecessary fights, to bring joy to our entire family."

Marigold's face flushed. "I do?"

"You do. When you were born, your mama was so happy. She wanted a big family. I think she was awfully lonely growing up. She said most of her family members only had one child, never three. But she thought a third daughter was exactly what our family needed. She was right. Whatever is going on with your sisters, we will find a way to get through this together, okay?" Daddy smiled at her.

Marigold straightened up as Daddy's words sank in deep. Even if Birdie and Lou wouldn't help her, things weren't completely hopeless. She still had people she could rely on. A plan was already forming, but she couldn't do it alone.

Sam was waiting at the boat ramp when she arrived that afternoon. She'd texted him a dozen apologies for yesterday, and he'd finally responded and agreed to meet her. The ramp itself was a concrete slab that slanted down into one of the creeks backing up to the forest. There was a weathered wood railing along the side. The creek water was still, and weeds clustered along the edges of the bank. On Sundays, at this time of day, no one else was around.

Sitting on the nearby dock, his feet dangling in the water, Sam turned as Marigold approached. He didn't wave or smile. Marigold's stomach dipped. He obviously wasn't over yesterday. But at least he was giving her a chance. She had to show him how sorry she was.

Marigold took a seat next to him, thinking of all the times she'd sat in this exact spot and watched him put his two-person kayak into the water. They hadn't gone kayaking since school had started, and she hadn't realized until now how much she missed it. He'd hold it steady as she clambered in. Then they'd be off, exploring the creeks, usually with a fishing rod draped across Sam's lap. Sam did most of the paddling, but he never complained. She'd notice the marsh grass undulating and the silver glint of a fish tail flicking out of the water. And especially last summer, it was their kayak rides that had helped her remember there was more to her world than Daddy's accident and Mama's silence and the town's hatred of their family.

"Thanks for meeting me," Marigold said.

Sam nodded but kept quiet.

Marigold had no choice but to dive right in. "Sam, I'm so, so, *so* sorry about what I said about the band. Please forgive me. I didn't mean it."

"You did."

"No, I—"

Sam held up a hand to stop her, and Marigold clamped her mouth shut. The water lapped against the side of the dock in a gentle rhythm as the silenced stretched on.

"It wasn't what you said," Sam continued, staring out at the water and not looking at her. "It was that you said it to Lauren behind my back. You were making fun of me to other people. People who had said mean things about *you*. That . . . hurt."

Marigold gulped. "I feel awful."

Sam shrugged.

"Can I make it up to you?" Marigold asked. "I could bake you some cookies or help you with algebra or go to your extra band practices—"

"That's okay." Sam ran a hand over his purple hair. "I know you feel bad right now. But Lauren is not a nice person. She'll make you think . . ." His voice faded into the breeze.

"I was the one who was mean," Marigold said.

Sam raised his eyebrows without commenting.

All of a sudden Marigold wondered why she *had* made the mean comment about the band. She knew what it was like when Lauren made fun of her behind her back. It had made her feel small and unimportant and sad. And yet now Marigold had done the same thing to Sam, her very best friend. All because she'd wanted to impress a few girls? Marigold swallowed. That was not the kind of person she wanted to be.

"I won't do it again, Sam," Marigold said. "I won't let myself talk about other people like that, especially you. I promise. And just so you know, *you* sounded really good when you were playing yesterday."

Sam half smiled down at his lap. "Thanks." He finally met her eyes. "Let's forget this whole thing."

"Really?" Marigold asked.

"Really," Sam said, but his smile wasn't as bright as usual.

Marigold felt her whole body sigh in relief. It was her fault if Sam doubted her. She was lucky to have him as her best friend and would work to earn back his trust.

For now Marigold only swung her feet above the water. "I saw Daddy today. He came back for a few hours."

"Really? How was it?" Sam leaned forward.

Marigold thought about his question for several seconds. "Weird."

"Good weird or bad weird?" Sam asked.

"Okay weird." Marigold wasn't sure how else to explain it.

Yet Sam nodded as if he understood, and she knew he did. He always got what Marigold really meant.

"I came up with an idea for destroying the malediction. But—" Marigold hesitated. "I can't do it on my own. I know the timing is terrible, and I feel bad even asking after what I did yesterday."

"How can I help?"

Tears welled up behind Marigold's eyes at Sam's immediate response, but she blinked them away. Instead she let out a shaky laugh. "You'd better brace yourself. This might be tricky."

CHAPTER EIGHTEEN

Sprinkle mimosa for purification before breaking a curse.

On Monday afternoon Marigold and Sam stood outside the visitor's center. Luckily, she wasn't missing anything. Ms. Ballard had cancelled rehearsal after a leak in the roof of the town auditorium had damaged the stage over the weekend; more of the vex at work, but at least no one had been hurt.

The visitor's center was located inside a weathered gray cottage, surrounded by a white picket fence with manicured violets. Beside it the Old Salt Lighthouse reached high up to the blue sky. Patches of white paint flaked off the brick sides of the lighthouse, and small square windows looped around the top. A metal catwalk circled the highest point, two hundred feet from the ground.

Edith Markel cracked open the door of the visitor's center. A few leaves from the nearby oaks fluttered to the ground, already yellow around the edges. She jumped at the sight of Sam and Marigold.

"Samuel and Marigold, what a surprise." Miss Edith's voice did not make it sound as if it were a good surprise.

Though Miss Edith had worked at the visitor's center forever, she didn't particularly like visitors. She liked quiet and order, and wore the same crisp white button-down shirt and navy-blue pants every day, hot or cold, rain or sun. Whenever visitors climbed the Old Salt Lighthouse, she usually stood at the bottom with a scowl on her face the entire time.

"Did your bikes break down?" Miss Edith asked.

"Nope. We're here to look around. We want to learn more about our heritage," Sam said, and smiled his winning smile that usually melted any grown-up into a puddle.

"Why?" Miss Edith asked suspiciously.

"For, um, fun?" Marigold said.

"It's too late in the afternoon for fun," Miss Edith said, and frowned.

"Well, then not for fun. We're here for serious research,"

Sam said in a cheerful voice, climbing the wooden stairs that led to the front door of the visitor's center.

Miss Edith sniffed and moved out of the way, realizing she couldn't prevent them from entering but clearly wishing she could.

The visitor's center was one long room with a grouping of postcards, fake pirate swords, and T-shirts in the front next to a small desk and cash register. The island relics lined the back walls in locked, glass display cases. Marigold and Sam needed to find the bowl, steal Miss Edith's keys to unlock the case, *and* destroy the bowl itself.

Marigold rushed over to the cases. In each one was an array of objects. There were small knives, ceramic jugs, an old quilt linked to Molly Allerton, a few books, and a couple of maps that belonged to the Spencers.

"I don't see a bowl," Marigold whispered after she'd scanned every object in the first case.

"It must be in the next case," Sam whispered back, pretending to read a plaque about a rusted fork.

Marigold glanced over at the front. Miss Edith watched them from the register. A line formed between her eyes. She picked up the phone and spoke quietly into the receiver. Marigold tried to ignore her. She needed to focus. Her eyes roamed over the objects inside the second case. There was another quilt, a plate, a few pewter cups. There! Tucked in the left-hand corner between a yellowed map and a stack of old books was a bowl.

The bowl was a large vessel of graying ceramic. The sides were chipped, with a faint design of red poppies intertwined with green vines. Marigold took a deep breath and bent closer. Off to the side of the case were small plaques describing each object. Sure enough, the bowl was attributed to Martha Willard from the early 1800s. This was it.

"Found it," Marigold silently mouthed to Sam.

Miss Edith was off the phone. Her arms crossed, she continued to stare at the two of them. Sam edged down the room toward the small desk with the cash register. The keys were visible on top of the desk. Marigold stepped into the center of the room and smiled at Miss Edith, drawing her attention and distracting her from Sam.

"Miss Edith, did you hear I got the lead in the school musical?" she asked.

Miss Edith walked over to Marigold, her face relaxing. Her back was to the desk. "I did hear. I'm a big fan of our productions. I always go see the show," she admitted.

"It's called *The Magical Town of Oz*." Marigold clasped her hands together. "I was hoping we could put some flyers up here for publicity. This is such a popular spot."

"I suppose we could," Miss Edith said, looking pleased.

Sam was at the desk now, reaching for the keys. Miss

Edith took a step sideways as if to walk back to the front desk. If she caught Sam now, they'd never get the bowl. Marigold panicked.

"Would you like to hear my big solo?" Marigold asked, and without waiting for an answer, she burst into song.

Miss Edith looked understandably confused but stayed put in the center of the room, listening to Marigold. Meanwhile, Sam grabbed the keys and held them above his head in triumph behind Miss Edith's back. Marigold finished the song with a flourish.

"That was . . . quite something," Miss Edith said.

"I can come back and sing anytime," Marigold offered.

"That won't be necessary," Miss Edith said firmly.

Miss Edith headed toward the front, passing Sam, who had stuffed the keys into his pocket. He slipped Marigold the key ring. They went straight to the glass case with Martha Willard's bowl. The front door chimed opened, and Mr. Jackson strolled in.

Marigold froze. Of all the rotten luck. The *law* was here, right now! How was she going to destroy a priceless artifact with the director of public safety watching her every move?

Mr. Jackson wore his white shirt with the Luna Island emblem on the left pocket. He strolled over to Marigold and Sam.

"How are y'all doing this fine day?" Mr. Jackson asked.

"Okay," Marigold said. Her gut clenched as tight as a fist.

Mr. Jackson gestured to the display case. "Pretty interesting stuff. You kids like history?"

"I do," Sam said at once. "I've always wanted to learn more about this island's past, especially about the founding families like your own."

"The Spencers were an interesting bunch, that's for sure. Did you know they say my great-great-great-great-grandfather could tell when trouble was coming by a red haze that would spread across the horizon just for him?" Mr. Jackson said, chuckling.

"That's cool," Sam said.

They keys were warm in Marigold's pocket. She clutched them tightly. The metal bit into her skin.

"Be careful in here now," Mr. Jackson said. "Lots of valuable artifacts."

"We will," Sam said.

Mr. Jackson sauntered away, as relaxed as anything, and stopped in front of another case. Was he ever going to leave?

"This is your chance," Sam whispered. He angled in front of her, shielding her hands from view.

Marigold's entire body tied itself into knots. Her hand shook. She pulled out the keys and fit the smallest one into the lock on the glass case. It didn't work. She tried the next key, but it was too big. She could hear Mr. Jackson's foot-steps near the front of the room. How much time did she have before he realized what she was up to? Her palms were clammy. She jammed the final key into the lock and turned. The lock clicked. Fitting her finger into the notch on the glass door, she slid it open.

The bowl was inches away. All she needed to do was pick up it up and smash it on the ground, but how was she going to do that in front of Miss Edith and Mr. Jackson? But then how could she not? She didn't know how much longer she had left before the curse took one or both of her sisters away. This was life or death! Her eyes flicked from the bowl to Miss Edith to Mr. Jackson, and back once more. Meanwhile, Sam was pointing his chin toward the bowl in increasingly jerky movements.

Marigold reached into the display case. Her arms trembled.

"Marigold Lafleur, what are you doing?" Miss Edith yelled.

"Now!" Sam cried.

Marigold didn't stop. She didn't think. She grabbed the bowl, squeezed her eyes shut, and slammed it to the floor.

Smash!

The bowl broke into a thousand pieces.

Miss Edith yelled, "What did you do?"

Mr. Jackson hurried toward Miss Edith. "Let's all stay calm."

Miss Edith kept on shouting, but Marigold beamed at Sam. Her chest expanded as if someone had blown up a giant balloon inside her. She'd done it. The curse was broken. She threw her arms around Sam in a hug. "Thank you."

When she pulled back, Sam's face was red. "I didn't do anything."

"Yes, you did." Marigold hoped she would have had the courage to steal the keys and destroy the malediction on her own, but it had been a whole lot easier with Sam by her side.

Miss Edith huffed over, her face suffused with rage. Marigold took a step back from the anger radiating off her. She looked like a furious chili pepper, all wrinkled red face and pointy chin.

"You children ruined a piece of Luna Island history! Mr. Jackson, arrest them immediately!" Miss Edith screeched.

"Sam had nothing to do with it," Marigold said, putting up her hands in protest.

"It's okay," Sam whispered. "I'll handle them."

Marigold turned to Miss Edith. "I'm sorry. It was an accident."

"It was a priceless artifact," Miss Edith snapped. "It's vandalism, plain and simple. How did this case even get open? What are my keys doing in the lock?"

Mr. Jackson looked at the shattered bowl and Miss Edith's face. He reached for his phone clipped onto his belt. "I think we'd best call your parents."

Marigold knew she needed to stop smiling, but the corners of her lips would not turn down. She'd endure Mama and Miss Edith and Mr. Jackson. It was all worth it because she'd destroyed the malediction. Her sisters were safe.

CHAPTER NINETEEN

Geranium offers protection against danger and dark magic.

Marigold flung open the door to her house. Her heart lifted as she smelled a blend of gardenia and vanilla. Birdie and Lou! They were both here together, waiting for her. She'd done it. She'd actually done it!

After sprinting up the stairs, two at a time, Marigold burst into Birdie and Lou's room to find Birdie standing in the middle right where she belonged. Marigold's entire body sparked with joy. She covered the space between them in two gigantic leaps and threw her arms around Birdie.

"It's over now. I missed you," Marigold said, squeezing tight.

Birdie stepped back and turned to her closet.

Marigold frowned, expecting more of a reunion. "What did it feel like when it happened?"

"When what happened?" Birdie didn't turn around.

"When the curse broke," Marigold said impatiently. "Did you suddenly sense things were different? Do you feel like yourself again?" It was then that Marigold registered the half-packed suitcase on the ground. "Are you going somewhere?"

"I'm moving in with Gram."

Marigold's pulse stuttered. She sank onto Lou's bed. "But I broke the bowl," she said, more to herself than to Birdie.

Birdie pulled out several shirts. "I'm not sure what you think you did, but nothing is different around here."

Nothing is different. The words slowly sank in.

"I don't understand," Marigold said.

"It's simple. I need to focus on school and applying for college scholarships. Gram lives a mile from Eastport High. This way I won't have to ride the ferry back and forth twice a day. It will give me more time for studying and extracurricular activities."

A coldness settled into Marigold's bones. Birdie was leaving.

Birdie sighed at Marigold's face. "I'm sorry you're upset, but I have to do what's right for me for once. Besides, I think a little separation from each other is for the best right now. We need some time to heal from this constant fighting."

"That's not true. What happened to us sticking together through anything?" Marigold asked.

Birdie had *promised* her after Daddy had left; she'd promised they would always have one another. She'd promised she wouldn't leave. Marigold's heart was cracking apart like ice on top of winter leaves.

"It's time for you to grow up, Marigold. We're individuals who want different things. Did you really expect we were all going to live together forever in the same place?" Birdie asked.

"No." *Yes*.

Marigold had imagined that someday the three sisters would live in an apartment together in New York City. She would go on auditions and come home to Birdie's soups and Lou's jokes, and they would go for walks in Central Park every night. But maybe that was Marigold's dream and not Birdie's or Lou's; maybe her sisters fit perfectly inside that dream only in her head, not in real life.

Birdie bustled around in her closet, placing the shirts

neatly into her suitcase and wincing at the movement. She gingerly touched her upper arm.

"Did something happen to your arm?" Marigold asked. Goose bumps dotted her skin in warning.

Birdie frowned. "Actually, yes. It was the weirdest thing. I was in the Moon Market this morning, and a whole row of shelves collapsed and hit me."

Marigold gasped for air. "Was anyone else hurt?"

"It was mostly bruises and cuts. I think Mr. Mercer may have broken his leg. I had to get five stitches. A part of the shelf broke off and sliced open my arm. The doctor said if the metal had gone in a millimeter to the left, it would have hit my brachial artery and I'd have died in minutes." Birdie patted her arm. There was still a jagged red line on her forehead where the shingles had struck her last week. "Such a freak accident."

Bile slithered up Marigold's throat. The curse had almost killed Birdie today.

"Does—does Mama know you're leaving?" Marigold managed to ask.

"It was her idea." Birdie's mouth twisted into the shadow of a smile. "She hardly seems to care. She's already back down in the basement working on her latest concoction that will probably mess up someone's life. At least this time I won't be around to see it."

Marigold stood, though the floor slid sideways under her feet. She reached out a hand to steady herself against the bed. Still swaying, she made her way back downstairs. Her heart hammered in her ears as if there were a construction zone inside her head.

Gram was waiting in the living room, seated on the couch. "Your mother wants a word with you. I heard about what happened today. Do you have an explanation?"

Marigold ignored Gram's question. It wasn't important. "Birdie almost died."

Gram rose to her feet. "I'm aware, Marigold. Why else do you think I'm here?"

"You can't take her away!" Marigold exclaimed.

"Taking Birdie with me is the only option. I've warded my entire house with a powerful charm strengthened with geranium. Your mother will focus all her energy on the problem of your other sister. I saw Lou when I arrived. She is most certainly ill. We know she's misusing aromagic."

"Mama knows?" Marigold asked, astonished. Mama had been in her own world even more these last few weeks since the smell had first arrived; Marigold hadn't thought she had any idea what was going on.

"Of course she knows. She has eyes, doesn't she? She's committed to stopping it, but it will be easier to address without the distraction of constant arguments. And . . ."

Gram hesitated. "If we separate you ourselves, it may keep something worse from happening."

"So that's it. We're just going to stay apart?" The dingy yellow walls blurred in Marigold's vision. "Why isn't everyone trying to fix what's really happening? Why won't anyone help me break the curse?"

Gram leaned on the arm of the couch, suddenly looking exhausted. Her face was drawn, and her cheeks drooped down toward her chin. "Don't you think I tried?"

"You did?"

"Of course I did." Gram drew in a long rattling breath. "When I was young and first married, I knew I wanted children. I tried to find the malediction. I searched this entire island, every corner and crevice I could think of. Every book I could find."

"You never said—" Marigold's body was as taut as a wire.

"I didn't want to take away your hope." Gram's face softened to a gentle expression Marigold had never seen before. "You were desperate to do something."

"I thought I'd found the malediction today, but I was wrong," Marigold said. Tears gathered behind her eyes.

"I am sorry," Gram said sadly.

Birdie came into the room then, holding her bags. In a matter of minutes Gram and Birdie were down the hall and out the front door. Marigold trailed behind. Lou was standing beside the porch in the garden where they'd spent half their lives together. She looked miserable. Her hair was stringy, and her shoulders hunched over her body as if to protect it from unseen forces. Her black eye had turned a sickly purple. The bruise on her cheek was yellow tinged with green.

"I'll give you a moment," Gram said, and walked toward the edge of the yard.

The three sisters stared at one another. There was a chill in the air, and Marigold shivered against it.

"Well, good luck," Birdie finally said. "I'm sorry to go, but I have to do this for my education."

Lou snorted. "What a farewell."

"Would you rather me leave without saying anything?" Birdie sniped.

"I'd rather you be honest," Lou said. "You don't want to leave because of school. You can get into any college you want."

The rotten smell hung over everything. The roses by Lou's side had shriveled up, the leaves blackened. When had that happened? No one had worked in the garden in weeks, and it showed. The thorns stood out among the twisting branches. Leaves littered the ground at her feet. The garden was dying.

"You know what? You're right. I want to leave because I can't stand being around you." Birdie pointed at Lou.

"You don't even see what's happening. You've turned into a cold and selfish person. You push people away and lash out against anyone trying to help you, because deep down you know the truth."

"And what's that?" Lou challenged her.

"If someone knew the real you, they wouldn't want you. No one wants to stay friends or sisters with a self-centered brat. So there you go. You got your wish. You're alone."

Lou inhaled sharply. Something shattered behind her eyes.

"Don't say that," Marigold said, her voice thick with tears. "She's not alone!"

Birdie rounded on Marigold. "And you're not the younger sister I thought you were if you think you need her in your life. There are some people you can't fix."

Marigold recoiled as if Birdie's words had pierced her heart. Even if this was the curse, Birdie still believed what she said, deep down in some part of her. The curse was only making her say it.

Lou plucked a branch by her side. A thorn pricked her thumb, drawing beads of crimson blood. Her voice was low, venomous. "As if you should talk, Birdie. You think you're so much better than us. You're boring and a tyrant and always have your head in a book. You try to act all perfect as if that will make people like you, but it doesn't work.

Everyone can see what a loser you are. They're all laughing at you behind your back."

"It's not true. She doesn't really mean that," Marigold said, frantic as she looked from one sister to the other. She had to stop this. These were words that could wound their relationship forever. They were possibly the last words they'd ever speak to one another.

"I do mean it," Lou sneered, and flicked a disdainful glance at Marigold. "Stay out of our business. You can't turn everything into some dramatic scene that ends in happily ever after; you can't solve this."

Marigold's lip trembled, and tears slid down her cheeks.

Birdie spun around and stalked off down the path. Her arms were rigid by her sides and her head was high. She didn't look back once.

Lou growled and punched the side of the house. Marigold gasped. Lou's knuckles were bleeding, and her face was furious.

She rounded on Marigold. "Don't look at me," she hissed, then swirled back and ran into the woods.

Marigold stood as if in a daze, Clemence's poem filling her brain. *Misfortune and hate tear apart. Dark magic stole a sister's heart.*

Time was up.

The curse had won.

• • •

Marigold's eyes were nearly swollen shut the following morning from the constant flow of tears the night before, but she washed her face and got dressed for school anyway. When she left, Lou's door was shut tight, as was Mama's. Their house was silent.

At school Marigold pretended to listen in class and forced herself to smile at her classmates. She was too upset to even talk to Sam. She felt like a robot. None of it sank in, not the faces or teachers, certainly not her schoolwork. All she could think of was her failure to stop the curse.

Marigold was standing at Lauren's locker with Kendall and Julia, trying to look interested as Lauren rambled on about her pool party.

"And we're going to rent a karaoke machine," Lauren continued.

"I can't wait," Julia said. "Two girls in my science class heard about it. They already want to know when you'll start inviting people."

Lauren smiled. "I guess I need to finalize the guest list since the entire school will know soon. I feel bad, though. I can't invite everyone."

But Lauren's smile said she didn't feel too bad.

"Marigold, I heard what happened in the visitor's center. Did you get in trouble?" Kendall asked, her brown eyes soft.

"Not too much. It was an accident." *And one more thing to worry about.* Marigold wondered how many people were gossiping about her smashing a priceless artifact.

"You're the star of the play. That's a big deal around here. No one will care if you break some old relic," Lauren said, and rolled her eyes.

Except Marigold was the star of nothing right now. The vex was continuing to ruin the entire play.

"Hey, looks like the cowboy wants to talk to you," Lauren said, nodding her head at Sam, who stood across the hall waving. She giggled. "I still can't think about their band without laughing. You should do him a favor and tell him they're not ready for a concert yet, or ever."

Marigold frowned. "Sam is a good guitar player."

"I guess I heard a different band last weekend," Lauren said, smirking.

"I have to go," Marigold said abruptly.

"Don't forget this." Lauren held out the purple scrunchie Marigold had pulled out of her hair because it scratched at her earlobe. It matched the ones Lauren, Kendall, and Julia were all wearing.

"Thanks," Marigold said, and shoved it into her pocket before walking over to Sam.

Sam was hopping from one foot to the other. "Where were you this morning and last night? I called and texted you! You never responded. Did we break the curse?"

Marigold focused on her shoes, realizing for the first time all day that she'd worn two different-colored socks. "It didn't work."

"It didn't work?" Sam asked, his forehead wrinkling in confusion.

"We didn't break it."

A large group of eighth-grade boys pushed past them. They were talking and laughing too loudly, and their back-packs jostled one another. The hallway smelled like pencil shavings and peanut butter. It was the usual smell, the usual kids. Marigold didn't understand how everything could smell the same and look the same when her entire world had altered.

"But—you smashed the bowl," Sam said.

Marigold raised one shoulder. "I guess the bowl wasn't the malediction, or smashing it wasn't enough to break the curse."

"There's got to be something we can do. We can go back to see if Gram has any more information, or we can do bet-ter research. I don't think I'm allowed back into the visitor's center again, but we could go check the library for more books or—or something."

Marigold hit her forehead with one hand. "Gosh, Sam, I'm an awful friend. I can't believe I forgot to ask. Did you get in trouble with your parents?"

"They weren't happy with me. But it's okay."

Marigold could see he was holding back from telling her the whole truth. "That bad?"

"Let's talk about this later," Sam said.

"Tell me now," Marigold demanded.

Sam sighed. "I'm grounded for the next month, which means no hanging out after school, no band practice, no pep rally."

"But you're supposed to perform next week."

Sam looked miserable. "I know. I'm hoping I can talk them into letting me play."

Marigold closed her eyes, feeling sick. "This is all my fault. If I hadn't roped you into my dumb scheme, you wouldn't have gotten in trouble. I'm sorry. I'll talk to your parents. Tell them the whole thing was my idea. I should be the one in trouble."

"You're not doing that," Sam said. "Anyway, it won't matter. You know my parents. They will only say I should have known better and not gone along with you."

"But you were only being a good friend," Marigold said.

"It was worth it. We were trying to save your family. We still are. What can we do next?"

Marigold wished she could take back everything that had happened the day before. Smashing that bowl and getting Sam in trouble had been for nothing. All she did was mess things up for anyone who cared about her.

"*We* aren't going to do anything next," Marigold said. "This isn't your problem to solve anymore." She hurried down the hallway, pushing through the crowds.

Who cared if Marigold was late to class? Who cared if she got in trouble? Nothing mattered.

"Hey, Marigold." Anna's voice rang out from the side of the hall. Anna hurried to catch up with her.

Marigold tried to smile, but seeing Anna reminded her of the ruined play.

Anna was breathless. "I wanted to talk to you—" She stopped and peered more closely at Marigold's face. "Are you okay?"

"Not really," Marigold said. "I don't feel very well. I'm going home."

"I could bring by your homework assignments later if you want."

Marigold waved away the offer. Homework was the last thing she cared about.

"Okay, if you're sure." Anna frowned. "Anyway, I was thinking about the play and how we haven't had a good rehearsal yet. Let's hold a cast meeting and convince everyone to really work hard. What do you think? We don't want this play to be a bust. Everyone needs to see how good you are."

Marigold's eyes pricked with tears. Anna was willing to set up a cast-wide meeting to try to convince people to work harder because she believed in Marigold. Anna, who was too shy to speak in class. The pit in Marigold's stomach deepened. She hadn't even earned the lead. She'd stolen it *from* Anna.

"I'm not sure we can fix this," Marigold said.

"That's not true," Anna protested.

Marigold leaned over and pulled Anna into a quick hug. "You're a good person, Anna."

Anna's eyes were wide. "Thank you."

"I'll see you later," Marigold said, and started back down the hall.

"I hope you feel better," Anna called after her.

Marigold didn't say another word. How could she when the truth was too painful to admit? She was never going to feel better again.

CHAPTER TWENTY

Honeysuckle will draw friends home.

The school nurse called Mama, who agreed Marigold could be sent home for the rest of the day. The sun was shining but it seemed too bright. The sickly-sweet rot still hung over the island, and the scent turned Marigold's stomach. Her sisters were gone; Birdie had left the island for who knows how long, and Lou had disappeared into her own problems. Marigold had run out of ideas, and she was too upset to come up with another plan at the moment.

Miss Iris was sitting on the steps of the Dolphin Gift

Shop, cradling a mug of tea. "Marigold," she called out.

Marigold stopped, shielding her eyes from the sun. Miss Iris stood and met her on the sidewalk. The deck between the Dogwood Coffee Shop and Dream Pies was deserted. The yellow umbrellas over the tables looked like wilted daisies today, leaning to one side or the other.

"Are you all right? Shouldn't you be in school?" Miss Iris asked, looking concerned.

"I'm feeling a little sick," Marigold said honestly. "Mama said it was all right for me to go home and rest."

Miss Iris raised her eyebrows. "And how is your mama?"

Marigold shrugged. "Oh, fine. I guess."

Miss Iris sipped her tea, gazing out at the endless water. "I miss her."

Marigold stared at Miss Iris, certain she must have heard her wrong.

Miss Iris chuckled softly. "I can see you're surprised. It wasn't my choice to stay away from Lilac Cottage. Your mama told me not to come around for a while. She wanted her space while she . . . processed everything." She took another sip of her tea, her eyes glassy. "I wondered many times if I was doing the right thing. She's looked—"

"Strange," Marigold finished for her.

"I was going to say 'lonely,'" Miss Iris said. The ferryboat horn blared in the distance, and the wind off the water rattled the flags hanging from the shop doors. "I hope you know that not everyone blames your family for the earthquake."

Except it was their fault; it was her fault.

"I think most people blame us for a lot of things, and maybe they should," Marigold said.

Miss Iris wrinkled her brow. "Marigold, that's not so. Your family has done so much good. Your mama helped many of us when we were ill. I can't count the number of times she came into my shop, exhausted from staying up all night to make and deliver her healing mists to folks around the island. Or the happiness charms she mixes to lift people up when they're feeling down. She's given us protection charms to keep our children safe at college or bring family members home from journeys. Why, Miss Eugenie said the protection charm your mama made to keep her home secure was the only thing that helped her feel safe after her husband died."

Marigold dropped her backpack, astonished. "Miss Eugenie? She would never use one of Mama's mists. She thinks we're all dangerous."

Miss Iris shook her head, frowning. "You're wrong. After your daddy's accident, Miss Eugenie brought over enough meals to stock your whole freezer. As did Linda Fitch, Lizzie Abernathy, Jessica Willard, Abigail Monrow, Mr. Goodman, myself, and many, many others. We organized a big meal-delivery service for y'all for weeks."

Marigold thought back to those first weeks after Daddy's accident, rushing home to eat and change clothes before heading back to the hospital to sit at Daddy's bedside. She'd never stopped to wonder where the suppers of chicken casseroles and lasagnas had come from, how the cold cuts, bread, and fruit had appeared in their pantry. She'd never thought people cared enough to do that for her family.

"I didn't know," Marigold said softly.

Miss Iris patted her arm. "My dear girl, there are certainly people who don't trust your mama's gifts or who don't believe magic is real, but there are many others who do. I'm one of them. Your mama found me my husband. I was lonely and unhappy, and I couldn't seem to do anything about it. Your mama—" She stopped and swiped at her eyes. "She knew I needed help, and mixed up a love charm for me. My Bobby got off the ferry a week later."

A memory slipped into Marigold's mind, as clear as the cloudless sky above her. She saw herself, Birdie, Lou, and Mama in the basement; Mama was mixing up a classic love charm of rose, daffodil, and ylang-ylang. A cloud of velvety red tapering out to the palest pink had risen from the charm. They held hands as Mama told them to blow on the brew with the clearest intention: *Bring love to Miss Iris*. That one charm, which Marigold had not thought of since, had worked. She had helped change Miss Iris's life for the better.

Miss Iris continued, "Now, I know there are people who love to talk, who say some of the charms don't end how they should, but you know what I say to that?"

Marigold swallowed. "What?"

"I say all of life has its risks. Some of your choices will be good and some won't. Everyone makes mistakes, but that doesn't mean you stop trying to make things better. In the end, you've got to do what feels right to you, and you can't worry too much about what other folks think." Miss Iris laughed a little. "Listen to me, going on like this." She waved Marigold down the road. "Go on home and rest now. I hope you feel better, and tell your mama I asked after her."

Pulling on her backpack, Marigold nodded and started back down the path, dazed by Miss Iris's words. She thought of the town bringing them meals after Daddy's accident, Mr. Goodman giving her free ice cream, Miss Jessica dropping off a chocolate pie, and Miss Linda insisting she stay for supper with Sam at least twice a week over the summer.

Marigold thought about what her family had done for Miss Iris, what Mama had done for so many people on the island to help them. How Mama was always paying atten-tion to the people of Luna Island. Marigold had thought Mama was being nosey, but perhaps she had looked at in the wrong way. She remembered how aromagic made her feel, as if she were doing the exact right thing at the exact right time. Yes, the charm to keep Daddy on Luna Island had been a mistake, but she'd learned from that, and she would always keep trying to do better. It seemed she'd misjudged her town. She'd thought everyone couldn't accept her and her family. But that wasn't true. Perhaps the truth was that Marigold couldn't accept herself.

Marigold's whole body lightened. For a moment she felt as if she could float into the air, up past the masts of the marina boats and filmy bits of clouds, straight up to the lemon-colored sun. She breathed in, smelling honeysuckle and ocean brine. She was tired of denying who she was and what she could do, even if she was different from most other people, even if people couldn't understand.

Aromagic was a part of her, it was in her blood, and it was maybe the only thing that could save her family.

It was well past eleven that night. Marigold had waited until Mama and Lou were fast asleep. She turned out all the lamps in her room and lit three candles in a row on her windowsill. Their flames gave off an eerie, thin glow as if the room were trapped underwater. Mama said the cover of darkness was best for performing enchantments.

Marigold gripped Clemence's diary in her lap, feeling

the smoothness of the leather under her hands as she opened to the first page, the one with Clemence's name inscribed in her loopy, now faded handwriting: *Diary of Clemence Lafleur*. Taking a deep breath, Marigold closed her eyes. Through her eyelids, she could see the candlelight flickering. She put her hands on the paper, covering Clemence's writing. *Clemence Lafleur, show me your secrets*.

Nothing happened.

Marigold tried again, breathing in as deeply as she could, waiting for the acrid sting in her nose. She had no idea if she could smell Clemence's secrets from only her diary, but she had to try. Seconds passed; still, she smelled nothing. Marigold shifted in her seat and opened her eyes. The diary had grown heavy in her lap, the corners of it pressing into her knees. Perhaps if she read a few of Clemence's entries, it would help get her into the right mindset.

After flipping through the pages, Marigold stopped at the entry right before the Great Hurricane, the one with the ripped-out page. She'd forgotten about the missing pages. The back of her neck prickled, like a sewing machine tracing tiny stitches in her skin. What if those pages contained something important? Like who had cursed the Lafleurs? What if this was the secret she needed to locate?

Once again Marigold breathed in deeply, but this time she kept her eyes open. She stared down hard at the ragged edges of the binding. The burning smell was there before she could blink, stronger than ever. Instead of pushing it down, she inhaled more deeply. Her head filled with an image of a fragile and torn piece of paper. It was wedged into a dark spot with splintered wood planks above, where only a crevice let in slivers of light. *Where is this?* The candles flickered. Marigold closed her eyes, narrowing in on the paper, seeing its ripped edges and wrinkled sides. Then she made herself pull back, through the crevice until she was above the paper in her mind. Her eyes turned to the left and right inside the dreamlike image, and she gasped. She was in her very own living room. The paper was trapped beneath the floorboards by the window overlooking the garden.

Marigold's eyes snapped open and she leapt to her feet, tossing the diary out of her way. She tiptoed down the stairs, two at a time, and reached the bottom in record speed. She raced into the living room and knelt beneath the window. The wood was scratched and swirled with knots and discoloration. She felt around the edges of the floorboards. They were nestled tightly together except for a gap between two of the boards.

Spying the fire poker beside the fireplace, Marigold grabbed it. Then she wedged it beneath the edge of one of the floorboards and tipped it backward, using all her strength until the board lifted along one side. She pried the board off the floor, staying as quiet as possible. There, in the narrow gap, was a single sheet of paper, folded up.

She reached down and lifted the paper with trembling fingers. It was yellowed with age, and one edge was rough and ragged. After resecuring the floorboard, she rose to her feet and settled herself onto the couch before flipping on the table light.

The writing was faint but familiar; it was Clemence's slanted cursive. The first part of the page was a recipe for a charm, but it was unlike any Marigold had seen. At first glance she assumed it was a power charm, by the mixture of flowers and herbs. Yet the scents were all overly strong—yarrow, rose, star anise. It called for boiling each step of the way. She had never heard of boiling every scent or combining so many dominant scents into one. It must have smelled awful. Even odder, beneath the recipe, Clemence had written one word—*Take*.

Marigold frowned. She had no idea what this charm was designed to do, but she didn't need a charm right now. She needed to know what had happened to the sisters before the Great Hurricane. She began to read:

I've done something horrible.

Elise fell in love with Jacob Spencer. She intended to marry him. I begged her not to. She said things wouldn't change, but I knew better. She would move in with Jacob, and I would be alone. Our entire practice would become an afterthought, something to do between her wifely duties. Worst of all, I would become an afterthought.

Jacob wasn't enough for Elise. He only wanted her aromagic, to use her powers. His heart never recovered from his fiancée's departure. I could smell it on him every time he was near. I tried everything to make her see reason, but nothing worked. I thought if I took away her powers, he'd cast her aside. I would help her recover. I always intended to give the powers back. I swear it. I never wanted to hurt her.

A shiver went through Marigold's body. She swallowed and put down the page, knowing where this entry was going. Her delight from minutes before had evaporated.

I mixed up the charm. I didn't fear the consequences. I would save Elise from a terrible marriage, and if there was a price to be paid, then surely I would be the one to pay it, not her. I believed that nothing would harm her. How very wrong I was.

As soon as I sprayed the charm on Elise, the heavens darkened overhead. The candles in the house extinguished. Thunder rolled in, ominous and loud. The heavy rain began, as if the waves themselves were washing over our cottage.

Elise stared at me for a long moment. Her blue eyes turned cloudy. She clutched her stomach and doubled over, collapsing to the floor. I will never forget her last words to me, "Clemence, what have you done?"

I cannot write what happened next. I cannot bear to put the words on the page. I did pay the price. The price was my entire heart.

I lost Elise forever.

The writing stopped there. Marigold put a shaking hand to her throat as she realized the truth of Clemence's dark secret. She thought back to the poem. *Bound by blood and born as friends. The rot foretells the bitter ends. Misfortune and hate tear apart. Dark magic stole a sister's heart.* The dark magic had been of Clemence's own making. There was no curse against the Lafleur family. There never had been.

Clemence had taken Elise's powers, and fate had taken Elise's life. Then fate had demanded the ultimate price from every generation since.

Marigold tucked the paper into her robe pocket and sank back into the couch cushions. She looked up to the ceiling where above, Lou lay in a fitful sleep, her face looking more hollow and empty every day. Turning her head toward the water and Eastport, Marigold imagined Birdie up studying in Gram's guest room, alone, separated by her choice, though for her own protection too. Marigold had to find a way to pay back her family's debt to fate and save her sisters from losing one another for good.

Mama appeared in the doorway. "What are you doing up?"

Marigold didn't want to tell Mama what she'd discovered about Clemence and the real reason for the Lafleur misfortune. Mama would feel terrible if faced with actual evidence of the vex. Marigold had given her enough to worry about by breaking into Miss Jessica's house and destroying the bowl in the visitor's center. Besides, Mama couldn't help with this. Only a sister could pay the debt to fate.

"I couldn't sleep," Marigold said.

Mama sat down beside her on the couch. "Me neither."

"Are you okay?" Marigold asked.

Mama rubbed her hands together as if to ward off a chill. "Not really. How can I be, when one of my daughters has left and another seems determined to hurt herself?"

"Have you talked to Lou?" Marigold asked.

Mama lifted one shoulder. "Your daddy and I had a long discussion with her. She's promised to stay away from aromagic for the time being until she can better . . . stabilize her desires."

Lou had promised. Yet without Birdie to temper her wild ideas and Marigold to jolt her out of anger, would Lou keep her word? Marigold feared she would not. The vex had brought out her sisters' worst tendencies.

Mama continued, "You know, I was always so aware of other people's fears. I've been able to smell them since I was young. Perhaps in some ways it made me ignore my own. I did things without bothering to consider the consequences."

"What do you mean?" Marigold asked, scooting a little closer. Mama's voice had the particular rhythm to it that meant she had a story to tell. Marigold realized she'd missed that voice.

"I had you girls, all three of you. I knew it was a risk, but I truly didn't believe there was anything to Gram's superstitions about the Lafleur curse. I thought three was a powerful number, and three sisters the most powerful of all. I suppose I was afraid that if I didn't have three children, your childhood would be like mine. I didn't want you to feel like I did growing up."

"How did you feel?"

"Alone." Mama laughed a little like she was embarrassed at the sentiment. "I never saw eye to eye with Gram. We're so different, and I had no siblings to play with or confide in. My father died when I was young. I was . . . peculiar. No one else had aromagic. I thought if I gave each of you sisters, you'd have others who understood you, to keep you from feeling lonely. That certainly backfired, didn't it?"

Marigold took Mama's hand. If Daddy could forgive her for the accident and Sam could forgive her for acting cruel and the town could forgive them for the earthquake, Marigold could certainly forgive Mama for wanting a family, for wanting *her*. "Birdie and Lou were the best things that ever happened to me."

Mama squeezed her hand. "Thank you for saying that, Marigold. I'm doing everything I can think of to mend this and keep you all safe. I know you may not trust every word I say. I've been absent a lot these last few months."

The dim light of the room cast Mama's face in shadows. Her lashes dipped to her cheeks, and her burnished red hair covered one side of her face. Marigold stared, suddenly understanding. Her strange, unreadable mama was sad. She was desperately, hopelessly sad. How had Marigold not seen it before? All those times Mama had been in the basement late into the evening and stayed in bed through the morning, she hadn't been avoiding her daughters. She'd been avoiding her life, for Daddy hadn't just left the three of them; he'd left Mama, too.

All these months, Marigold hadn't wanted to remember the truth, that things had been broken between Mama and Daddy for a long time. She'd ignored the fights and the slammed doors and the stomping out of the house. She'd wanted to imagine everything would go back to normal when Daddy came home from the hospital, but that wasn't realistic. Daddy and Mama had drifted apart for reasons Marigold would never understand and couldn't fix.

"I'm sorry Daddy left," Marigold said.

"I knew he was going back to Asheville on Sunday," Mama said.

"I didn't mean on Sunday," Marigold said simply.

Mama stayed quiet, her hand resting in Marigold's. Though Marigold knew she should go to bed or start brainstorming what to do next, she couldn't make herself leave Mama's side. Instead they sat together in silence for a long time, neither of them wanting to be alone.

CHAPTER TWENTY-ONE

Pansy will give you the courage to make changes
in your life.

The next day Marigold paused in the entrance to the cafeteria. The long tables were jammed, and she wasn't hungry. All she wanted was to return home so she could figure out how to fix her family, now that she knew what had happened all those years ago with Clemence and Elise. She wasn't giving up.

Marigold noticed Sam sitting at a table with Will and Charlie. She still sat with them sometimes. Today Will was waving his hands in the air, in the middle of a story, and Charlie was wearing one of the band's cowboy hats. It looked completely out of place in the lunchroom, but he didn't seem to care.

"Marigold," Lauren called from a nearby table. "We saved you a seat."

Marigold walked over, wishing Lauren hadn't spotted her. All Lauren wanted to talk about was her party, and Marigold was tired of pretending that mattered when everything was spiraling out of control with her family.

Lauren patted the seat beside her. "We're trying to decide what to wear to the pep rally next Friday." She looked up at Marigold and frowned. "Did you forget to brush your hair today?"

Marigold reached up and ran a hand through her tangles. "I guess I did. I didn't sleep much last night. Things aren't great at home."

"I'm sorry," Kendall said, leaning forward in her seat. Her rings caught the light and splashed an arc of color over the table. "What's wrong?"

"My sisters are fighting, and Lou is . . . sick," Marigold said, unable to think of another way to describe what was happening to her sister.

"Ugh, stop. I'm having a good day. No depressing talk," Lauren said.

Marigold clenched her jaw. Lauren didn't want to talk

about anything painful unless it was about her. It didn't matter that Marigold was upset. Her sadness didn't fit into Lauren's perfect world, and Lauren's perfect world was all that mattered to Lauren.

"Do you think Lou's illness is serious?" Kendall asked.

"Maybe," Marigold said, grateful that at least Kendall was concerned. Lou had looked awful that morning when Marigold had left for school. Her face was a sickly white. She'd barely raised her head off the pillow when Marigold had checked in on her.

Lauren cleared her throat. "I'm sure Lou is fine." She gestured to the seat next to her once again. "We're thinking striped shirts."

Marigold frowned. "What?"

"For the pep rally," Lauren said. "If we all wear striped shirts, we'll stand out. I want to finally make Todd Robinson notice me."

Marigold stared down at Lauren. She was still talking about what to wear to a dumb pep rally after Marigold had confided that her sister might be seriously ill. She'd probably have the same reaction if Marigold said her other sister had left and was never coming home. Marigold suddenly realized she didn't want to sit with Lauren.

"Well, are you going to sit down?" Lauren asked in a snippy voice.

"No," Marigold said. "I'm going to sit with Sam today."

Lauren's eyes widened. She glanced over at Sam, Will, and Charlie before turning back to Marigold with a look of disbelief. "Did you see that Charlie is wearing the band cowboy hat? People are staring."

"So what? I like his hat. I think it's cool that Sam started a band that wears cowboy hats. And I'm going to sit over there because I know none of them will call me strange behind my back in the girls' bathroom," Marigold said. Her hands shook as the true words spilled out, but she stood straighter than she had in days.

Lauren blushed. "I don't know what you're even talking about right now."

"I think you do," Marigold said. "See you around."

Lauren crossed her arms as Marigold walked away.

Maybe it wasn't fair to blame Lauren for not taking her problems seriously. Marigold hadn't told her about the vex. Yet Marigold couldn't forget what Lauren had said in the bathroom. And even if Lauren did share a few of her secrets and have the most fun parties and make Marigold feel special with her attention, she wasn't a very nice person most of the time. In the back of her mind Marigold had never stop worrying whether Lauren would think she was strange or scary or worse if Marigold told her about what was happening to her sisters. Marigold didn't want a friend she couldn't trust with her problems.

After crossing the room, Marigold stopped behind Sam.

"Can I sit here?" Marigold asked.

"Sure," Charlie said. "We're discussing band names again."

"I still like 'Big Fish,'" Will said stubbornly.

"Well, I like 'Three Dudes in Hats,'" Charlie said.

Sam looked up at Marigold. "Is something wrong?"

"Nothing more than usual," Marigold said, sitting beside Will.

"You look wiped out," Sam said. He handed her his extra sandwich, and though she wasn't hungry, she took it anyway. After taking a bite, she realized maybe she was the tiniest bit hungry after all.

"Heard we're getting a big storm later today," Will said.

Charlie groaned. "That means I'll have to help my dad tie up the boats at the marina." He turned to Marigold. "Couldn't you do a spell and make the storm go away or something?"

Marigold froze, the sandwich halfway to her mouth.

Sam glanced at her, then back at Charlie. His face went dark. "You know, that's really offensive. Marigold isn't a witch—"

"Who can make storms stop," Marigold finished for him, setting the sandwich down. She smiled at Charlie and

Will to show them she wasn't upset. "But if you need help with gardening, I'm the person to call."

"That's the one chore I'm not responsible for at my house," Charlie said.

"Can't help you, then," Marigold said cheerfully.

"Yeah," Sam said, looking relaxed and happy. "She can't help you."

Marigold smiled at Sam. He'd always stick up for her, even if she didn't need him to.

Charlie shrugged. "Was worth a try."

"You're an idiot, dude." Will shoved Charlie with his elbow.

"An idiot who hates tying up boats," Charlie said, shoving him back.

Marigold leaned her elbows on the table and pointed to Charlie's hat. "Got any more of those? I was thinking I might like one to show my support for the band."

Charlie beamed at her. "You bet! I've got ten more at home."

Marigold finished her sandwich. Their laughter calmed the anxious churning of her stomach, at least for the rest of lunch.

Later, on her way out of the cafeteria, Marigold heard someone calling her name. Ms. Ballard hurried up to her. "I'm glad I caught you. Do you have a minute to talk?"

"Sure," Marigold said, and followed Ms. Ballard a few doors down. She had barely thought about the play and had missed practice the day before. There was simply too much going on at home.

"I hate to tell you this, but we may have to push back the date for opening night." Ms. Ballard pressed her lips together and sat heavily down in the chair behind her desk.

Marigold dropped into the seat across from her. Ms. Ballard's office was painted a pretty light blue, and posters of past school plays were framed along the walls. Ms. Ballard herself looked like a wilted flower, bent over her desk with her head sagging to one side.

"We're dreadfully behind. We haven't even managed to have one real rehearsal yet," Ms. Ballard said. "I don't want you to worry. I know we haven't gotten to any of your scenes, but I was hoping to get some of the big cast-wide numbers done first. I'm not concerned about your songs. You were incredible at the auditions."

Marigold wanted to hide underneath her chair. Her face flamed with shame, remembering the charm that had made her incredible. "Thanks."

"I can't seem to motivate anyone. Just yesterday Robert and Leila both said they couldn't sing because their throats were closing up. Even the set keeps collapsing for no reason, although our volunteers are already working on it."

"Um, about the volunteers." Marigold cleared her throat. It was time to tell Ms. Ballard the truth about her sisters. "Birdie and Lou can't help with the painting. I—I signed them up without checking first, and they're going through a lot right now."

"It's—"

"There's more," Marigold interrupted. Her face was hot. "Mama doesn't want to be on the planning committee. She could help with flowers if you even do those. I'm sorry. I know you were counting on us, and it's my fault for saying yes on their behalf."

Ms. Ballard only smiled a little. "I understand."

"You do?" Marigold looked at her in astonishment.

"Yes, and I don't need you to justify anything to me. I think flowers are a great idea if your mama has time. Between us, I wouldn't join that planning committee either." Ms. Ballard leaned in close and whispered, "Too much drama."

Despite everything, Marigold lifted her mouth in a return smile.

Ms. Ballard continued. "Back to the play. I'm going to add some extra rehearsals, do a bit more work with the smaller roles. Even if we have a few rocky songs in the end, at least we'll have your solos to carry us through."

Marigold swallowed hard. She didn't deserve to be the star. The cast was struggling because of what *she* had done.

She owed it to everyone to at least put the best person in the lead role, and the best person was not her.

"Actually, I'm not sure I'm right for the lead," Marigold said, the words tumbling out of her mouth before she could stop them.

Ms. Ballard's head jerked back. "Excuse me? You want to give up the lead?"

Marigold gave her a small nod. "I think Anna will do a better job." She smiled so Ms. Ballard knew she meant it.

"She's very good but—" Ms. Ballard stopped and shook her head. "I'll have to think about this."

Marigold stood. "Okay, but please consider this my official resignation."

Ms. Ballard's forehead wrinkled up. "I don't think this has ever happened before."

Marigold didn't trust herself to say anything else. Of course it had never happened. No one wanted to give up the lead role.

Despite knowing she was doing the right thing, quitting the play wasn't easy. Maybe kids at school would start avoiding her again. Some of the committee members might shun her family because they weren't helping out. But she didn't need to impress people by being the lead in the play, and if there were townspeople who didn't like her or her family because they were different, then she didn't need them as friends. Still, she had to admit that being the star—the admiring looks, the compliments, the applause after her solo—well, she was going to miss it all the same.

They both turned at the knock on the door. Robert and Leila stood in the doorway. They were grinning widely.

"I feel way better," Robert said. "I'm ready to rehearse this afternoon."

"Me too," Leila said. "I'm sorry about yesterday. I don't know what was going on with me, but I feel like a different person today. The medication the doctor gave me worked! I can even stay late on Thursday if it would help."

Behind Robert and Leila eight more cast members appeared, trickling in one by one. They were all talking over one another excitedly, offering to spend extra hours the next day and on Saturday rehearsing. They were telling Ms. Ballard they no longer felt sick, that they couldn't wait to start practicing, and asking if they could go onstage later that afternoon.

Ms. Ballard was laughing. "This is the kind of enthusiasm I've been waiting for!"

Marigold used the confusion to slip past them and out of the office. Ms. Ballard met her eyes from across the room. She mouthed, "Are you sure?"

Marigold nodded with a sad smile. She passed Anna at the edge of the office.

"Congratulations," Marigold said to her.

"Congratulations on what?" Anna asked.

"You'll see," Marigold said, and continued down the hall.

As Marigold walked away, more cast members lined up at Ms. Ballard's office. Marigold counted at least twenty kids. She couldn't believe it. The cast-wide problems seemed to have magically ended just as she'd dropped out of the play.

Marigold stopped short, nearly tripping over her feet. Of course! She'd paid back the debt to fate. Suddenly Marigold knew exactly what she needed to do to fix Clemence's vex.

CHAPTER TWENTY-TWO

Lily of the valley inspires loyalty and devotion.

Marigold raced home after school. Mama had left a note on the kitchen countertop. *Went to mainland for ingredients, home late.* Perfect. Marigold had a plan, and she needed to be alone.

After hurrying to the basement with the torn page from Clemence's diary, Marigold halted in surprise. The cabinets were open, and ingredients were spilled along the table. This was unusual; Mama always left the basement immaculate. It didn't matter. This was Marigold's only idea for fixing the vex, and she had to begin. She began measuring ingredients.

After some time had passed, Marigold registered the silence in the house. She'd been so intent on beginning the charm, she hadn't thought to wonder about Lou. Lou was probably resting, but Marigold knew she should check on her anyway. She had time while the ingredients soaked.

Marigold pushed open the door to Lou's room and stopped. Lou's bed was empty. She leaned into the hallway. "Lou."

There was no answer. Marigold called her name again, but there was only silence in return. Her heart beat a little faster. Where was her sister?

Grabbing her phone, Marigold texted Lou. She waited several minutes with no reply, texted again, then called. No answer. She called Mama and got her voice mail. Texting Lou's two best friends didn't help. Neither had spoken to her in days. She then sent a group text to her classmates, asking if anyone had seen Lou around the island. Charlie responded that his father had seen her getting off the ferry hours earlier. But she was still grounded and sick. Where had she gone on the ferry?

Marigold slumped onto Lou's bed as her gaze searched the room. Then her eyes landed on a corner of Lou's pillow case. There was a lump under the pillow. She reached beneath it and pulled out Lou's phone. Marigold shifted uneasily. Lou took her phone everywhere. There was no way she'd leave it behind . . . unless she wasn't thinking straight.

Marigold powered on the phone and punched in the password to unlock the phone. It was a combination of her sisters' birthdays, the same code Lou used for everything. The same one Marigold and Birdie used.

Opening up the messages, Marigold peered down at the recent texts. They were from John Bradbury, which made no sense. John was a known bully and was as mean as a raccoon. He was the one Birdie had exposed as the vandal who'd drawn graffiti down the school hallway last year. He hated the Lafleurs.

Marigold clicked on the text chain and scanned the messages. John had sent Lou cruel texts about her getting kicked off the field hockey team, calling her weird and creepy, over and over. There was a single response back from Lou.

You will regret this.

Marigold froze at the ominous words. A chill scuttled down her arm like spiders along her skin. Suddenly she knew why the basement was a mess. It was Lou. She must have mixed up a charm to enact revenge against John. But revenge would do more than harm John; it could harm Lou even more. Marigold had to find her.

"Hello?" Birdie's voice echoed through the house. Her footsteps came up the stairs. She stalked into her room. "What are you doing in here?"

"Shouldn't you be at Gram's?" Marigold asked. The vex

wasn't fixed yet, and Birdie could get hurt by merely being around Marigold.

"I forgot some of my calculus notes and have a test tomorrow," Birdie said, rummaging at her desk. "I guess Lou isn't back yet. I swear she's going to get herself kicked out of school entirely. She isn't allowed to set foot on campus right now with her suspension, but I saw her heading into the swim and dive meet earlier. Not that she cares about following any rules."

The swim and dive meet? John Bradbury was captain of the swim and dive team. That might explain what Lou was doing at school. Pulling out her phone, Marigold navigated to the Eastport High website and the online newspaper with its team updates. Sure enough, there was a recap of the meet. Her body went colder at what she read.

"I'm worried that Lou is in trouble," Marigold said.

Birdie straightened and narrowed her eyes. "What makes you say that?"

"I think she meddled in that meet today. I just checked online. John Bradbury forfeited every single one of his dives. He's the reason the team lost."

"What does that have to do with Lou?"

"John sent Lou some mean texts. He was gloating about her getting kicked off the field hockey team, and she said he would regret it. My guess is she mixed up a charm to make him lose."

"Nothing she does surprises me these days," Birdie said, sniffing.

"Didn't you hear what I said? Lou is missing and she used a charm to alter the outcome of a competition. Don't you realize what that means?"

Birdie's angry mask slipped, and her blue eyes widened as the realization struck her. "Fate demands its price," she whispered.

"Exactly," Marigold said. "And I'm not sure where she could have gone. Charlie's dad saw her get off the ferry hours ago."

"I guess we have to find her before she makes a bigger mess," Birdie said.

Marigold hesitated, then nodded. At least if Birdie was with her, she could keep an eye on her sister until she finished her plan.

When they stepped outside, the sky was already darkening to dusk. Charcoal clouds filtered out the remaining bits of sunlight. There was a bite to the air. Marigold shivered and tugged her jacket closed. The temperature had dropped off a cliff, a sign as ominous as the clouds that had suddenly rolled in.

Marigold looked wildly around the yard. Where should they start? Lou could be anywhere, and while the island wasn't that big, it wasn't that small, either.

"Who is that?" Birdie pointed to the edge of their yard.

A group of figures hovered beyond the trees. It was impossible to see their faces in the dimming light until they were headed right up the path to Lilac Cottage. It was Sam and Charlie, Will and Anna, Julia and Kendall, and a few other cast members.

"W-what are you doing here?" Marigold stammered.

"We're here to help," Sam said.

"We know Lou is missing," Anna added.

"We didn't want you to look for her alone," Julia said.

"But it's cold and getting dark," Marigold said in disbelief.

"Should have brought my paddleboard," Will said. "I could have covered a wider area that way."

"Except you always fall off," Charlie said.

Will shoved him. "Dude, no I don't."

"We need to focus," Julia said. "Now isn't the time to talk about paddleboards."

"I think we should split up," Sam said, taking charge. "I'll go to the marina with Will and Charlie. Anna, you and Kendall take the Allerton Shore. Julia and Leila, you can go through the woods on the south side of the island." Sam continued talking and pointing until everyone had an assignment.

They were all here to help her. Even with the play, Marigold had continued to worry that no one liked her, that everyone was afraid of her and the entire island was just waiting for her family to mess up again, but it seemed she was wrong. Miss Iris had told her there were people who'd supported them after Daddy's accident and who appreciated Mama's help. It seemed those people weren't the only ones who cared for the Lafleurs. Marigold had friends who showed up when she needed them. They didn't mention the weird rotten smell that was strongest in her yard. They didn't mind that she wasn't the lead in the play or that her family was a little different. They still wanted to help, and it meant everything.

Minutes later they were calling out planned routes and trotting down the path in different directions. Marigold stood still, watching them go.

"We'll find her," they called.

"Don't worry," they said.

She was afraid that if she tried to thank them, she'd burst out sobbing.

Sam turned back, sensing how she was feeling, the same way he always did, and gave her his signature smile. He didn't hug her or make a mushy comment. Instead he said, "Ready to go?"

Marigold only nodded, her eyes resting on Sam's kind face. She was lucky to have him as her friend. She pushed back her hair and motioned to Birdie. This time Birdie didn't hesitate.

Birdie and Marigold headed to the beach by way of the path through the south woods. The wind tore at their hair, gathering in intensity. The longer they walked, the more Marigold's panic grew. She pictured Lou lying alone on the ground, her face pale and still. Marigold shuddered at the thought. Her phone kept chiming with texts from the search party:

Not at the marina.

North woods are empty.

Shops are closing—no sign of Lou.

Ferry is deserted.

Lou was nowhere. Sticking close to the edge of the road, Marigold peered into the underbrush every few steps.

By the time they reached the beach, the dark had well and truly set in. The wind howled, making it difficult for them to hear. The waves crashed in curves of white foam like froth at the mouth of an angry animal.

"She's probably on a—a run or something," Birdie offered as they stared at the empty expanse of beach. The sand gusted around them in mini tornadoes.

"I don't think so," Marigold said. Somehow she knew that Lou needed their help and needed it now.

"This is hopeless," Birdie said. "She'll never hear us in this, and I'm having trouble seeing anything."

"Nothing is hopeless," Marigold said, but her insides clenched up tight.

Birdie stopped. "Let's think. What exactly happened during the meet today? It might give us a clue about what happened to Lou."

"The online newspaper said the team lost their first meet of the season because John forfeited all his dives. Apparently, he climbed back down the ladder rather than go off the diving board. The reporter wrote that it looked as if John was suddenly afraid of heights."

"Okay . . . so, what if Lou's charm did make John afraid of heights? Would a vex make her like heights?" Birdie asked, wrinkling her brow. "That doesn't make much sense."

Marigold stared at Birdie. "Maybe it does. What if— what if the vex made it so she had no fear at all? What would she do then?"

Birdie swallowed. "What's the highest point on the island?"

They realized it at the same time. "The Old Salt Light-house."

Marigold's knees threatened to buckle as she considered what Lou might do. She grabbed Birdie's arm. "We need to run."

They ran straight there, crashing through the trees. Marigold immediately spotted the light glowing from the windows high up on the lighthouse. It illuminated the cat-walk and the lone figure standing on it. Marigold sucked in a breath when she saw how small the figure was—how high the figure was.

Marigold pointed. "We have to get up there now."

Somehow Lou had managed to smash the lock on the door at the base of the lighthouse, and the door swung open on its rusted hinges. Marigold pulled Birdie through the doorway. They clattered up the stairs, taking them two a time; one flight, two flights, three flights, higher and higher. Marigold's lungs burned from the effort, but she didn't slow down.

They climbed the final ladder leading up through a hatch in the ceiling to the top of the lighthouse, with its small circular room surrounded by windows. One of the windows was open. They could see Lou clearly, leaning over the railing of the metal catwalk. She looked tiny with the vast night behind her. Beyond her the ocean churned and the twinkling lights of Eastport winked in and out. Below her was the cold, hard ground.

"Lou," Marigold said in a strangled voice. She could hear the pounding of her heartbeat inside her ears.

Lou turned, catching sight of her sisters. Her eyes were empty. "Whatareyoudoinghere?" she whispered, slurring the words into one messy rush of syllables.

"We're here to take you home," Marigold said gently, not wanting to startle her.

Birdie crossed her arms. "Get down from there, Lou.

This is ridiculous. You're going to hurt yourself."

Lou lurched backward then. Her elbow hit the railing and she stumbled, careening to one side. Her feet scuffled against the metal bars along the floor. Birdie gasped.

"Watch out," Marigold yelled.

Lou straightened and grabbed the railing, swaying back and forth. The wind was wild up there, yanking at the catwalk as if it wanted to tug the entire thing down, and Lou along with it. Sinister clouds gathered behind her, blotting out the moon. The deadly vex was demanding its price.

"Please come back inside, " Marigold begged.

Lou turned, and her hand drifted up. Her profile was calm, dreamy even, as she pointed a finger outward. "You can see Eastport from here. It's beautiful up this high, like being a bird. Soaring above everyone." Her voice sounded disconnected from her body, as if she were in a trance. She stepped closer to the railing, until her hip rested against it.

"Lou, I'm afraid. Come away from the edge. Please," Marigold said. She glanced back at Birdie, her eyes insistent, mutely asking what they should do next. Yet Birdie was as white as a lily and frozen in place.

"I've always wanted to fly," Lou said in that same eerie voice. "Witches in stories can fly, you know. Maybe I can too."

Marigold trembled at her words. Lou was not coming inside voluntarily. Birdie couldn't go out there. She might get hurt too. No, Marigold had to get Lou herself. She opened another window and climbed out onto the catwalk, Glancing down between the metal grates of the catwalk's floor, her stomach dropped. No one was allowed up here for good reason. The ground was impossibly far away. If Lou fell, there was no way she'd survive.

"I don't think you can fly. You can barely cook," Marigold tried to joke. Her vision blurred as she considered how close Lou was to the edge. The guard rail was only waist high. One wrong step . . .

"You don't know what I can do. No one does," Lou said faintly. Her skin glowed in the darkness.

"You could tell me," Marigold said, gliding farther down the catwalk and closer to Lou, her back pressed against the wall of the lighthouse. "Why don't you tell me now?"

"I'm not afraid," Lou murmured. She leaned forward over the railing, reaching out her hands to the darkness engulfing her. If she tipped another inch, she'd flip over the side. Marigold had seconds, maybe less.

Marigold exchanged a look with Birdie through the glass panes. Birdie dipped her chin once, acknowledging the plan. She stepped up to the open window closest to Lou, a look of grim determination that matched Marigold's own. Lou leaned out again, rising onto her tiptoes, teetering on the railing. Marigold rushed forward and yanked Lou's arm hard, pushing her toward Birdie. Birdie reached through the open window, wrapped her arms around Lou's torso, and hauled Lou over the windowsill without a second breath. Marigold bounded inside behind her.

Marigold couldn't stop her body from shuddering. Birdie was crying in great gulping sobs. Lou lay still on the floor inside, her eyes closed. It was as if the night air had sucked every bit of life from her. Marigold knelt down and lightly stroked Lou's face. Her cheeks seared Marigold's hand; she was burning up with fever.

"We need to get her home," Marigold said.

"How are we supposed to do that? She broke into the lighthouse. If we call for help, we'll get in so much trouble." Birdie's voice thickened with tears. Her blue eyes were big and round in her pale face.

"We'll each take an arm and support her between us," Marigold insisted. She pulled out her phone. "I'm texting Sam, Charlie, and Will to meet us here and help get her home. Come on."

Birdie and Marigold boosted Lou up to their shoulders. Lou leaned heavily on her sisters, her legs barely supporting her. Marigold bowed under the weight but didn't let herself fall. They had to get Lou home, safe. There was one last charm she had to brew.

CHAPTER TWENTY-THREE

Yarrow banishes evil from one's home.

The five of them carried Lou to Lilac Cottage and laid her on the sofa in the living room. After the boys left, Birdie piled the blankets from their beds on top of Lou. Yet Lou still shivered hard enough to shake the couch. They didn't know how long she'd been on the catwalk. Her breathing was shallow, and she hadn't spoken a word or opened her eyes.

Birdie pulled Marigold into the hall. Her brow furrowed. "She's burning up. We should call Dr. Scott or Mr. Jackson."

"I think we both know this isn't some ordinary illness," Marigold said.

"Don't say it's the curse," Birdie said, glaring.

"This isn't a curse. It's a vex."

"Because of Lou doing aromagic," Birdie said.

"Partly. But I think Lou has started using charms again because of Clemence," Marigold said.

Birdie squinted in confusion. She opened her mouth to speak, and Marigold cut her off. "I don't have time to explain. We have to get Lou to the basement right now before she gets worse."

Birdie tapped her foot against the cracked boards of the floor. "I don't have the patience for whatever scheme you've cooked up this time. I'm not going down there."

"This won't take long," Marigold said, refusing to let herself get drawn into Birdie's frustration.

Birdie sighed. They helped Lou to her feet and half dragged her down to the basement. Marigold wasn't sure if Lou even knew where she was.

In the basement they settled Lou onto the old sagging couch in the corner. The dim overhead lights illuminated the charm Marigold had already begun. The torn page from Clemence's diary was centered on the table.

Birdie leaned over to peer down at the glass. "Did you combine rose and star anise and yarrow? Is that cedar too? Those are all dominant scents. They don't belong in one charm. What are you making?"

Marigold ignored her and clicked the flame of the burner on beneath the brew. She lit the white pillar candles scattered around the room. The space lit up with an eerie glow, casting shadows into the corners and monstrous shapes along the walls. The liquid inside the glass began to bubble.

"That's way too much nutmeg," Birdie continued, her eyes fixed on the page. "Whatever you're brewing will smell terrible, and why are you boiling them all? Ugh! It smells like burned trash."

Marigold stared down at the glass. Her stomach roiled with fear. This had to work.

Lou stretched on the couch, her eyes half-lidded. "What's that awful smell?"

Lou's voice was slurred and quiet, but Marigold nearly wept at the sound.

"You're awake," Marigold said, and rushed over. She put a hand to Lou's forehead. Lou was still much too warm.

"What am I doing here?" Lou mumbled, pushing Marigold's hand away.

"Marigold is mixing up some weird charm," Birdie said. She paced back and forth in front of the long table. "You're wasting Mama's ingredients."

Marigold gritted her teeth and continued, holding her own nose against the smell. She stared at the ingredients, which had turned a muddy brown. It was time to add the intention. She blocked out Birdie's complaints and Lou's mumbles. Focusing on the glass container, she blew softly across it and sent her mind spinning down into the charm itself.

Give. Give. G—

"This isn't working." Birdie's whine cut through Marigold's thoughts. "The smell is getting worse because you're burning it."

Marigold straightened. She shook her head and refocused, imagining she was alone. Blowing softly again, she sent her intentions straight into the charm and . . . nothing happened. She tried once more, breathing deeply, clearing her mind. Yet despite her efforts, the charm remained the same muddy-brown, horrible-smelling, and decidedly not magical mixture. Whatever she was doing, it wasn't working.

Rubbing her eyes, Marigold exhaled. She knew this was the way to break the vex, but how to convey her intentions into such a powerful charm? Marigold didn't have enough strength to reverse a centuries-old vex. It wasn't possible for one person to pacify fate for such an injustice.

Marigold stared blankly around the room, at Lou draped across the couch, at Birdie pacing the floor. This charm needed more than she alone could give. She needed more strength, more luck, more power. She needed . . . her *sisters.* Marigold lit up as the answer to everything reverberated through her. Of course, she needed her sisters.

Three was a powerful number among aromages, and Mama had believed three sisters was the most powerful of all. They did not belong apart. They were not safer alone. They were more powerful together, always.

"I know what we need to do," Marigold said urgently. "But both of you will need to help."

"I'm not helping with this," Birdie said. "We made a pact to stop doing aromagic."

"We should never have done that," Marigold said. "We can't deny who we are."

The dim light illuminated Birdie's face, highlighting the shadows under her eyes and the turned-down corners of her mouth.

"Tell me what you're doing," Birdie demanded, "or I will leave this house. Is this some kind of strange healing spell for Lou? Because it's not going to work with a charm that looks like that, and even if it does, it could hurt her. We know aromagic is dangerous. Remember what happened with Daddy?"

Marigold slipped around the side of the table until she was closer to Birdie, staring straight into her eyes. She needed Birdie to see how much Marigold cared. "I'll never forget what happened with Daddy. But aromagic is only dangerous if it's misused. We loved working on charms together. Remember? We would come down here with Mama and mix up the ingredients. I would press the rose petals, and you would distill the violets."

"I always had to use the mortar and pestle," Lou said softly from the couch. "I didn't know how much cedar root one person could grind."

"That's because you have the most upper-arm strength," Marigold said.

Birdie cracked a smile. "I usually pretended my hand hurt to get out of it."

"I knew your hand couldn't have that many cramps from writing papers," Lou said, her eyes drifting closed.

Birdie's genuine smile slipped. "Those times are over, for good."

"Please," Marigold said. "I need you. Both of you."

Birdie hesitated, then nodded once.

Marigold grabbed the glass container and set it carefully on the floor next to the couch. She placed a candle on either side and took a seat on the floor, motioning for Birdie to join her. Lou slid down beside them, forming a small circle with the bowl at the center. Marigold grabbed her sisters' hands, and Lou and Birdie followed her lead, clasping the other's fingers.

"You'd better not do anything dangerous," Birdie said, eyeing the container.

Marigold took a deep breath. What she was about to do

was the most terrifying thing she'd ever attempted in her life. She looked at Birdie and Lou, at the familiar curves to their jaws and the matching specks of green in their blue eyes. Her beloved sisters. She would never get tired of seeing them, not in a million years. It was worth any sacrifice.

"Focus your mind on me and only me," Marigold said. "No matter what happens."

Birdie and Lou grumbled but quickly went silent.

Marigold stared at the charm. She set her mind to its very depths and infused the charm with the same intention over and over. *Give.* Her head crowded with images of Lilac Cottage, of flowers in full bloom because of the sisters' hours spent in the garden, of days picnicking at the beach, of fierce hugs, of the familiar comfort of vanilla and gardenia, of joy from one another's laughter and words of support, of a love so strong that it reached to her very core, of how happy she was when she was around her sisters. She felt light with laughter and heavy from heartache in equal measure.

Give, give, give.

The flames of the candles rose, sparking until they doubled in size. A breeze blew through the room, ruffling Marigold's hair. The charm boiled stronger of its own accord into thick black gusts that filled the room.

"What is happening?" Birdie asked, her voice rising.

Yet Marigold didn't stop staring at the glass; she didn't

stop squeezing her sisters' hands. A huge boom of thunder sounded outside. At once the lights flicked off, plunging the house into darkness but for the flickering candles. A heavy rain lashed against the windows.

"Marigold?" Lou's voice was a question.

Not breaking eye contact with the charm, Marigold asked, "Do you trust me?"

Birdie exhaled a stream of air. "Yes."

In a quiet, but unmistakable, whisper Lou said, "Yes."

Marigold's heart surged with hope. She broke her hold of their hands, lifted the charm, and tossed it high up toward the ceiling. Birdie and Lou gasped. The mist spilled out in a stream toward the ground as the glass plummeted to the floor and shattered. All around them the overwhelming smell of earth and smoke and wet stone melded together and burst upward.

A sharp pain cracked open Marigold's chest. She doubled over, feeling as if someone were tugging her inside out. Her sisters' cries of alarm barely broke through the aches clouding her vision. She screwed her eyes shut, trying not to cry. Every one of her senses faded away before Marigold fainted.

CHAPTER TWENTY-FOUR

Hyacinth is known to restore self-esteem and rebuild trust.

The first thing Marigold saw was Birdie, bent close to her face. Her skin was blotchy as if she'd been crying.

"Oh, thank goodness," Birdie said, stroking Marigold's brow. There were bright tears in her eyes. "I thought you'd died."

Lou was close too, holding Marigold's hands in her own. "You completely freaked us out, you lunatic. What was that charm?"

Marigold struggled to sit up, realizing she was upstairs on the living room couch, tucked beneath the blanket from Birdie's own bed. "How long was I out?"

Birdie patted Marigold's back in a soothing way. "An hour or so." She ducked her head. "The worst hour of my life."

Marigold took stock of her body. All fingers and toes still appeared to work. Her vision was cloudy but sharpening by the second. Her head pounded like there was a jackhammer inside her skull, but even that seemed to lessen as the minutes ticked by.

"You brought me up here?" Marigold asked.

"We had to do something," Birdie said. "I tried calling Mr. Jackson, but the storm knocked out our cell reception." She glanced down at her phone. "It's back up now. The storm just stopped."

Marigold looked beyond her sisters to the darkness outside the window. It wasn't menacing any longer, not with the moon hovering low over the trees and the pinpricks of starlight above. She could see the faint outlines of the garden, the white dahlias blooming amidst the shadows. The clouds had well and truly fled, leaving behind a clear night sky.

"You should know I feel robbed, with you fainting the way you did," Lou announced.

"What do you mean?" Marigold asked.

"You stole all the attention. I'm supposed to be the sick one everyone is worried about," Lou said, and smiled a little.

The thing was, Lou didn't look so sick anymore. She was sitting up. Though her face was still wan, there was a hint of pink to her cheeks. When she stretched with her usual loose grace, her hands no longer shook, and the dazed bleariness was gone from her eyes.

"I'd prefer to not worry about either of you," Birdie said, shaking her head.

The sisters sat in silence for several moments, none of them looking at the others. The air inside the house was still.

"Are you going to tell us what happened downstairs?" Lou finally asked.

"Was it a healing spell?" Birdie asked.

Marigold opened her mouth, then closed it. How to explain? "I was trying to help all of us."

After unintentionally fixing the vex on the play's cast, Marigold had realized how to end the vex on the Lafleurs. It required sacrifice. Clemence had taken Elise's powers, and Elise's life in the process. The only way to stop the Lafleurs from continuing to lose their sisters was to pay the debt to fate caused by Clemence taking Elise's gift, and the only way Marigold had been able to think of doing this was to give up her own powers. She'd recreated Clemence's spell. Yet instead of the intention to take, she'd infused the charm with the intention to give.

Marigold hoped it was enough. It certainly seemed to have taken away her ability to smell anything. She couldn't smell the incense Mama burned beside the front door, or the ghost scent of mint tea that usually wafted from the kitchen. There was no lingering smell of firewood from the living room or a hint of rose from the sachets in their drawers. She couldn't smell anything. A small part of her shriveled up inside. She'd never realized how much she'd loved the smell of her house before.

Without her ability to smell, aromagic was impossible. Smelling secrets was impossible. Just as Marigold had realized how much she wanted her powers, she'd had to give them up for good. Yet it was all worth it if her sisters came back to her.

"I'd better make some chamomile tea," Birdie said, standing and smoothing back her hair. "I think that will settle us down. Mama texted a little while ago. She'll be home soon too."

"Don't you have to get back to Eastport?" Lou asked.

Birdie froze. Marigold held her breath, waiting for Birdie's answer. There was an enormous lump blocking her throat.

Birdie looked down for a moment, then met her sisters' eyes and smiled—it was the big, heartbreaking, wonderful Birdie smile that brightened everything around her. It was a smile Marigold hadn't seen in weeks. "I'd rather stay here if you don't mind. Gram's house is too quiet and empty . . . and I miss you both so much."

Marigold leapt up and wrapped her arms around Birdie's waist. Lou wrapped her arms around Marigold. The three of them stood perfectly still, not moving, not talking. Marigold wished she could stay in this moment forever.

For the first time in weeks, she felt truly happy and safe. Her sisters were home.

The following day Marigold sat at lunch with Charlie, Will, and Sam. She'd also flagged down Anna, who usually ate lunch by herself at a table in the back. Marigold was hoping another person might stop the constant band talk. Apparently, they'd decided to name the band "Big Fish in Cowboy Hats" as a compromise. She hoped the decision also included a little more practicing. Sam didn't know it yet, but he was playing in the pep rally next week.

Lauren and Kendall walked by with Julia. They stopped beside Marigold. There were students packed in on either side of their table in long rows, and the small windows along the far wall left squares of golden light on the floors. It was bright inside the cafeteria, or maybe it was just bright inside Marigold.

"I heard the craziest rumor. Someone told me you dropped out of the musical," Lauren said.

"I didn't drop out," Marigold said. "I'm still in the chorus." She'd gone back to school that morning and asked Ms. Ballard if she could rejoin the play as a chorus member. Her cast mates had shown her the night before that they cared about her and wanted her around even if she wasn't the star.

Lauren blinked several times in a row. "But what about the lead?"

"I gave it up," Marigold said cheerfully. "I felt like there was someone better qualified than me." She looked at Anna and smiled.

Anna blushed. "I still can't believe it."

"I can't either," Lauren said, flipping her hair over one shoulder.

"It actually wasn't too hard a decision, especially after last night," Marigold said.

"Oh right," Lauren replied. "I heard Lou went missing. Sorry I couldn't help look for her, but it *was* dark and about to pour, and my mama said no way *was* I going out in that weather. She always warns me about how I have a delicate constitution and could lose my life if I'm not careful with my health." Lauren spoke this last part in a hushed, dramatic voice. She was making Lou's disappearance all about her, the same way she did with everything else.

Marigold only shrugged. "It's okay." She turned to Julia and Kendall. "Thanks for showing up to help. It made a big difference."

Kendall nodded. "I'm relieved you found her."

"It was kind of exciting," Julia said. "I felt like a detective or something."

"Me too!" Kendall exclaimed. "And it was fun when we all got hot cocoa after at Leila's house."

Lauren sniffed. "I don't think looking for Lou qualifies as detective work." She crossed her arms, a sour look on her face. "I still don't get why you gave up the lead."

"There were a lot of things that happened this past week that made me realize I don't need the lead," Marigold said.

When she had woken up that morning in the nest of blankets between her sisters' beds, it had felt like the most magical place on earth. Birdie had bustled around, making everyone oatmeal, and even Mama had come down from her room to see them off to school. Lou had called her coach and apologized for the fighting. She'd asked him to give her another chance on the field hockey team, and he was considering it. The nightmare of the past few weeks was finally over, though the outcome didn't look the way

Marigold had expected. It wouldn't include Daddy coming back to live at Lilac Cottage, even though she'd believed him when he'd said he would still be a part of her life. It wouldn't mean everyone in town suddenly accepted the Lafleurs, but those who did were the only ones she wanted to call friends anyway. And Mama wouldn't start joining committees, although Marigold hoped Mama would continue to talk to her as they had the other night. Best of all, Marigold had her sisters back. They could face any new normal together.

"Anyway, I want to spend more time at home too so I can help Mama and my sisters with their charms." Marigold couldn't use aromagic herself anymore, but she still wanted to be a part of that world in even the smallest way.

Lauren gasped. "I don't know if I'd say that, Marigold. After the earthquake some people are a little nervous around your mama." She looked around the table for confirmation, but everyone just stared at her.

"Mama didn't do anything wrong," Marigold said. "Besides, if people don't want to be around me because of my family, then I guess that's their loss."

"I want to be around you," Sam said cheerfully.

"Me too," Anna said.

"Me too," Will and Charlie said in unison.

"Me too," Kendall said, as Julia smiled and nodded.

"I didn't mean it that way. *I* obviously don't care what other people think," Lauren said, her face red. She turned to Kendall and Julia. "We should get in the lunch line before they run out of fries."

Kendall sat next to Marigold and held up her lunch bag. "I'm going to sit. I already have my lunch."

Lauren's mouth tightened, but she merely nodded once, grabbed Julia's arm, and got in the back of the line. Julia waved as Lauren pulled her away.

Marigold watched them in line. Lauren was talking and brushing back her long, blond hair. She wore a ruffled skirt that hit at the exact right length, and a striking jangle of bracelets that slid up and down her arms. The girls in front of her turned to laugh at something she said, and the boys behind her leaned in closer to catch her next words. Her classmates would always want to stand near Lauren and go along with her plans. But that didn't mean Marigold had to be one of them.

Sam looked down at his phone and straightened up in his seat. He pumped his fist in the air. "Oh man! This is unbelievable. My mama texted that I'm not grounded anymore so I can practice with the band!"

"Are you serious? That's phenomenal, dude!" Will said.

Charlie high-fived Sam. "We're going to crush the pep rally next week."

Marigold looked down at the table and smiled.

They talked about the new Dirk Thomas and the Wailers album and the upcoming pep rally. They talked about Kendall's plan to design shell jewelry, and Anna's online yoga classes. No one mentioned charms or aromagic, though Marigold knew they wouldn't care if she brought the topic up. Soon the bell rang, signaling the end of lunch. They all cleared up their trash and started off to fifth period.

Sam kept stealing glances at Marigold as they walked down the hall. When they were finally alone at their lockers, he asked, "Did you have something to do with me getting out of my punishment early?"

"Me?" Marigold said in mock astonishment, putting a little emphasis on the word just for fun. Her tone would have conveyed the perfect amount of surprise to an audience. "What would make you say that?"

"When I saw the text from my mama, you got that look on your face. The one that means you're planning something or planned something," Sam said. "Come on, spill."

Marigold shrugged, her arms swinging at her sides. The hallways were full, but they didn't seem hostile. No one cleared out of her way, or if they did, she chose not to notice.

"I called your mama and apologized. I told her the truth. That you were only there because I begged you to go and it was a matter of grave importance."

"Grave importance, huh?"

"That's what I said. Well that, and I told her you were helping me because you're my best friend and I needed you." Marigold pulled a book out of her locker. "That really seemed to work. But she did spend a good fifteen minutes lecturing me afterward."

"I bet she did." Sam ducked his head. "You didn't have to do that."

"I did," Marigold said firmly. "You've gotten me through the last few weeks. This is the least I could do."

Sam grinned. "I'm really glad I can rehearse again."

Marigold smiled at him. "I'm really glad you can too. But y'all are going to practice a lot before the pep rally, right?"

CHAPTER TWENTY-FIVE

The magical uses for rose include strengthening friendship, bestowing happiness, and securing love.

Mama was on the porch when Marigold got home, sitting in her rocking chair, a blanket tucked around her. She lifted her hand in a wave as Marigold started up the walk. The rotten smell was finally gone.

"What are you doing here?" Marigold asked. She'd hadn't seen Mama relax in these rocking chairs in months.

"Waiting for you," Mama said. She patted the rocking chair beside her. "Sit."

Marigold took a seat and rocked back and forth for a moment. From her chair she could see the ocean beyond the dunes and make out the gentle roar of the waves. But she couldn't smell the salt on the breeze or the dirt below them.

"You broke the curse," Mama said.

"How did you know?" Marigold asked.

Mama hadn't returned home the night before until after Marigold had already gone to bed. She'd gotten stuck on the mainland during the storm. They hadn't yet told her what had happened at the lighthouse or the aromagic afterward.

Mama smiled a little. "I overheard Lou talking to her coach this morning, and Birdie told me that she'd moved back home. More than that, I could smell a difference as soon as I walked through our front door last night. It smells clean again."

"I figured out how to fix it," Marigold said. Her eyes burned with hidden tears when she thought about having lost her aromagic forever.

"Why aren't you happy?" Mama asked.

"I am," Marigold insisted.

Mama shook her head. "I can tell there's something wrong," she added, but she didn't breathe in deeply to smell Marigold's fears. Instead she waited.

Marigold wanted to repair things between her and

Mama, and she couldn't do that if she wasn't honest. So Marigold went inside to retrieve the page from Clemence's diary. She explained about the vex and the way she'd fixed it.

Mama was still and silent. Marigold finally peered over at her and saw tears streaming down her face. "Are you crying?" She'd never seen Mama cry, not when Daddy had left, not when Birdie had moved out, not when Lou had gotten suspended, not when people had whispered as she'd walked past. Mama was stoic, but it seemed she wasn't made of stone.

"I'm grateful," Mama said. There was a catch in her voice. "Changing fate is a dangerous path."

Marigold looked down at her lap. Mama was right. It was dangerous, and Marigold wasn't sure she would ever attempt to do so again, even if she had her aromagic back. Marigold might not have always agreed with Mama's choices to help people in the way she did, but Marigold now understood that there were reasons why people took the risk; there were reasons why Mama helped them. After losing her sisters, after Birdie had moved away and Lou had nearly died, after Daddy—Marigold knew better than anyone else that sometimes people made decisions to do what they thought was best for the people they loved.

"When I think of what could have happened to you . . ." Mama swallowed. "I know I haven't really been there for you, but you should have told me. I could have helped."

"You couldn't pay back the debt. Only a sister could do that."

"That's not necessarily true. Vexes are tricky things to break. It's possible I could have sacrificed for you, much like I did with—" Mama pressed her lips together.

"Much like you did with what?" Marigold asked.

Mama bit her lip and looked away. "It's nothing."

"Mama, please. No more secrets," Marigold pleaded.

Mama sighed and smoothed back her red hair. "After your daddy's accident, when you told me what you'd done, I was afraid the outcome of your charm might kill him, so I made a charm of my own."

"But you must have given something up in return?" Marigold questioned, for she knew now that fixing a vex wasn't easy. It involved true sacrifice.

Mama rocked back and forth. The breeze lifted the corners of her old plaid blanket. Marigold watched the steam curl up from the top of her tea. For a moment she thought Mama might remain silent on this subject forever.

Finally Mama lifted her hands in a gesture of surrender. "I didn't want your daddy to leave either. I hoped . . . it doesn't matter what I hoped. Deep in my heart I knew he wanted to go. He no longer wanted to live on Luna Island with me."

"You gave him up," Marigold whispered. She remembered Mama in the emergency room, hovering over Daddy when he was lying still in the hospital bed. She remembered the smell of honey and eucalyptus. Of course. Marigold should have suspected all along that Mama was the one who saved him.

"It's more complicated than that, Marigold. I had already lost him. I found the strength to recognize that, and I set him free," Mama corrected. "I'm glad I did. It was time."

Marigold's eyes watered. "You saved his life."

"I'm not always so oblivious to my family," Mama said matter-of-factly.

"No, you're not," Marigold said, realizing that she had a lot to learn about Mama.

"Now close your eyes," Mama said.

"Why?"

Mama didn't reply but waited patiently, as was her way. Marigold exhaled and closed her eyes.

"Breathe in," Mama said.

Marigold breathed in, feeling the air fill her nostrils, but there was no scent.

"Again," Mama said.

Marigold took a deep, long breath. And there, right at the edges of her nose, tickling, was something. It was minty and faint and would be barely noticeable to anyone else. Well, to anyone who wasn't a Lafleur.

"I smell pine," Marigold whispered.

"Yes," Mama replied.

"But—but how?" Marigold's eyes flew open.

"Did you forget Clemence's original charm? The purpose was not to take Elise's powers away permanently. It was intended to be temporary until her fiancé left her. You reversed the charm and gave up your powers to fix the vex, but it's only temporary."

"My aromagic will return," Marigold said.

"It will," Mama said.

Marigold leaned her head back and sniffed the air. She'd get her aromagic back, and this time she would learn to appreciate it.

Marigold met her sisters at the ferry later that afternoon. Lou was still looking a little frail but was standing on her own. Birdie was carrying Lou's backpack. Their heads were inclined together, and they were talking animatedly. They spotted Marigold at the same time and waved, faces bright.

"What are you doing here?" Birdie asked when they caught up to her.

"Waiting for you. I thought we could walk home along the beach," Marigold said. She grabbed Lou's backpack from Birdie.

"Thank goodness," Birdie said. "That thing was getting

heavy. Lou has a lot of makeup work for us to get started on."

Lou mumbled something that resembled a curse word under her breath.

"I don't mind carrying it," Marigold said.

"Get used to it," Lou said. "I'm still sickly, you know. In fact, I suspect you'll have to meet me here to carry my backpack home for the next few weeks. I might also need you to make me supper, bring me tea in bed, clean up my room . . ."

Marigold cracked a smile. "That sounds a lot like me working as your servant."

"It does sound a lot like that, doesn't it?" Lou said, smirking. "Okay, if you insist, I'll agree to let you work as my servant. I'm going to need some serious care and recovery before I'm ready for practice."

"The coach is letting you back on the field hockey team?" Marigold asked.

"Not varsity. He said I had to earn my way back, but he's going to allow me to play on junior varsity and he said we'd see how it goes. I did a lot of apologizing," Lou said ruefully. "And I'm going to have to work really hard, since I won't have aromagic to help me."

"No more aromagic?" Marigold asked.

"No more aromagic that helps me and hurts other people," Lou amended.

A weight lifted from Marigold's chest.

Marigold tore off her shoes and let her toes sink into the sand. The ocean sparkled with bits of crystallized sunlight, and the sky was as blue and clear as her sisters' eyes. They walked in silence, but it was the lovely kind of buoyant silence that makes sense when you're strolling on the beach on a sunny day.

"I talked to Daddy this morning," Birdie said. "I told him I moved back to Lilac Cottage and that Lou is better. He said he's feeling stronger too. He's excited to see us next week, and I think he might even come home soon."

Marigold held up a hand. "You don't have to say that. I know he's not."

Birdie opened and closed her mouth. "He—he might."

"He might, but it's more likely he might not," Marigold said. "I can handle it. And yeah, I wish Daddy still lived here, and I wish he and Mama were still married so we could see him more. But they weren't happy together, and that's not our fault. We're still a family, even if Daddy lives somewhere else. We all love each other, and that's what matters."

Birdie put a soft hand on Marigold's shoulder and squeezed. Marigold's eyes pricked with sudden tears. She'd miss Daddy every single day.

"I'm glad you're growing up and all that, but we don't have to keep talking about this, do we?" Lou asked, rubbing her neck and looking distinctly uncomfortable. "Can't we go on a normal walk without sharing our feelings about everything?"

"We can share our feelings if Marigold wants," Birdie said primly.

"I'm okay right now," Marigold said, and found that she meant it. "Sometimes people have to leave Luna Island to figure out what's next." She gave Birdie a knowing look. "Like you. Are you still applying to college?"

"Yeah, that's a good question," Lou said.

Birdie sped up. "I said that when I was mad. I already promised you I wasn't going to leave Luna Island."

"That wasn't a fair promise," Marigold said. "You should go. I'll miss you, but I shouldn't expect you to stay until I can leave."

"I guess I'll . . . I'll think about it," Birdie said, blinking rapidly as the sand shifted under her feet.

"Don't think too long, or I'm liable to bar the door and keep you here," Lou said, shoving Birdie gently on the arm. "We're going to have a tough time surviving on my cooking, M."

"I can learn," Marigold said.

"I'd say you're too young, but honestly, that may be the only way we make it to Christmas," Lou said.

"Mama will help too," Marigold said.

Both sisters looked at her in astonishment.

"She will," Marigold insisted. "You'll see."

"I think the curse might have affected your brain waves," Lou said, smirking at her own joke.

Birdie stopped and took Marigold's hands. "I have to say something."

Lou groaned. "Not again. You're about to get sappy on us."

Birdie ignored Lou, still staring at Marigold. "What you did—" She stopped and swallowed twice. "What you did saved me. I didn't even know how unhappy and empty I was without you both until I had you back again. There is no way to really thank you, M, but . . . thank you."

Marigold squeezed her hands.

"She's right," Lou said after a moment, suddenly serious too. "You saved me too." She clamped her mouth shut, and Marigold knew she wanted to say more but couldn't.

"It was only fair. You've both saved me a million times over," Marigold said, thinking of all the times they'd protected her from their parents' fights, stood up for her in town, made her meals, forced her to laugh, and kept her safe, especially after Daddy left and Mama went quiet. They'd saved her again and again because that's what sisters did. They rescued one another, and protected one another, and in the darkest moments they were the ones standing beside you, guarding you against any curse.

"Are you ever going to tell us what charm you made last night?" Birdie asked.

"Let's just say I vanquished the curse like a leading lady would," Marigold said. She was wearing a long scarf tied around her braid—the brilliant pinks and purples matched her mood—and she flicked it behind her like a cape.

"I'll get it out of you eventually," Lou said.

"Not when you can't smell secrets like me," Marigold said. "Speaking of that, I do need more help practicing my aromagic. The other week I was at the Moon Market in line behind Miss Lizzie and Miss Eugenie. They were talking about Miss Eugenie's famous lemon pie, and I burst out Miss Lizzie's secret—she hates that pie. Miss Eugenie looked as if she wanted to kill us both."

Lou snorted in laughter.

Birdie sighed. "I'll help you, but there will be rules."

"Of course there will," Lou said, and rolled her eyes at Marigold. "Weirdly, I wouldn't mind a few rules before I use aromagic again."

"You're finally coming around to my way of thinking," Birdie said, dusting off her hands.

"And you're coming around to mine," Lou said.

"Did you forget this was all my idea in the first place?" Marigold said, raising her eyebrows.

Birdie and Lou exchanged a look before nodding. "You're right, Little Sister," Lou said.

"Finally," Marigold declared. "Someone acknowledges the truth!"

The three of them looked at one another and laughed. The vex was gone, the emptiness was filled, the world was right again. They sat down on the sand, facing the ocean, none of them in a hurry to go anywhere. They already had everything they needed right beside them.

There were many powers in their world. There were vexes, curses, and charms. There was the courage of leaving home and finding new friends. There was the strength of letting go while holding on tight. There was good and evil and secrets and sacrifice, and there was power in all of them. Yet with sunlight wrapped around her and salt tickling her nose, Marigold believed one thing for certain: nothing was more powerful than the heart of a sister.

ACKNOWLEDGMENTS

Thank you to my editor, Krista Vitola. Your vision for this story improved the book in more ways than I can count. I am grateful for your brilliance, your patience, and your kindness. It is a privilege to work with you.

To my agent, Katie Grimm, your wisdom, loyalty, and encouragement mean the world to me. I cannot thank you enough for the brainstorming phone calls and calm advice. I am incredibly lucky to call you my agent and my friend.

Krista Vossen, your stunning cover design perfectly captures the story. Jen Bricking, you are a wondrous talent, and I'm honored to have your beautiful illustrations in my book. Thank you to Chava Wolin, Katrina Groover, Emily Hutton, Mary Nubla, Catherine Laudone, Bara MacNeill, Shivani Annirood, Devin MacDonald, Nadia Almahdi, Nicole Benevento, Amy Beaudoin, and the entire team at Simon & Schuster for everything you've done for my books. I'm so appreciative of your energy and enthusiasm.

Thank you to all the friends and readers who have supported my writing. I cherished every text, direct message, e-mail, and positive review. The outpouring of encouragement and excitement has been one of the bright spots of my life.

To my wonderful family—Pop Pop, Grandma, Ginna, Barry, UG, Ashby, Lori, Jeff, Pope, Erin, Alston, Claire, Parker, Lucas, Scarlett, Miles, Gus, Benny, Reese—you mean the world to me. To Dad, your constant support and love convinced me I could do anything and for that I'm truly grateful.

I set out to write a book about sisters. I could never have done that without the inspiration of my own sister. Sarah, I can't begin to capture how much you mean to me in the pages of a book, but you certainly deserve a story where the little sister saves her big sister since you are always the heroine to me.

Gray, Colter, Bo, and West, your humor, curiosity, and kind hearts have provided me with more happiness than you could ever know. I'm endlessly proud of you.

Roby, thank you for taking the boys sailing so I could write a book during a pandemic. Our family is probably the closest thing to magic I'll experience in this life, and you are at the center of it. I love you dearly.